It's the End of the World
as
We
Know
It,
and I Could Use a Drink

A work of fiction that, incidentally, happens to be true

Scott Sherman

WORDSEARTH PRESS
Los Angeles

WordsEarth Press
P.O. Box 261331
Los Angeles, CA 91426-1331

Contact: Wordsearth@aol.com

Or visit our website at www.wordsearth.com

This book is a work of fiction. However, several people portrayed in this book are actual real-life visionaries and heroes who are making a tremendous difference in the battle to save the Earth. These people include Sharif Abdullah, Dave Foreman, Alan Durning, John Todd, Nancy Todd, Kirkpatrick Sale, Riane Eisler, Bill Mollison, Bill McKibben, Lester Brown, and William McDonough. All other names and characters are fictitious. (This includes the characters of Scott Sherman's parents who are much nicer in real life than the imaginary people portrayed in this book.) Any resemblance to real people, living or dead, is purely coincidental.

The incidents portrayed in this book are also products of the author's limited imagination. However, much of the factual information in the book is true. The author has done his best to accurately represent the viewpoints of the visionary heroes listed above. Where there are discrepancies, these are entirely the fault of the author, and he apologizes sincerely. Please forgive him.

Cover designed by Chris Lauer
Lauer Design Studios
San Francisco, California

Printed in the United States of America
on recycled, non-bleached, non-chlorinated paper

ISBN 0-9679029-0-8

Library of Congress Card Number: 00-190331

Prologue #1
Fictions

Once upon a time, I hated fiction.

This was back around the end of the second millennium, when the world was falling apart. Scientists were abuzz with reports of global warming, telling us that the polar ice caps would melt, and the oceans would rise, and half the continent would flood, and suddenly people in Iowa would be living on beachfront property. If you asked me, it was time to start building an "ark nouveau." (We could send out frilly little invitations to all the animal species that we humans hadn't already killed off: "RSVP, two by two.")

Meanwhile, other scientists were talking about the ozone layer disappearing, and how all of us white people would get cancer -- which was kind of like our karma, because of all the oppression and imperialist stuff we did to darker-skinned people. (And I thought, hey, that's kind of unfair, 'cause I was Jewish, and all these thousands of years we got oppressed with the best of them).

At the time, I was reading all these very serious, important books about nuclear bombs and disappearing rainforests and starving people in Africa. So when I looked at all the people who read fiction, I got on my self-righteous soapbox. "How could anyone waste their time with novels?" I bristled with indignation. "There are all these real emergencies we've got to address, and people are just consuming their hours reading about the imaginary problems of imaginary people. None of it matters a bit."

I was incensed. We needed to save the world. We couldn't fritter away these crucial hours wondering whether Heathcliff would triumph in love.

But lately my views have changed. I no longer harbor hatred and disdain for the world of make-believe. For, recently, a slithering suspicion has coiled around my mind:

Perhaps I, too, am nothing more than a work of fiction.

*　　*　　*

My physical existence is not in doubt. Hold me and you will feel my warmth. Cut me and I will bleed. My flesh inhabits the earth, as substantial as your own.

It is my deeper identity which remains in question. My personality is fictional, built on shams and little white lies. I have created so many masks for myself that I no longer remember my own true face.

I am a storyteller. I spin yarns about my life to boast, to entertain, or simply to impress my sense of importance upon the rest of the world.

Recently I decided to write a novel. It was about one heroic young man on a daring, adventurous crusade to singlehandedly save the world from all the forces of evil. The book was, of course, based on my life.

Yes, it was an autobiography, thinly disguised as fiction. Only the names had been changed to protect certain individuals. I didn't want to place an undue burden on all the people who might have felt the curious compulsion to sue me for defamation.

My novel started out with a dramatic opening line:

I was conceived in the Summer of Love, but grew up in a season of fear.

This was certainly an auspicious beginning to my work. After pouring hours of blood, sweat, toil, and tears into authoring such immortal words, I rewarded myself with a much-deserved rest. Proud of my magnum opus, I showed it to my mother.

"What's this mean?" she asked quizzically. "What's the Summer of Love?"

"You know, Mom, the summer of '67! All the young people were going to San Francisco, and wearing flowers in their hair!" I lost myself in a romantic, nostalgic air for a time I had never known. Psychedelic visions paraded before my eyes. "It was the dawning of a new age, when everybody was sure that peace would reign on the earth. The sun would shine in, and we all would live in a spirit of harmony and love."

My mother, who had three children already by the summer of 1967 and was living in suburban Los Angeles with no more than dandruff in her hair, protested. "You weren't conceived in the Summer of Love. Your birthday is in November. That means you were conceived in February -- in the Winter before the Summer of Love."

My ears were offended by such revisionist history. "Sure, I was first conceived in February," I conceded, "but I was still being conceived for the nine months until I was born."

"No, no, no," corrected the woman who had conceived me. "Conception happens in one moment of time. You were actually gestating for the next 9 months."

"Oh, mom! I can't say *I was gestating in the Summer of Love*. That's not very poetic or romantic. Where's the drama? Where's the irony?"

"Oh, just use some artistic license," she scoffed. "No one really cares when you were conceived anyway. Who's going to

3

read a book about your life? What have you ever done to publish your memoirs by age 27?"

I struggled to respond. I could have told her that I was on a secret mission to rescue the world from the forces of darkness. But then it wouldn't have been secret anymore. Plus, it wouldn't have been true.

Sometimes I get the distinctions blurred between me and my fictional shadow.

*   *   *

You see, everyday life is kind of boring. What do I actually do on the average day? I wake up around 8:00, still pretty sleepy. Then I'll read the paper, and eat some Wheaties, and pore over the classified ads, and even pay the bills, if there's any money in my account. Maybe I'll turn on the TV, or go to the gym, if I can muster the resolve. Pretty soon the day's half-finished. I don't exactly understand how my life is draining away so fast. I can't really account for it. When you're unemployed, you just sit around and mostly do a lot of nothing. It's extremely time-consuming.

I have to laugh when I ponder how different my current existence is from the movies. Real life isn't like anything that happens on television or in books.

I'll give you a good example: My mom has probably read about 5,000 murder mysteries in her life. She reads them at the rate of at least one a day. But I'll bet she's never seen a real murder. And she most certainly would be horrified if she did. Still, she mows through these tales of mayhem and mutilation as light entertainment, seeing if she can solve the case before Miss Marple saves the day.

It's just so far removed from reality -- this stuff doesn't happen to the ordinary person, not to any of my friends, that's for sure. There was this strange, eccentric, really brilliant kid who went to my high school for a while, until he was found blowing up electrical sockets and stealing power tools from construction workers. Anyway, he ended up murdering his father when he was 16, and he was put away in a juvenile detention center for a number of years. He's probably out of jail by now, maybe jostling your shoulder on the street corner. (Warning: Don't get him too mad.) But that's the exception. It wasn't this great murder mystery anyway. There weren't a dozen suspects, all with ambiguous motives. Everyone knew that this kid had blown away his father and buried him in the backyard. The case was open and shut.

Real life is sure a lot more boring than movies, television, and books. Nothing much interesting ever happens at all.....

Prologue #2
Truths

OK, maybe <u>one</u> interesting thing happened in real life:

In 1992, the world's leading scientists got together and declared that the end of the world was at hand.

Now I know what you're thinking: You think I must be suffering from apocalyptic fever. You think I simply made up this story as a result of the millennial flu. You think this is all just another fiction.

But, I swear, every word is true:

In an urgent *Warning to Humanity*, the scientists declared that the environmental crisis was escalating out of control. As few as 10 years remained before the earth would be "irretrievably mutilated" and "the prospects for humanity immeasurably diminished."

These were not doomsdayers or religious fanatics who sounded the alarm. These were not wild-eyed, white-bearded street corner prophets, ranting and raving about the imminent end of the world. No, these were the world's most respected scientists.

104 of them had won the Nobel Prize, the highest award bestowed on people who have expanded the frontiers of human knowledge. And the remaining 1566 scientists included some of the most distinguished names in the field: Carl Sagan, Stephen Hawking, E.O. Wilson, Stephen Jay Gould.

These were men and women of great integrity and distinction -- perhaps the greatest collection of geniuses ever assembled together. They were trained in the scientific method, where all data must be empirically proven and verifiable. In other words, these were not the types of people to make wild, unsupportable claims. They would not make conclusions without a mountain of evidence behind them.

Overall, the 1670 women and men who had endorsed the *Warning to Humanity* were among the most brilliant minds in the world. These were experts in the study of life on earth. They came from 71 different nations, including many from Africa, Asia, Latin America, and Europe. They came from the largest 19 economic powers and the 12 most populous nations. Yet, despite their differences in race, religion, culture, and creed, they had all apparently come to a consensus on a threat more immediate and more dangerous than even nuclear war:

The earth had as few as 10 years left.

Of course, this was the most important news of our lifetimes. But most people never even heard about this event. Others simply ignored it and went on with business as usual.

Now it was 1997, and nothing had been done to solve the ecological crisis. In fact, the situation was only getting worse. Five years had already passed.....

Time was running out.

Chapter 1

It was a typical, boring, average afternoon when I decided to save the world.

I went to tell my parents about it. "I'm going to save the world, Mom," I said to my mother, who was reading a mystery.

"Mmmm," she consented pleasantly without looking up from her novel. "That's very nice."

"Didn't you hear me, Mom?" I pleaded. "I'm going off on an international adventure, full of danger and intrigue, trying to find the solutions to all the world's problems."

"Well dress warmly," she counseled, her attention still focused on the book. "Will you be home in time for dinner?"

A bit discouraged, I decided to leave my Mom and seek out my father.

"I'm going to save the world, Dad."

"There's no money in that," he warned. "Saving the world's all fine and dandy, but it's not going to put any bread on the table."

"But Dad, I want to make a difference. I want to stop the spread of evil in the world. I want to reverse the tide of ecological destruction, violence, poverty, and suffering."

"All you think about is yourself, isn't it? Always thinking about what <u>you</u> want."

He started mimicking my voice in a sing-song fashion: "'<u>I</u> want to make a difference. <u>I</u> want to stop evil. <u>I</u> want to save the world.' It's always me, me, me. You just want <u>everything</u> to go your way, don't you?"

Looking for more encouragement, I turned to my closest friends.

Ellison was an intellectual. When I approached him in the university library, he was poring over Kant's Critique of Pure Reason. Every few seconds, he would nod approvingly, jot down some notes in the margin, and mutter to himself "How true!" When I interrupted him, he was chuckling over the absurdity of a certain metaphysical leap of faith, and arguing out loud, to no one in particular, "Yes, but what must Wittgenstein have thought?"

With great enthusiasm, I informed Ellison of my plans.

"Very interesting," he responded. "It leads us the obvious question of whether there really is a world out there which we can save. According to Hindu philosophy, this world is like a dream -- insubstantial, unreal, a product of our delusion."

"Huh?"

"Let me quote Emerson on this point...."

"Um, really, no thanks, I've got to get going."

Ellison chased after me. "Wait, wait!" he called out as I fled the room. "If you're really going to attempt to save the world, just keep in mind the words of H.L. Mencken: 'For every complex problem, there is a simple solution. Unfortunately, it is wrong.'"

*   *   *

You may ask why I decided to save the world. It's rather simple:

I just didn't have anything better to do.

You know, some people like to do crossword puzzles to whittle away the hours of their life. Other people prefer to waste

9

away in front of the television set. Some people even enjoy reading novels to escape the grim reality which lurks outside their door. (But we won't get into that.)

As for myself, I prefer to indulge in a relentless battle against all the forces of evil in the world.

Before I made the momentous decision to save the world, I had found myself lost and confused. Like most young people today, I was among the "vocationally challenged." I had no idea what to do with my life, a problem that was exacerbated by the fact that I have no talents or skills of any kind. You might call me a jack of no trades.

When I was a child, I thought I would become a famous baseball player, the king of stolen bases. Unfortunately, as my little league coach soon pointed out to me, I actually had to reach first base in order to steal second. Thus ended my dreams of becoming a major league hero.

I then imagined I would become a great singer. At age seven, I was convinced that I was the reincarnation of Paul McCartney. My mother was not very supportive of my dreams; she had the insensitivity to observe that the legendary Beatles singer was still alive and thus incapable of being a candidate for reincarnation. I was undeterred.

In my room, I would play the Beatles records at full volume, and sing along. It was uncanny how I sounded exactly like Paul.

One day, I decided to give a concert for my fellow first-graders on the playground. I launched into my rendition of "A Hard Day's Night," but, without the benefit of a record player to drown out my voice, I suddenly didn't sound so good. All the dogs in the neighborhood started barking and squealing in pain. I gave new meaning to the word cacophony. Thus ended my dreams of becoming a musical genius.

So it went. For the next several years, everything I touched turned to pyrite. I barely passed through school, having achieved an unparalleled record of mediocrity. Then I went to work, got fired, went to work, got fired, and repeated the cycle each three to four months.

So I was 27 years old, unemployed, and living at home with my parents. I had failed at every job I had tried. In a dog-eat-dog world, I was a miniature poodle.

I had no idea what to do with my life. I attempted to get a job flipping burgers at McDonalds, but I flunked the intelligence test. I next went to look for work at Burger King, but they suspected me of trying to overthrow the monarchy. Nobody else would hire me either. So without any jobs on the horizon, I had a lot of free time on my hands.

That's when I decided I might as well save the world. I had nothing better to do.

* * *

My father burst into my room with some exciting news: "I've been thinking about it, son, and I've decided to give you my permission to go ahead and save the world. You can start after polo practice on Wednesday."

"Thanks, Dad. What changed your mind?"

"Well, your mother and I discussed this, and admittedly at first we thought it was a waste of time. But then we started thinking about what's really important:

"Money."

"What?" I responded in disbelief.

11

"You know, I think I was wrong when I dismissed the idea so easily before. You actually could make lots of money off of this. You could write a book about how you saved the world. Just imagine the profit potential! You would be famous, you could go on television, we could start giving tours of our home." My father looked like one of Pavlov's dogs, salivating on cue every time he mentioned money.

I protested vehemently against this ludicrous idea. "Dad, I have absolutely no writing talent."

"Who says you need talent to sell books? Look at half the authors on the New York Times bestseller list."

Looking around suspiciously to make sure no spy would alight to steal his ideas, my father revealed his marketing plans to me:

"Think about it -- you could offer all the solutions to society's problems. Everyone's tired of hearing about all our troubles. There are too many books out there with pessimistic titles like: *America: What Went Wrong*. Your book could be an antidote to despair. You could provide us with all the answers. You could show us a better vision of the future."

"But, Dad," I protested to deaf ears, "I'm no expert. I'm just a young person worried about the future. I just want to go out and find the real heroes: visionary people who are transforming the world, men and women who have developed innovative models of success in education, in economics, in the environment, and in justice. I thought I might tie all their ideas together into one big picture."

"Good! That's good! One young person on an adventurous search for all the solutions to the problems of the earth! I like it! It has movie potential. People are really interested in your generation. Just imagine the possibilities: 'One young slacker

12

throws off his chains of apathy and rises up in righteous anger to confront the hydra-headed demons that threaten Generation X.' Could you put some sex in it, some violence, you know, spice it up a bit?"

"Well, whatever, nevermind." I started to respond, but figured it wasn't worth it.

"You could sell a whole new line of personalized merchandise! Think about Scott Sherman action figures!"

"What, you think kids are going to get excited about the figure of a person sitting at his desk, doing research, and writing a book? Anyway, I don't want a million plastic dolls that look like me in every home in America, where a whole new generation of inquisitive toddlers is going to be pulling off my clothes to see if I'm anatomically correct."

"Why are you limiting yourself to America? You know the markets are opening worldwide --we could have every youngster in Zimbabwe vying for a 'Save the World' poster to put on their bedroom wall."

"Dad, there are a lot of children in Africa who don't even have a bedroom wall. They don't have a shelter over their heads or food enough to eat. That's precisely the point -- that's why I want to explore if there's a path to a better future."

"Oh, don't start preaching at me," said my father, who looked somewhat hurt and betrayed. "You need to take yourself a little less seriously. Have some fun. My God, you'd think the world was about to end, the way you go off on your self-righteous sermons." And with that, my father stormed out of the room, vowing never to return until I was ready to negotiate the foreign rights to my story.

*   *   *

13

When you're thinking about saving the world, it's a good idea to plan ahead.

How many times has this happened to you? You're about to save the world, but then there's a good show on television, and then you remember a few phone calls you have to return, and then you decide to go for a little snack. Before you know it, the day is over, and the world is still on a course for sure damnation and ruin. I hate when that happens.

So now I make sure to pencil it in on my schedule. You see, there it is, scribbled in my datebook: 2 to 4 p.m. -- SAVE THE WORLD. I managed to sandwich it in between my golf game in the morning and happy hour in the afternoon.

Boy, won't we have something to celebrate over drinks!

*   *   *

I had just entered the bar when I saw my friend Schadenfraude -- or "Shoddy," as I like to call him. It was not a happy hour for him. He looked to be in poor spirits, having just received some devastating news.

"Ellison won a prestigious scholarship," he lamented, as he poured his beer. There were seven empty beer bottles already littered on the table where Schadenfraude had been drinking alone.

"That's wonderful!" I exulted at the news about our mutual friend.

"Why do good things always happen to him?" Schadenfraude sulked. "He has all the luck. This scholarship is going to be paying him $40,000 a year to go to some exotic tropical island in the south Pacific. I'm smarter than he is. I should have gotten that scholarship."

"But you didn't even apply," I insisted. "You're not even a student."

"Oh, don't bring up such irrelevant little details," snapped Schadenfraude, who was a temp worker at Burger King. "The point is: everything good happens to Ellison." He downed his beer quickly, pouting about his relative misfortune. Then, all of a sudden, a little smile danced onto his face as he was struck by a hopeful thought: "Maybe he'll get malaria over there. Or maybe the oceans will rise because of global warming, and his little island will be submerged."

"Ellison is your friend!" I protested. "Aren't you happy for him?"

"I'd be happier for him if he wasn't always so successful. That's a really annoying quality in a person." Shoddy glared at me for a moment, then thought to himself how lucky he was at least to have me as a friend. I was never a threat. He could take comfort in knowing that he was always superior to me.

"Oh by the way," I changed the subject. "I almost forgot to tell you: I'm going off on a mission to save the world."

Schadenfraude almost lost his beer. "What?!?" he asked indignantly.

"I'm going to save the world," I repeated.

"Oh yeah?" he challenged, regaining his composure. "That's nothing. I'm going to save the universe."

"You can't save the universe!" I cried. "What are you going to do about entropy?"

"What's that?" he asked with a puzzled look on his face.

"You know, entropy. The second law of thermodynamics. It's something we learned about in ninth grade.

15

All things tend towards chaos and disorder. Things fall apart, the center cannot hold. Everything ends in the heat death of the universe."

"Don't be such a pessimist," Schadenfraude scolded me. "How do you expect to save the world with such a negative attitude? If you're going to let a few little obstacles like chaos, death, and disorder get in your way, you'll never get anything accomplished."

My friend started to barrage me with homilies about the power of positive thinking. "If you believe it, you can achieve it!" he insisted. I wondered if it was this self-confident motivational attitude that had earned him a minimum-wage job serving up burgers and fries. "You create your own reality," he added.

I decided to create the reality of my exit from the scene, fleeing a rapid fire of platitudes and clichés.

* * *

I have an embarrassing confession to make: I'm a virgin when it comes to saving the world. I've never done it before. So I'm not exactly sure how to do it. Where do you start?

I thought maybe I could look at a book and follow the diagrams, step-by-step. But, if there were any books like that in the library, they've either been burned or banned for being too controversial.

A few years ago, some people in the community were advocating that the schools should offer a class on the subject, but others argued it would corrupt the youth. They said that if you teach children about saving the world, they might actually go out and do it. So now what mostly happens is that kids have to figure out how to do it on their own, which can be rather dangerous.

16

A memory floats to me on the waves of the subconscious: When I was six years old, beginning to get very curious about the mysteries of life, I went to my Mom in search of answers.

"Mom, where do better worlds come from?"

She had an embarrassed, awkward look on her face.

"John, the boy's asking about... well, you know... the facts of real life," she called to my father.

"Well, you'd better deal with it," he called back from the living room where he was too busy watching TV and drinking a beer to handle such mundane matters.

"Well, you see," she began clumsily, "there comes a time when two people love each other very much. In fact, not just two people -- millions of people, all living in a spirit of love for each other, and brotherhood and sisterhood, where differences based on race and religion don't seem to be so important anymore...."

My father was listening in from the other room and was growing very concerned at this radical talk. "What kind of trash are you teaching this kid?" he asked, as he rushed into the kitchen. "You want to pervert his mind at such an early age? Listen, kid, it's the stork. The stork delivers a better world, and everyone lives happily ever after."

That's all I ever learned. I still don't really know how to save the world.

*   *   *

On the street outside the bar, I had a chance encounter with my old friend Rainbow. She and I had grown up together, but we had lost touch when she went off to college at Berkeley. There she had become a modern-day hippie, a refuge from the 1960's, invariably attired in tie-dye shirts, cut-off jeans, and

Birkenstock sandals. I even heard rumors that she had joined a cult.

After she left Berkeley, I didn't receive news about Rainbow for several years. Then one day, when passing a newsstand, I saw her face gracing the cover of Fortune Magazine. She was now a multi-millionairess. In fact, she had become one of the richest women in America by starting her own business, selling men's perfumes.

At the time she came up with this entrepreneurial idea, everybody thought she was crazy. "Most men don't wear perfume," her critics assailed the idea.

"That's why I'm going to develop a line of perfumes that have no detectable odor," Rainbow patiently explained. "I'm going to call it 'The Emperor's New Colognes.' Men won't have to worry about giving off some musky, artificial scent."

"So why would anyone buy it?" asked her investors.

"Status," she replied.

Her advertisements spread a mystique: Men who wore these scentless perfumes would become more masculine, sexy, and successful. Wearers of the cologne were irresistible and invincible, if not quite immortal. Anyone who dabbed on the Emperor's New Colognes would find instant popularity, prosperity, and happiness.

Many of her advertisements did not even show the perfume at all. She would offer scenic photographs of rugged cowboys on horseback in Monument Valley, with the strong, individualistic slogan underneath: "An Empire of His Own." To attract adolescent boys, she created cartoon billboards that showed a very hip, bohemian unicorn surrounded by beautiful women. The message was subtle, but as powerful as a pheromone: Joe Unicorn, the horny ungulate, was so popular

18

with the human females for one reason and one reason only -- he wore the Emperor's New Colognes.

Within a year, Rainbow had earned $100 million dollars.

The nouveau riche entrepreneur insisted that she was a businesswoman with a conscience. For instance, she was quick to point out that no real unicorns were harmed in the making of her product. She also touted her perfumes as non-toxic, non-fat, and non-denominational. All the ingredients were natural. In fact, there was just one ingredient -- water -- and it came straight from Mother Nature, by way of the tap in her bathroom.

It had been years since we had talked in person. I was afraid that, with her newfound fame and success, she might disregard her old acquaintances. But she seemed genuinely pleased to see me.

"Who are you again?" she asked.

I explained to her how we had lived next door to each other from the time we were four years old, how we had dated for three years in high school, and how we had gone to the senior prom together, where she had unceremoniously dumped me for another man. A dull glimmer of recollection slowly dawned upon her face.

"Yes, of course -- Steve!" she said.

"Scott," I corrected her.

"Yes, of course -- Scott. It's so good to see you. I think about you all the time. So what are you doing with yourself nowadays?"

"I'm going to save the world," I told her with glee, unable to contain my excitement.

"Been there, done that," she yawned, unable to hide her ennui.

"What?!?" I exclaimed.

"That's so passé," she informed me. "I mean, like, I don't wanna be rude or anything, but saving the world is getting pretty mundane nowadays. It's just so trite. It's like you're still living in 1995. Don't you know that it's not hip anymore to be an activist? It's like totally out of fashion. Get with the program."

I apologized for my apparent inability to keep up with the latest trends. "What's the current vogue?"

"Shopping," she smiled. "It's an oldie, but a goodie. A classic that never seems to go out of fashion. Yes, there's nothing quite like the thrill of the hunt -- catching the unmistakable scent of new clothes, new toys, new gadgets and gidgets, gizmos and gazoos!"

"Gazoos?" I asked.

"Yes!" she exclaimed. "It's the American way of life: Shop until you drop! It doesn't matter what sorts of useless or frivolous items you buy: they'll probably all be obsolete, out-of-date, or out of fashion in a year, anyway!" She winked at me conspiratorially, as if we were privy to some wonderful inside joke.

Before I even had time to respond, she was already preparing to leave.

"This was fun," she said with all the sincerity she could possibly fake. "We'll definitely have to get together again soon," she added, which I interpreted as a clear signal that she never wanted to see me again.

"Now if you don't mind me, I have to get to a sale at Macy's. If the end of the world is really coming soon, there's a lot of shopping I still need to get done." And with those final words, she left me for the mall.

*　　*　　*

I went off searching for solutions to the environmental crisis.

I began at the university -- the ivory tower where we send our best and our brightest. I myself had never been smart enough to attend college. I had always imagined it as the place where the finest young minds were cultivated and the most important knowledge developed.

When I arrived on the campus, a party was in progress with twelve full kegs. A fraternity was busy welcoming its new recruits by trying to induce early cirrhosis of their livers. In an apparent attempt to expand the frontiers of human knowledge, they were performing dozens of empirical studies of the effect of alcohol on adolescent males. Many of the young college students were generously donating their own brain cells for the advancement of science.

I hurried past the inebriated crowds, and rushed to the School of Natural Resources. There I stepped into a class called "Introduction to Environmental Issues," taught by the respected Professor Phineas Smogg.

Professor Smogg was the world's leading authority on transgendered voles in the Tasmanian outback. He had published over 250 articles on this subject, two of which had even been read by other scholars in the field. He carried himself with a supercilious air, as if his expertise on Tasmanian voles made him brilliant enough to make definitive pronouncements on every other subject from the national health care policy to the future of the stock market.

Now he stood in front of the class, reading the contents of the course.

"The first week we're going to talk about toxic waste," he said, "followed by a review of species destruction, then we're going to air our dirty emissions. We'll spend the next several weeks speaking about global warming, the ozone hole, habitat destruction, loss of biodiversity, and the disproportionate impacts of environmental problems on poor people and people of color. Any questions?"

I raised my hand from the back of the class. "Yes, are we going to talk about solutions at all?"

"I don't know what kind of rabble-rouser you are," the professor shouted me down. "This class is about critical thinking. It's not our aim to present constructive solutions, which would only be an imposition of my white, male, patriarchal ideas upon the rest of the classroom. Instead, I am presenting a Marxist critique, a feminist critique, and a deconstructionist critique on the causes of the environmental crisis."

"Well, after we're through deconstructing, can we start to construct a vision of something better?"

"I'm afraid we just don't have time for such an academic exercise."

The teaching assistant was in tears by now. "This is a really hard class to get through," he admitted to the students. "We're going to form a support group to get us through the semester, if anyone wants to deal with their unresolved feelings of despair, hopelessness, and rage."

"What about guilt?" asked one woman eagerly. "After all, we are the cause of most of the environmental problems, aren't we?"

"Excellent point," suggested the T.A. "That's the kind of insightful thinking we like to encourage here."

A bit disappointed, I left the university and went to the local library to browse through the environmental literature. I had a range of titles to choose from: "The Population Bomb," "Our Stolen Future," and "Silent Spring," to name but a few of the more upbeat selections. I half-expected to find a book called: "The End of the World in 80 Days."

I opened up a book at random. It looked like it could have been written by Professor Smogg. Chapters 1 through 19 detailed the extent of the environmental crisis in excruciating detail with statistics, charts, and pictures to exacerbate the reader's despair. Finally, in the concluding chapter to the book, the author proposed solutions. He called for a worldwide revolution in values, a new ecological consciousness, and a dramatic change in the way we think.

It was brilliant. It was bold. It was totally unrealistic.

I searched all the other books for anything more than lofty ideals and vague proposals. I came away defeated.

Finally, I made a pilgrimage to meet Robert Cassandra, a prominent leader of the environmental community. I was desperately seeking some answers.

As I sat down in his office, I noticed a poster of Kermit the Frog on the wall. The caption underneath read: "It's Not Easy Being Green."

Cassandra caught me looking at his office decor. "Kermit doesn't realize how bad it's become," he caustically remarked. "It's bad. It's worse than bad. It's catastrophic, titanic, disastrous, egregious, horrendously horribly bad!"

I wondered to myself whether Cassandra had to pay a royalty to Roget's thesaurus every time he spoke.

"Our current society is completely unsustainable!" he preached with all the hellfire and brimstone he could manage. He proceeded to chant a litany of complaints about the world being hopelessly screwed up.

"Yes," I agreed enthusiastically, already a convert to the cause, "but what can we do about it?"

"Send more money to our organizations," he instructed. "Then we'll send you lots of junk mail and newsletters, telling you about how the world is getting even worse. We'll keep you abreast of all the latest tragedies, calamities, and disasters."

"Isn't there any good news?" I prayed. "I already know that humans are on a collision course with nature. Don't you have any vision of what a sustainable society might look like? Do you know how we can create solutions to the environmental crisis?"

"We can't waste our time with that," he bellowed. "We have to bankrupt the World Bank, battle the multinational companies, and combat the Misfortune 500 corporations. We've got to fight the powerful forces who are destroying the world. We can't indulge in trivial matters like proposing better alternatives."

As Cassandra looked at me, he just shook his head with pity and compassion. "Solutions," he chuckled to himself. "How very naive."

"I'm very sorry for interrupting your busy day," I apologized to the environmental leader, as I rose to leave. "Now if you'll excuse me I've got to catch the last train to Armageddon. Have a nice day."

*   *   *

A funny thing happened on the way to the apocalypse.

The night after I met with Cassandra, I had a really strange dream. Now I don't usually like to tell people about my dreams, because you might start to psychoanalyze me, telling me that I've

24

got some sort of oedipal complex or delusions of grandeur. But, against my better judgement, I'm going to reveal to you my reveries. They may prove to be important to the story:

You see, I was at a train station, trying to get a one-way ticket to Armageddon. Unfortunately, everybody seemed to be headed in that same direction. All the tickets were booked.

Looking for an alternative means of transportation, I found myself at a stable, where a shadowy figure with a large scythe was renting horses. He was completely enshrouded in robes of black, probably to avoid too much exposure to the sunlight. With the hole in the ozone layer, you have to be pretty careful about getting skin cancer nowadays.

"I need to get to the apocalypse," I said.

"You're in luck," he said jovially. "We have a group of three who were headed right that way. We were looking for a fourth horseman. Pestilence just came down with the flu."

I jumped upon a blood-red steed, which quickly started galloping on the road towards doom. Looking at the horseman next to me, I noticed he was gaunt and anorexic, all skin and bones.

"What's your name?" I asked. He glared at me for intruding into his personal business. Finally he replied with a single word: "Famine."

"What kind of parents are cruel enough to name their kids Famine?" I thought to myself. Just imagine all the teasing he must have had to endure in school when he was growing up! It's no wonder he was so thin, probably feeling like he had to live up to a certain svelte body image -- impossible standards of beauty which his parents had clearly imposed. I dared not voice these thoughts out loud at risk of offending my new friend.

"So, got any hobbies?" I asked, just to make conversation. I mean, there's no reason why riding off to certain doom and destruction should be boring. As long as we were all going on the journey together, I thought we should get to know each other better.

"Starvation, drought, inequitable distribution of resources," he started to make a list.

"Oh, so you're into that whole S & M scene, are you?" I asked. I had never met a sadomasochistic before. This was all getting rather exciting.

I looked at the horseman on the other side of me. He was carrying several nuclear warheads and intercontinental ballistic missiles, weighing down his stallion.

"You really should pack more lightly," I offered a bit of friendly advice. "I mean, I'm sure you can get most of these things when we get to Armageddon. They may be a bit more expensive there -- you know, they raise the prices for tourists and all, but you can always haggle."

The horseman just glared at me. I swear, some people just can't take a bit of constructive criticism. I was only trying to help.

My belligerent travelling companion opened up his heavy flak army jacket to reveal an extensive personal gun collection that would have made Genghis Khan look like a pacifist by comparison. "Isn't this a bit of overkill?" I thought to myself. "This guy must be suffering from a real sense of insecurity and paranoia." Then I noticed that he had a spear protruding from his chest that stuck clear through his body.

"Uh, you might want to look into that," I stuttered. "I'm sure there must be a hospital in the next town. You want to get that treated before it gets infected."

"My name is War!" he roared with anger.

"Yes, yes, enough with the formalities. We'll have plenty of time for personal introductions later. I really do think our first priority is to see a doctor about your condition.

"Does anyone know of a medical center around here?" I asked the other two horsemen. Famine was secretly eating a spam sandwich, which he tried to conceal when I caught him in the act. The last rider, the Grim Reaper himself who had sold me on this package deal to Armageddon, came galloping along to see what was the matter. Suddenly he threw off his shroud, only to reveal his true identity.

"Dad! What are you doing here?" I exclaimed.

"Shhhh!" he whispered. "I've come to rescue you."

"Rescue me?" I asked. "I was going off on a little weekend getaway to Armageddon. They say it's hotter than hell down there, but the brochures looked pretty nice: Heavenly angels blowing trumpets. God himself coming to pass judgement on us all. A climactic battle between the forces of good and evil. You don't get that kind of entertainment in many other places, outside of Las Vegas. And I've heard the food is pretty good, too."

"Don't surrender to the dark forces of doom and gloom," my father urged.

"Yeah," I said, "like I should take advice from a guy who's dressed as Death."

"I've come to take you home," he insisted.

"Dad, you're embarrassing me in front of my new friends!" I complained.

"Don't worry," interrupted Famine. "This is just a dream you're having. You can always escape from your father's voice of responsibility. Just imagine yourself someplace else."

Suddenly I dreamt myself on an airplane, still headed straight for the end of the world. My father had disappeared, but the horsemen of the apocalypse were still on my flight. I peered straight into the face of Death, to make sure it wasn't my Dad in disguise again. All I saw was a skeleton with a huge smile on its face.

"I love modern technology," said Death merrily. "It's so much more comfortable than riding on a horse all day."

I wasn't so sure about this. I was stuck in the economy class, sandwiched in a tiny seat right between Death and Famine. There was only enough arm room if you were the Venus de Milo.

Death continued to prattle on and on. He was a non-stop talker. "I'm really not as grim as rumors would have you believe," he said to me confidentially. "Actually, I can be just as much fun as the next guy." I thought to myself that this was certainly true, since the next guy happened to be Famine.

"I wonder if I should have bought airline insurance," Death pondered aloud. "I'm a little nervous about flying, to be quite honest, but you wouldn't believe how hard it is to get insurance coverage for someone who's already technically dead. I can't even get health coverage because they tell me it's a pre-existing medical condition.

"You know, being the Reaper is not as easy as you might think. Sure, you probably imagine all the glamour, the fame, the nightlife, the women. Well, let me tell you, it's not all fun and games." He began to list an entire catalogue of his hardships, clearly unaware that he was boring me to death.

Meanwhile, Famine started complaining about the scanty portions the airline was serving for its meals. "I'm starving here!" he said in a thick New York accent as he picked at his miniature bag of peanuts. To appease him, I offered him my microscopic bag of pretzels. I wasn't really hungry anyway. There's nothing like the imminent end of the world to put a damper on your appetite.

War was sitting by himself on the other side of the row. He was still surrounded by several nuclear missiles. A flight attendant was quickly alerted to the crisis, and she came running over.

"I'm sorry, sir," she said. "But you'll have to stow those atomic warheads underneath the seat in front of you, or in an overhead compartment." War blushed, his pale face turning red, and meekly complied with the orders.

We were getting closer to the end of the world when, suddenly, the plane was hijacked and taken back towards Los Angeles. I was indignant at this act of terrorism.

"It's OK," reassured Death. "L.A. really isn't all that different from Armageddon."

This was little consolation to me. I rushed to the front of the cabin to see who was responsible for this act of terrorism, only to receive the shock of my life. Sitting in the pilot seat was none other than my father. He had abruptly returned to my dream, seized control of the plane, and forcefully steered me away from the apocalypse.

"Dad!" I complained. "You keep embarrassing me!"

"Son, I only want the best for you," he informed me. "If I'm hijacking a plane, it's for your own good. You have to remember that this certainly hurts me more than it hurts you."

"Why won't you let me go to the day of judgment?" I whined. "Everyone else is doing it!"

"If everyone else jumped off the Empire State Building, would you do it too?" retorted my mother, who was sitting in the co-pilot's seat.

I did not have enough time to consider the possibility before my father leaped in with a lecture on filial duties: "I thought you were going to save the world," he reminded me. "After all the money your mother and I have invested in you, that's the least you can do for us."

"I gave up on saving the world," I explained. "It was just too hard. I went looking around for solutions, but all I found was a lot of negativity and despair. I finally figured I might as well just join the bandwagon to the apocalypse. After all, if the earth is being flushed down the toilet, why should I fight the flow?"

Indeed, I had made a firm decision to no longer rescue the planet. Of course, I realized it might require all the willpower I could muster. I had heard stories of so many people who had vowed not to save the world, but who kept slipping back into the activity in times of weakness.

But I had made a reputation as a quitter, and I wasn't about to change now. In even the easiest battles, I was always the first person to raise the white flag of surrender. I could give up faster than anybody I knew. As soon as I encountered any troubles in my life, I immediately hightailed into retreat. (Mind you, one is not born with such extraordinary cowardice. It's a skill that can only be cultivated with lots and lots of practice.)

"Let me tell you a story," said my father. He hadn't told me a story since I was a little child. "I once knew this radio broadcaster in San Francisco, a guy by the name of Scoop Nisker. Everyday he would come into the radio station, report the news, and get depressed. The day's headlines were full of death, disaster, devastation, and sorrow. But Scoop didn't want his listeners to get too swept up by despair, so at the end of every broadcast, he urged everyone out there to take action. 'If you don't like the news, go out and make some of your own,' he always used to say." My Dad looked at me with a sense of satisfaction, as if the message were self-evident and I would be roused to action.

"That's the whole story?" I asked.

"Well, I didn't say it was a good story! The point is that you've got to go out there and make a difference. Don't give up. I still think you should write a book about the solutions to the ecological crisis. The answers are out there, Scott, but almost nobody knows about them. Just go out and find them."

"Dad, I don't understand you," I said, a bit baffled and confused. "I thought you were only interested in profit margins."

"It was all an act," my father confessed. "Most children rebel against their parents' wishes. So I thought if I were very materialistic and consumed by thoughts of money, you might turn out to be socially concerned and dedicated to doing good for the world."

It was as if a revelation had come to me. Suddenly all my parents' behavior over the past two decades made sense -- the frequent trips to the shopping mall.... the profligate, wasteful spending on things they did not need.... the worship at the altar of the almighty dollar.... Oh, what sacrifices my parents had made for my sake! What noble, selfless souls they were to indulge in the pursuit of money for 25 years, just so I would rebel!

I now realized what I had to do: I bid my travelling companions farewell and I parachuted out of the plane. The next morning, I woke up refreshed, motivated, and ready to start anew on my mission to save the world.

At breakfast, I told my parents all about everything I had seen -- Death, Famine, War, and my father. "You were in my dream," I told my dad. "And I learned your secret."

My dad quickly grabbed me and took me aside into the living room. "Whatever you do, don't tell your mother!" Then he looked me in the eye and insisted, "It was years ago when I was young and foolish."

"I'm talking about how you're using reverse psychology on me," I clarified. "You know, how you only pretend to be so obsessed with money because you wanted me to rebel against everything that was phony and materialistic about your lifestyle. And how you were always secretly hoping that I would go out and make a lasting contribution to humanity."

"Oh, well, yeah, of course," my father stumbled over his words, letting loose an audible sigh of relief. "Yeah, that's what I meant. Now, don't tell your mother," he winked. "It's our little secret."

I smiled and left the room, ready to resume my crusade to save the world. It was only after I left that my dad said aloud, to no one in particular:

"What a stupid dream."

*   *   *

That evening I went out to the local Chinese restaurant, where I would often see my friends. It was a popular hangout in the neighborhood, and I was always certain to run into some acquaintances. Much to my surprise, I came across Rainbow inside, frequenting the haunts where we had spent so much time as teens. She was sitting at a table, catching up with a few of our mutual friends from high school. I went over to the table, relishing the opportunity to unveil my exciting plans.

"Hey, Steve, how are you doing?" asked Rainbow. "You look excited about something. If you were glowing any more, I'd mistake you for nuclear waste."

32

"I'm going to write a book!" I told my friends with great enthusiasm.

"A book?" asked Schadenfraude. "Do they still make those anymore?"

"I was watching TV last night," replied Rainbow, "and I saw a report that the average American is more likely to be eaten alive by jackals than to read a book this year."

"I find that difficult to believe," protested Ellison. "I have known countless scholars who were insatiable readers of Derrida and Foucault, but only three of them were ever eaten alive by jackals."

"Hey, it was on TV," Rainbow argued in her own defense. "It must be true." As always, her impeccable logic silenced the critics. Nobody contradicts a millionaire.

"Anyway," I attempted to return to my subject, "I want to make this a blueprint for a better America. I want to find the best ideas for improving this country and making it into an ecologically sustainable nation."

"You want to tackle a serious problem?" challenged Schadenfraude. "I've got 289 channels on my TV, and there's never anything good to watch. Try solving that, Mr. Wizard!"

"That's so true!" Rainbow leapt back into the conversation. "Last night I had to watch 2 hours of reruns of America's Funniest Home Videos."

"Oh, that show is so funny!" exclaimed Ellison, letting drop his erudition. "Did you see that one where some guy was playing baseball and he got hit in the crotch? That was a classic!"

"Yeah and then there was the one with the three-year old driving the car," Schadenfraude laughed, then added with a confidential whisper, "Personally, I think they staged that one."

Suddenly the conversation became heated and passionate, as everyone started comparing their favorite episodes. Twenty minutes later there was a break in the conversation when a waiter brought us dinner.

"Oh anyway, I wanted to tell you a bit more about my book," I said, seizing the moment. Everyone did their best to feign interest, pretending to pay attention while they served themselves some szechuan chicken.

"You see, it starts out with this adventurous scene where the world's leading scientists get together -- almost 1700 of the most brilliant people in the world, including a majority of the Nobel Prize winners still alive today. This is a true story. This really happened back in 1992. And they said -- and these are the real quotes here -- that as few as 10 years remained before the earth would be 'irretrievably mutilated' and 'the prospects for humanity immeasurably diminished.'" I looked triumphantly around the table with a smug sense of satisfaction that comes with delivering terrible news.

"Huh, that's interesting," yawned Ellison. "Could you please pass the egg foo yung?"

I passed the Chinese food across the table. "I just saw this thing on TV the other night about some really brilliant scientists," said Rainbow. "They say that they may be able to develop this new type of material that lets you get a tan while you're wearing clothes."

The conversation took off from there. Over the mushu pork, my friends excitedly discussed the best tans they ever had, the worst sunburns they ever had, the time that Rainbow accidentally exposed herself when working on improving her tan-line at the beach, the prospects for surfing at the beach this coming week, the acquaintances they had met at the beach last week, the gossip about the acquaintances they had met at the beach last week, and a full blow-by-blow account of who was sleeping with whom among our mutual friends. Then the fortune cookies arrived.

"SMILE AND THE WHOLE WORLD SMILES WITH YOU," read Schadenfraude, frowning. "That's not a fortune!" he complained. "It's more like a statement of fact. And it's not really even true."

"CONFUCIUS SAYS: HE WHO LAUGHS LAST IS USUALLY THE SLOWEST AT UNDERSTANDING THE JOKE," Ellison read. We all broke into hysterics, except for Schadenfraude who was jealous that he hadn't chosen that fortune cookie.

"YOU WILL BE EATEN ALIVE BY JACKALS," read Rainbow. "Oh, that's rather unfortunate. I guess I won't be able to read your book, Steve."

I was the last to open my fortune cookie. Nothing was inside.

*   *   *

For the next several years, I went and did research. I discovered dozens of brilliant people who had fascinating ideas for solving our nation's problems. These were not utopian schemes or dreams. They were practical plans, forged in the crucible of experience. All the best ideas were out there. It was just that few people had heard of them.

I spent hours each day exploring in libraries, seeking out manuscripts with solutions. On a shoestring budget, I travelled across the country, interviewing some of the impressive visionaries. Then I toiled for countless hours each day, painstakingly composing my manuscript, a book about all the solutions. Finally, after four years of work, starving on my unsustainable savings account, in which I sacrificed everything for the book, I decided to send it to publishers and literary agents.

I was turned down by every one. I felt like I should be on a list of "America's Least Wanted." I calculated that 17 acres of trees had been cleared to produce all the paper for my rejection letters.

I'll give you an example of how hard it was: One day, I walked into the offices of one literary agent, a woman named Bess Bestsellerstein. She had legally changed her name from Elizabeth Jones in order to get the attention of publishers and clients. The strategy had evidently worked; she was inundated with requests for her services. Somehow, through a contact of my dad's, I had managed to get an appointment to meet her in her inner sanctum.

I was ushered into a room covered in the most chic postmodern art. In one corner was a toilet that had been painted bright green by Andy Warhol and sold for two million dollars. Directly across from it was a priceless work by the neo-nihilist master Buddha von Warburg: a blank canvas, expressing the essential meaninglessness of the universe. On the walls hung dozens of photographs of the distinguished Ms. Bestsellerstein, hobnobbing with celebrities. The only thing the room did not contain was books.

Behind the desk sat the agent, a no-nonsense woman who was famous for maximizing the use of her time. As she beckoned me forward into her room, she was smoking two cigarettes, drinking coffee, shuffling through papers, and haranguing a client over the phone. When she finally hung up, I had the opportunity to hand her my manuscript.

"This is a book about the end of the world," I said to her.

"Is it a comedy?" she asked hopefully.

The question caught me off guard. "Um, well, no, not exactly," I stuttered. "It's more like a book about all the visionary ideas for saving the planet from imminent destruction."

"Boooooring." She dumped it into the wastebasket without looking at it.

"What?" I asked incredulously.

"I just don't think it will sell," she explained. "There's not a market for a book on solutions to the most intractable problems of our age. Try again in ten years."

"But the world's leading scientists have warned that we may have fewer than ten years left before it's too late to save the planet!"

"OK, then try again in 5 years. No, on second thought, nix that plan. Those scientists are really good at predicting ecological catastrophes, but they're not very good at predicting what will sell. OK, kid, you want some advice: Try writing some romance novels. Those are a hot commodity nowadays."

"I was hoping to write something that would save the world," I insisted.

"Couldn't you produce a book on something more marketable?" she asked. "Here's an example: this one manuscript came across my desk this morning. It's about a werewolf who's a bulimic Roman Catholic. Now that's a great story! This guy eats people, but doesn't want to put on any weight, so he vomits them up, and then goes to confession. It's called *You Can Eat the Body of Christ, But Not of His Disciples*. The bidding for this book started out at 2 million dollars. Already, fourteen movie studios have inquired about the rights."

"Can't I do anything with the manuscript that I have?" I persevered.

"It's just such a dry topic. I wish you would come up with a more exciting idea. Let's see...." She pulled my manuscript from the trash can and started flipping through the pages. "OK, well, you start with all these brilliant scientists getting together to declare that the world only has ten years left, yadda yadda yadda..... Frankly, it's kind of trite."

"But it's true!"

"When does truth ever sell books?" asked the agent. "People don't want to read about truth. That's why they're reading books in the first place -- to escape from the truth. You want to entertain your reading audience, not lecture them. Here's an idea: Maybe you can get all these leading scientists together and slowly, one by one, they are murdered. That would be dramatic. And it turns out that one of the scientists is actually an alien from the planet Zorkon-B in the further regions of the Andromeda Galaxy. Now let's add a love interest into the mix: let's say the alien is in love with the heroine of the story, the woman who's about to solve the crime. And she suspects that her lover may be the killer, but she doesn't want to betray him. Yes, this is good. This is good!"

I could not conceal the look of disappointment on my face.

"The bottom line is money," she explained unapologetically. "You know that I'm as concerned about the end of the world as anyone, but I've got a business to run...."

*   *   *

Ten minutes later, I left the office of the literary agent with my manuscript in shreds. Her final prophetic words still echoed in my mind: "Sex sells, and violence sells, but the truth shall set you free to join the unemployment lines." Come to think of it, my book <u>was</u> rather boring. It was preachy and pretentious. The prose was prosaic. The interviews were dull.

The battle to save the world ought to be the most exciting epic ever to be written. It should be a great adventure, the type of book you can't put down -- a rip-roaring tale of danger, mystery, and intrigue.

Just imagine the possibilities.....

Chapter 2

The sign on the door said, "Scott Sherman, private investigator." He had rented an office in the back of a dingy apartment building, thirteen steps up a creaking, wooden staircase that threatened to collapse right under his blistering feet.

There had been a time when his surroundings were better. Back in the days of the communist threat, he had been a secret agent in the plush Virginia headquarters of the Central Intelligence Agency. Dispatched around the world to quell uprisings in Nicaragua and rebel movements in Angola, he had a résumé that would impress any foreign power. Of course, if you ever saw his résumé, he would have to kill you. Everything he did was supposed to be top secret.

Indeed, his international exploits would have all been confidential, except for the fact that some best-selling author kept writing books about him. It was rumored that Harrison Ford would play him in the movies.

But those glory days had long since ended with the downfall of the Soviet Union. No longer did Scott get sent to Berlin to match wits with East German spies. Gone were the good old days when he would infiltrate the command of the Russian communist party. It had been many a year since he had thwarted a sinister Soviet plot to destroy the Western democracies.

Now life was more mundane. After being downsized by the federal government, Scott had spent most of the next several years bumming around welfare lines and unemployment offices. It was only recently that he had gone back into business for himself, launching a one-man detective agency in the slums of San Francisco.

Now it was a late Friday afternoon, and the last golden light was filtering in through his windows, before the fog would roll in off the Pacific to obscure the setting sun. Scott was just preparing to leave his offices for the weekend.

Suddenly a sultry dame walked through his office door. He feared she might ask him to find her maltese falcon. He had fallen for that old trick before.

"Are you Sam Spade?" she asked.

"I'm sorry, miss, but I think you've got the wrong detective agency."

"How about Bond?" she pleaded. "James Bond?"

The woman seemed intelligent, but she had clearly never been informed about copyright laws. If Scott had ever attempted to appropriate the name of a fictional detective, he would have quickly found himself staring down the wrong end of a double-barreled lawsuit.

The woman sensed that she was not getting anywhere with her inquiries. She attempted a few more guesses, offering up the names of investigators from the best-selling works of Tom Clancy, Nelson DeMille, and Clive Cussler. Finally, exasperated by her fruitless search for a larger-than-life hero, she ventured up a last wild stab-in-the-dark: "Are you by any chance Scott Sherman?"

"You've heard of me?" he gasped. His veil of secrecy had fallen and left him indecently exposed.

"Of course," she claimed. "I know everything about you! I've heard how you stopped nuclear submarines from destroying the entire world. I've heard how you battled Soviet spies in Cuba during the heights of the Cold War. In fact, I've heard that you were single-handedly responsible for the collapse of the Soviet Union and the downfall of communism."

"All in a day's work," he humbly confessed.

"What have you been doing since the fall of the Berlin Wall?" she asked.

"Well," Scott replied, "you know, there aren't that many good spying opportunities for federal workers anymore. So I've gone private. I'm a detective now -- a gumshoe, an investigator. It's all pretty routine stuff: murders, kidnappings, and the occasional act of international terrorism. In my spare time, I thwart the sinister plans of evil Colombian drug lords. It's not all that glamorous, but it pays the bills."

"Very impressive, Mr. Sherman," she said. "But that's small stuff compared to the case I have for you."

"Let's start from the beginning," he cautioned her. "Who are you and what brought you here?"

"My code name is Potemkin," she replied. "I work for the United States government as an undercover secret agent. I've come to you with an important mission, personally authorized by the President himself."

Scott looked closely at his mysterious guest. She had an olive complexion, with dark piercing eyes and raven hair. There was something eerily familiar about her, as if he had seen her face in a newspaper somewhere. But he knew it was impossible; secret agents take pains to stay out of the public eye, no matter what the cost. He turned his attention back to the message his guest was about to deliver.

"Right now we're facing the greatest threat to national security since the nuclear arms race," the secretive woman continued. "But it's not from any foreign enemies. This time it's an inside job. We have reason to believe that there are underground forces within the United States that are working to destroy our country."

Scott was intrigued. "Tell me more," he urged.

"It all started a few years ago," she said. "At the time, everything looked wonderful in the country. America was at peace, our economy was prosperous, and the President was riding a tidal wave of popularity. We were not prepared for the bombshell that would hit us.

"The first sign of trouble came in a laboratory at Harvard University. Researchers had been conducting a study of men's fertility in this country. It should have been a routine research experiment. But it turned out to be disastrous.

"What the Harvard scientists discovered was shocking: sperm counts had dropped by 50 percent in just the last few decades. Even more disturbing was that many of the surviving sperms were mutated or defective. In other words, something was endangering the health of American men.

"Meanwhile, in research laboratories on the other side of the country, we were stunned to hear some equally troubling news about threats to the health of women and their children. Scientists were doing a routine study of the nutritional content of breast milk for babies. Yet their results caught them by surprise: They discovered that the average American woman has more toxic chemicals in her breast milk than is permissible in milk sold by dairies! If this were a product on the market, it would be banned by the Food & Drug Administration for jeopardizing the lives of our children!

"We started investigating further, searching for other evidence that something had gone terribly wrong in the country. We did not want to cause a panic, so we secretly began to look for scientific indicators of a problem. And, much to our dismay, we found them everywhere:

"For instance, when we did autopsies on a number of human bodies shortly after the time of death, we were alarmed to discover that they often contained excessive amounts of heavy metals and toxic chemicals -- so many, in fact, that they could officially be classified as hazardous wastes!

"In isolation, each of these incidents seemed strange. But together, they were downright frightening. They seemed to point to a much larger, deadlier crisis: In fact, we began to suspect that something -- or someone -- was poisoning the American public."

"Who would do something like this?" Scott asked. "It's psychotic!"

"We don't have any suspects," the woman confessed. "Indeed, this seems like the perfect crime. There are no witnesses. There is no smoking gun. There are no clues at all by which we could begin to solve this mystery. We're absolutely baffled. That's why we've come to you."

"What can I do?" the detective asked.

"Let me show you this videotape that the President has prepared for you. It will explain everything you need to know." She handed Scott a tape, which he placed in the VCR on his desk. The machine whirred and hissed, before projecting an image onto his small-screen television monitor. It was a warning from the FBI: "CLASSIFIED INFORMATION -- Top secret!"

Suddenly the familiar visage of the President appeared. He looked more haggard than usual, with his cheeks sallow and his brow deeply fissured. Scott hadn't seen him in several years, since the chief executive had presented him with the national Medal of Honor for his bravery in combat. As Scott watched the President prepare his text for the camera, he reflected on how much the commander-in-chief had aged from the stress of his office. He was not the same man Scott once knew.

"Scott, this is the most dangerous case we've ever assigned," the President began his confidential message. "We're dealing with forces like which we've never seen before.

"We're confronting an invisible crisis. Most Americans are completely unaware that we're in the midst of a threat far greater than the Soviet Union ever posed. With a foreign enemy, we can at least see their armed forces mobilizing on a border. We can intercept and decipher their secret codes, so that we can be prepared for their next attack. We can develop the best technology to locate their nuclear missiles and prepare ourselves for a full-scale confrontation. But the current crisis is almost impossible for the government to detect or diagnose -- let alone the average American. So we all go about with our business as usual, unaware that the blitzkrieg has already begun.

"Something deadly is happening to the human environment. This is not some wild theory, invented by an imaginative fiction writer. The information is all public, and it's been confirmed by the very best scientists in the world:

"I imagine that our agent has already described to you some of the toxic threats to humans. But there's substantial evidence that the dangers are far more widespread. There's a pattern of rapid ecosystem decay across the planet. All the lands on which our lives depend -- the lands where we get our food, our water, and our resources -- are deteriorating at an unbelievable rate.

"Last year, we lost an area of productive land the size of France. It simply vanished. Some of our most fertile soils have also disappeared, leaving only deserts behind, and these lands can never be recovered -- or at least not for thousands of years.

"Species are dying off faster than at any time in the past 65 million years. Some people says it's natural for certain types of species to go extinct each year, and that's true. But the current wave of extinctions is completely unnatural -- as many as 80 percent of all living creatures on the earth could be wiped out within the next few decades. It's like a hidden holocaust happening every single day, right within our borders."

Scott listened to the President's warnings with growing concern. Of course, he had heard about the environmental crisis earlier in the decade, back when it was the fashionable cause. But it had ceased to be much of a topic in the news anymore. It didn't seem to affect the detective in his own life. He couldn't feel global warming in his air-conditioned apartment. He couldn't see the forest for all the clearcut trees. Somehow, it didn't seem very real to him.

To be quite honest, Scott had mostly ignored environmental issues up until now. He always assumed that someone else would take care of the problems. Perhaps the situation wasn't as severe as all the scientists had predicted. Perhaps if he didn't think about the ecological crisis, it would just go away.

Now it sounded like the problems hadn't gone away. If anything, they were getting worse.

"We need you to investigate this crime immediately," insisted the President. "This assignment may not seem as serious or threatening as when you were sneaking into the Kremlin, stealing the nuclear secrets from the hands of a ruthless madman. But it's even more perilous than you think, precisely because you can't see the death and destruction in front of your eyes.

"According to our top scientific advisors, we have only one year left. If we don't solve the crisis within the next 12 months, it may be too late --"

Chapter 3

The screen went black. The room was flooded with silence, as the detective considered the impossible task before him.

"How can I start an investigation like this?" Scott finally inquired. "Do we have any leads at all?"

"In the Pacific Northwest, there's a man who claims he's discovered a crucial piece of evidence," Potemkin offered. "But be careful. The enemy already seems to know our every move...."

Far away, several people laughed as they eavesdropped on the conversation. The hidden tap in the detective's office had worked its usual magic; every word was being recorded, every plan would be revealed. Scott was about to fall right into their trap.

Chapter 4

"That was a very short chapter," remarked my mother.

"Well, you know how it is today," I attempted to explain. "The average American has a very short attention span."

My mother wasn't listening anymore. She had already turned her interest to a zany television sitcom about a bulimic Roman Catholic werewolf. It was based on an international bestseller.

"So Mom," I called to her, trying to win her attention back from the television show. "What do you think of my book so far?"

"Well, it's not very believable," she said, annoyed that I was interrupting her favorite program. "You think anyone is going to buy the idea that there are toxics poisoning our environment?" She popped some fluorescent orange Cheetos snacks into her mouth, and started watching the television again.

"Everything in the chapter was true!" I insisted. "I mean, sure, I'm not really a detective, but all the facts and statistics were taken from real life. Don't you realize that there really is a huge environmental crisis that threatens all life on this planet? It may only be a matter of years before the end of the world as we know it!"

"Well, I'll deal with that when it happens," my mother retorted. "I've got a lot more important things to worry about right now. Did you hear that Delilah has incurable cancer?"

"Who's Delilah?" I gasped.

"Oh, she's this character on *Days of Our Lives*. She's been on the soap opera for 22 years, and I'm so upset that they would kill her now. It just sets the stage for her evil twin, you know."

A tear formed in my mother's eye. I decided it was best to leave her to her television shows. I would return to my epic adventure....

Chapter 5

The twin-propellor airplane looked like a relic from the Second World War. It hummed and buzzed at it passed ten thousand feet above the Cascades.

Scott looked down upon the mountain range from his seat on the plane. Even at this height, he could see the damage done by clearcuts of the forest. Vast tracts of the mountainsides were barren of life, looking like fallout from a nuclear war.

Was there any description of how much destruction had taken place here? The detective reviewed the dossier that Potemkin had given him before sending him off on his mission. On the first page, he found a description by David Orr, a professor of environmental education at Oberlin College in Ohio:

> "If today is a typical day on planet Earth,
> we will lose 116 square miles of rainforest,
> or about an acre a second. We will lose
> another 72 square miles to encroaching
> deserts.... We will lose (up to) 250 species."

Scott tried to imagine what it meant to lose almost 200 square miles of productive land every day. But the figures seemed incomprehensible to him.

As the plane approached Seattle-Tacoma airport, he searched for information about Alan Thein Durning, the man he would be meeting. According to the file, Durning had been a senior researcher at the Worldwatch Institute in Washington, D.C. where he had increasingly become concerned about the dangerous trends that threatened the environment. He began investigating what were the forces causing this unprecedented destruction. As he slowly unraveled the mystery, he realized that he was putting his own life in jeopardy. There were powerful vested interests that did not want this information released to the public.

The file did not reveal anything more than this. What had Durning discovered? A veil of secrecy covered over everything, dimly obscuring the truth.

Two hours later, Scott was ready to hear the answers. Durning had greeted him at the airport, and they had driven in an unmarked car to a well-concealed underground laboratory in the mountains. It was deep in the old-growth rainforest, a hike of several miles from the nearest parking lot. As they walked to their destination through a sea of green tendrils, mosses, ferns, and vines, Durning said nothing, but kept looking behind him suspiciously, to ensure they were not being followed. Finally, they came across a grove of towering red trees, with trunks as thick as forty feet in diameter. Durning took out a small remote control device, pressed a button, and watched as a camouflaged door slid open in one of the trees.

"Follow me," Durning ordered, breaking his mysterious silence, as he entered into the doorway. To any observer, it would have seemed as if the two men had vanished into the tree trunk. The hidden door led to an elevator that whisked them 75 feet underground. They stepped out into a sleek, post-modern computer room, filled with strange futuristic machines.

"Welcome to my personal laboratory," Durning greeted his guest. "Right now we're standing under one of the last stands of virgin old-growth forest in the world. 98 percent of the original forests have been decimated, logged for cheap timber, and cleared for easy profits.

"Most people have no idea how drastic the situation has become," the environmental researcher continued. "It's not easy to see the increasing devastation that occurs so many miles from the arena of our daily lives. You may not realize the magnitude of the danger you're facing. So I've developed this virtual reality simulation."

He offered Scott some large goggles that covered half the detective's face. Then he connected electrodes to the arms and legs of his guest. Scott felt enveloped in darkness, floating in ethereal space.

"Are you ready?" asked Durning.

As soon as Scott assented, an entire new world suddenly surrounded him. He was transported into a veritable Garden of Eden, teeming with abundant life. Lush forest canopies rose over his head, while waterfalls poured forth in front of him into rushing river rapids. Brightly colored toucans and parrots fluttered through the trees above. Everything was a deep shade of green -- alive, vibrant, and dynamic.

Suddenly, in a split second, the forest disappeared around him as quickly as it had appeared. Death razed the scene: the trees were gone, the birds had vanished, and an ominous silence filled the empty desert landscape. Only a few stumps and stray logs remained as a reminder that a forest had ever existed in this vast, ugly wasteland.

Scott could see this destruction spreading like a virus across the landscape. As far as his eye could see, the forests were receding, dying, and evanescing into nothing.

Durning pressed a button, and Scott suddenly found himself looking down on the scene from the skies. Every second, he witnessed another acre swept barren by this unstoppable plague. A wall of flames 50 feet high consumed everything in its path, moving across the rainforests at speeds too fast for the human eye to follow.

A deafening scream filled the air. Out of the sky, a commercial airline jet came spinning out of control, hurtling towards the ground, and exploding upon impact. Human bodies were thrown everywhere, and then incinerated in the ball of fire.

"What was that?!?" Scott asked in a panic. Everything seemed all too real in this virtual simulation. He felt like a personal witness -- perhaps even a voyeur -- to this bloody, violent scene of human mutilation.

"Those are the human results of this ecological devastation," Durning responded. "Every day, thousands of people die of starvation as a result of the destruction of their productive lands. It's the equivalent of a full passenger airliner crashing every few minutes, and killing everyone on board."

"Stop this, please," Scott insisted. "I can't take this anymore."

Durning turned off the machine, returning his guest to the safety of the real world. The virtual nightmare was over.

Scott could not stop trembling from the experience, while involuntary waves of nausea churned his stomach. He could not speak, and his face had turned deathly pale.

"Don't think that, just because the virtual reality simulation has finished, those tragedies you saw aren't repeating themselves every second," Durning instructed. "What you saw was a dramatic re-creation of the tragedy that is ravaging the entire planet right now, as we speak, in countless invisible ways. This year we will lose an amount of rainforest equal to the size of this entire state of Washington. 60 million people will starve, suffering horrible, gruesome deaths, because of the degraded ecosystems.

"Now you've hopefully gotten an idea of the immensity of this tragedy. It's no longer an abstraction to you. The statistics have turned into real flesh-and-blood humans who are dying before your eyes. You've seen the hidden holocaust behind all the dry, lifeless numbers."

"But why?" Scott demanded to know. "I was told that you've discovered some clues as to who might be causing this."

"Indeed," replied the researcher. "Why don't you come over to my computer?"

The two men walked to a large video monitor with a colorful map of the Olympic National Forest displayed on the screen. The areas that had been clear cut and raped were clearly marked on the map.

"I've developed a series of images that show the regions of the state with the worst ecological damage," Durning explained. He pressed a few keys on his database, and other maps alternated on the screen. "Then I did an analysis of who owns the land, and who is responsible for the clear cutting.

"The largest private stands of old-growth forest in Washington are owned by the Millhouse family. They have signed a contract with the Greenleaves Corporation to remove trees from their lands for export to foreign nations...."

52

"Wait a second," interrupted Scott. "Are you talking about the family of Richard Millhouse, the billionaire who made his fortune in coal?"

"Yes," responded Durning. "They're listed in Fortune Magazine as one of the 50 richest families in the world. But wait, there's more: I started looking into the major stockholders in the Greenleaves Corporation. This was the list of names that resulted when I did a financial search."

Durning typed a few more commands on his computer, until the names of several individuals scrolled down the screen:

Arnold Rockefeller, Jr.

Robert Vanderbilt III

Henry Ford VI

"This are some of the wealthiest people in America!" Scott exclaimed. "All of these people are corporate executives or heirs to family fortunes."

"That's right," Durning nodded solemnly. "The trail of destruction leads right into the mansions of the wealthiest, most powerful people in the United States. We're exposing the members of this country's elite, the people who pull the strings of power on Wall Street, to a potentially devastating scandal."

"I can't believe this!" Scott exclaimed. "Our enemies are among the most respected, famous names in America. No wonder they're trying to stop us from revealing this information. This is shocking."

"It gets worse," Durning reported. "The major landholder in the Pacific Northwest is not a private individual at all. It's the federal government. When I started delving into the practices of the United States, I found something I could not believe. I checked the figures again and again, but the results were conclusive every time: the U.S. government is subsidizing the cost of clearcutting on federal lands. In other words, they're letting these major corporations strip away the forests and mountains for bargain basement prices. It's a form of corporate welfare. The rich are getting richer at the expense of the American public, and the government is in on the plan."

"So this could implicate all our political leaders in the crime," Scott cried.

"Unfortunately," acknowledged Durning, "we're taking on all the forces of political and financial power in this country. It's not just the barons of Wall Street, or the rich people who are listed in the Fortune 500. We're up against the members of Congress. We're up against the President himself."

"What?!?" Scott gasped.

Durning confirmed his deepest fears: "Yes, all the evidence points straight to the Oval Office."

Chapter 6

"This doesn't make any sense," complained the literary agent. "How could all the incriminating evidence point to the President? He's the person who hired you to solve the crime!"

"Well, that's why this is a mystery," I explained. "Just wait and see what happens."

What happened took even me by surprise. There was a loud knock on my door. "Open up!" a voice shouted. "This is an emergency!"

I rushed to the door, and found a corporate attorney standing on my front porch. He was impeccably dressed in a three-piece suit, and his hair was slicked back in the style of a Mafia don. His greedy, beady eyes peered out at me from above the gold rims of his bifocals.

"I represent the Vanderbilts, the Fords, the Rockefellers, and every other Fortune 500 family that you slandered in your last chapter," he said. "We're suing you for defamation."

"What?!"

"Here's the subpoena," the lawyer said. "You'll see all the indictments against you: wanton and willful misrepresentations of the truth; intentional infliction of emotional distress; heresy against the capitalist system; and arbitrary and atrocious writing."

"There's no crime against bad writing!" I protested.

"No, but there ought to be," the lawyer replied.

"You're suing me for 500 billion dollars?" I asked in amazement, as I read the subpoena in my trembling hands.

"You've irreparably harmed the reputations of my clients," the attorney insisted. "How can they go on with their international dominance of global markets after this? What will they say to their stockholders?"

"That's funny," I interrupted. "I heard that the stocks in their companies skyrocketed after I published all the details about how much they raped and pillaged the earth in the name of making a profit."

"OBJECTION!" the attorney screamed, as if he were in a court of law. "That's irrelevant! Immaterial! He's badgering the prosecution! Who's on trial here, anyway?" The attorney cast an evil eye upon me, before making his final pronouncement: "I swear we will not rest until justice has been purchased!"

"Maybe we can work out a deal," I pleaded.

"Now you're speaking my language," replied the lawyer, as we sat down for a negotiation. "Why don't you move on to the next chapter, while we figure out how you can remedy the situation...."

Chapter 7

This Chapter brought to you by Microsoft

Scott was troubled. He grabbed a pack of Marlboro cigarettes, and reached for a match. "There's nothing like a good smoke to relieve your tensions," he said to Durning.

"I didn't know you smoked," Durning looked at him quizzically.

"I don't," Scott whispered in a confidential tone. "It's just a product endorsement." He took a drag of the cigarette, and immediately launched into a fit of coughing, hacking, and wheezing.

"So what are you going to do about this crisis?" Durning asked, as he took a refreshing sip of Coca Cola. "How are we going to stop the President from his illegal actions?" The scientist leaned back in his chair, and kicked his stylish Nike shoes up on the table. He was dressed casually, yet elegantly, in Dockers pants from Levi Strauss, and a Calvin Klein original shirt (now on sale at your local Walmart). Even in the midst of a world-threatening crisis, Durning could maintain his impeccable sense of fashion.....

Chapter 8

I had not been writing for more than a few minutes on my new, improved version of the book (tentatively entitled "It's the End of the World as We Know It, and I Could Use an Absolut Vodka"), when my concentration was interrupted by yet another knock on my door.

This time it was a young man who looked like a respected scholar. He was tall and lanky, with big glasses perched upon his nose. He carried an unwieldy sheaf of papers under his arm, which threatened to blow away in the brisk wind outside.

"Can I help you?" I inquired. "I'm really very busy right now, working on my book."

"Actually, that's what I wanted to talk to you about," the polite young man responded. "You see, somehow I got dragged into your fictional plot against my will. Please allow me to introduce myself: I'm Alan Durning."

My jaw dropped. I sensed another lawsuit in the air.

"I just wanted to set the record straight," he said irritably. "I don't actually endorse all those corporate products in the last chapter. In fact, almost <u>nothing</u> you've written about me in this book is true. I don't have some sort of hidden underground laboratory, brimming with the latest technological wizardry....."

"Dramatic plot device," I explained innocently.

"I'm not actually hunting down corporate executives and corrupt politicians...."

"Allow me some artistic license," I pled.

"To tell the truth, I didn't even say any of the words you put into my mouth. You've never even met me before!"

"Oh, stop quibbling over such minor little details," I insisted as I threw up my hands in exasperation. "I dabbled with the truth, and it just didn't get high enough ratings from my reading public. Look at the results of this survey...."

I pulled out several pages of computer statistics, charts, and graphs that had been provided to me by the literary agent. "You see here, I lost 97 percent of my readers when I started talking about the ecological crisis. I was advised to drop that part of the book, and add more sex scenes."

"But your whole book is about the ecological crisis," Durning astutely pointed out.

His keen observation took the wind out of my sails. "So what do I do now?" I despaired.

"Here's an idea," he suggested. "You can continue to write the book as a dramatic adventure story, full of fictional plot devices and contrived, wild twists and turns. But every time you get to something that really happened, or that really was true, you could footnote it!"

"Like this?" I asked.[1]

"Exactly!" he said. "A bunch of people might have thought that you made up that opening prologue about the world's leading scientists saying we only have a few years left to save the planet.[2] But now, with a footnote inserted in just the right place, you'll alert your readers to the truth."[3]

"It's ingenious!" I exulted.

No sooner had I voiced these words than the telephone rang. I excused myself from the doorway where I had been talking to Mr. Durning, ran to the kitchen, and answered the phone.

---

[1]What are you doing reading the footnotes? Don't you have something better to do with your time?
[2]Union of Concerned Scientists, "Warning to Humanity," October 1992.
[3]As if they really care.

"Your ratings are dropping!" the literary agent scolded me from the other end of the line. "Those footnotes are scaring everyone away. It's like a law review journal or some stodgy academic publication; nobody wants to read such pseudo-intellectual tripe. According to the latest polls, you've only got one person left who's reading your book right now, and that's a frustrated English doctoral student in his tenth year at Stanford, who's procrastinating on his dissertation. You'd better get back to the plot of the book!"

Quickly I threw out the academic style, and reverted to the sensational....

Chapter 9

The evidence was damning: dozens of documents implicated the President of the United States. Scott read over the evidence of these horrible crimes: The government was subsidizing wealthy corporations to rape the federal lands.

Through the 1872 Mining Law, for example, any corporation could strip mine national property, paying nominal fees of just $100 to mine up to $10 billion in gold. Surely, the President must know about this. Why hadn't he done anything to repeal this law? Why was he supporting such environmentally devastating profit-making schemes for a few powerful billionaires?

Scott found evidence of conspiracy everywhere: Durning had files that implicated the richest, most powerful people in the United States of America.

The detective was busy making photocopies and stuffing them into his briefcase when Durning returned to the room a few minutes later. Scott was oblivious to everything around him. He was obsessed with getting all the information.

Durning tapped him lightly on the shoulder, startling him for a moment. "You caught me by surprise," Scott said. "I was just looking over these files. I can hardly believe any of the evidence you've accumulated. It's a total subversion of democracy -- the President, the Congress, and the wealthiest one percent of Americans are conspiring to cheat the rest of the people out of all their wealth. And the results are devastating to the earth. It just doesn't seem possible! Why has this information been covered up?"

"It's much more insidious than you realize," Durning said. "I don't think the President is in control. I don't think the Congress is in control, either. In fact, I'm certain that not even those rich Fortune 500 executives -- the Rockefellers, the Vanderbilts, the Fords, and everyone else -- are in control!"

Scott took a few seconds to digest what the young environmentalist was telling him. There was *someone else* who was directing this whole conspiracy! Perhaps there was one mastermind who was responsible for the destruction of the Earth. And somehow this one sinister villain had managed to get the wealthiest and most powerful Americans to work for him!

But who was it? Who was in control?

Chapter 10

Scott didn't have much time to figure out the answer. He had been given a doomsday clock with a big red digital readout that counted down the days and hours until the end of the world. The clock reported that there were only 11 months left.

"What's that?" asked Durning, looking at the clock.

"Oh this?" Scott replied. "It's a clichéd literary device issued to every action hero who's involved in a race against time. It's supposed to heighten the suspense."

"That's pretty cool," said Durning. "What other technological wizardry do you have?"

"I've got a car that turns into a boat; a potion that makes me invisible; and a cufflink that shoots poisonous darts. I realize that none of this is too original, but I take what the author gives me."

"I'm afraid that all these gadgets won't be enough for you to accomplish your mission," Alan said. "The forces allied against you are too great. You can't go out there alone!" He paused ominously for dramatic effect. Then, in an attempt at foreshadowing, he warned: "You'll be killed!"

"You obviously haven't read many adventure stories," replied Scott. "It's always one brave action hero who fights an impossible battle against hundreds of heavily armed villains. I always win in the end."

"But the battle to save the Earth is different," Durning insisted. "It can't be achieved by one heroic individual, while everyone else stands by and watches. You'll need the help of all of us."

Scott scoffed, as he bid his farewell. "Just sit back and enjoy the story," he said. "I can handle this all alone." He left the laboratory as confident as ever.

But Durning was worried. He remembered the words of Lester Brown, his old friend at the World Watch Institute: "Saving the world is not a spectator sport...."

Chapter 11

I had another strange dream last night.

I was in a huge stadium with 50,000 screaming fans. On the field, Lester Brown, Alan Durning, and a few other environmentalists were running around with butterfly nets.

"Hey Lester!" yelled out a beer-swilling heckler next to me, "My three-year old daughter can save the world better than you!"

A vendor came down the aisle, hawking food and drinks. "Hey buddy," I called to him, "How much are the peanuts?"

"Well, that's an interesting question," he replied. "You might want to take into account the costs of harvesting the nuts from a rainforest thousands of miles away, the social costs of disrupting the native culture there, the price of transporting the peanuts across the world, the untold ecological damage caused by the production...."

"I didn't ask for a lecture," I responded impatiently. "Just tell me the price."

"Oh, they're only 25 cents," he said. "We don't actually take any of the social costs into account when we figure out the price."

A roar went up from the crowd. I turned my head to look at the scoreboard, and saw the numbers skyrocketing: "HUMANS - 6,100,000,000, TIGERS - 200. Every second, the human numbers increased by three. The tiger numbers kept dropping.

"You suck, Tigers!" screamed the heckler next to me. He turned his three-hundred pound frame towards me, and stuck his stubbly face in mine. "That's another franchise that's going to go belly up," he complained. "I've got to stop betting on all these endangered species...."

While the players on the field raced around trying to save the world, many of the fans were starting to get bored. They began tossing around beach balls.

"We need to get everyone involved!" I insisted to the spectators around me. "We're the crucial tenth man on the team. We can't just sit back while our team loses the battle to save the planet. We've got to do something!"

"You're right," said the intoxicated heckler. By now, his five-o'clock shadow had reached about three minutes before midnight. "Let's do the wave!" he cried. Within seconds, all the fans were standing up, flailing their arms in the air, and sitting down again. "We've got the rowdiest fans in the league," the heckler boasted proudly as he tried to squeeze his immense body mass back into the stadium seat. After firmly establishing himself back on solid ground, he grabbed his "John 3:16" sign and tried to get the attention of the television cameras.

At this point, I saw some substitutes run on the field. I recognized them from somewhere, but I couldn't quite place it. A figure in a dark shroud came running onto the field, dragging a scythe behind him. Two other shadowy figures came galloping on horses into the stadium grounds.

It wasn't until I saw the close-ups on the DiamondVision stadium video screen that I recognized my friends from Armageddon. Death was wearing a baseball cap with the Nike swoosh logo across the top. He held up a bony finger at the cameraman, and mouthed the words "We're number one!" Meanwhile, Famine was doing a victory dance on the sidelines, where he got penalized for excessive celebration. He seemed to shrug off the foul, as he too grinned into the television cameras.

"Hi, Mom!" was all he said, as he waved to the audience. I saw War grow to three times his size, until he began to cast his shadow over everyone on the playing field.

That's when I woke up. I asked my psychiatrist about the dream today, but he couldn't find any symbolism in it. He told me that dreams are often quite meaningless. "Sometimes a cigar is just a cigar," he said, quoting Sigmund Freud.

What was he talking about anyway? There weren't any cigars in my dream. I decided to forget about it, and go back to writing my book....

Chapter 12

After leaving Durning's secret hideaway, Scott waited by an isolated pay phone in Olympic National Park. Rain was drizzling down as he stood in back of the ranger station, surrounded by towering evergreens, covered with dripping moss.

The phone rang precisely at the time that Potemkin promised she would call. Scott answered the phone with an accusation:

"You tricked me," he said. "You don't work for the United States government."

"That's true," Potemkin confessed. "I'm actually part of an underground movement of Americans who are trying to create a better world."

"So how did you get the video of the President?" interrogated the detective.

"It was a fake," she admitted. "Nowadays you can't trust photographs or video images to tell the truth. They can be easily doctored to the point where you can't tell fact from fiction anymore."

"But why did you go to such lengths to deceive me?"

"We wanted you on our side. We've heard that you are the best private investigator in the country. And we have very little time to find solutions to the environmental crisis."

"Well, now you've thrust right me into the middle of this mess," said the detective begrudgingly. "What do you suggest I do now? I'm fighting against an invisible enemy and I have no idea where to begin."

"There's one person who might know the answers," replied the agent. "He's already started the fight, but it's all been in secret."

"Who is it?" Scott asked.

"His original name was Sherwood Sanders, but he's taken on a new identity. Unknown to the American public, he's leading an underground movement of rebels against the current system. It's all a covert operation.

"If you join him, you'll also have to go undercover. You'll need a new name, a new identity, a new disguise -- everything must be different. We can't have anyone recognizing you.

"This is the most dangerous assignment you've ever undertaken. You'll be fighting against a system in which many powerful people have vested interests. So anyone could be your enemy. A lot of people will want to see you killed. You'll be surrounded by death and devastation everywhere you go.

"I don't envy you, Scott. You're about to take a journey into the bowels of hell."

Chapter 13

Sherwood Sanders knew about hell.

He was born, unwanted, unloved, in the worst ghetto in America. As an African American, growing up in the epicenter of poverty and squalor, he seethed with rage towards society. He was convinced that white people were the cause of all his problems. They were the ones who controlled the power in America. It was their racist conspiracy to keep the black man poor and in chains. "When whites wake up in the morning," he imagined, "they must plot how they can oppress blacks each day."

By the age of twelve, he was an alcoholic. A few years later, depressed with his existence, he had become a hardened drug addict, too. He had seen people killed in his neighborhood for the price of a fish sandwich. It was a desperate, bleak existence.

This was the late 1960's, when the world seemed like it was about to explode. Riots erupted in ghettoes throughout America, and fires raged out of control in Watts, Chicago, and Detroit. Sherwood, smelling revolution in the air, joined the Black Panthers to fight for the rights of his people. He was a militant, angry youth.

It was in this turbulent time that fate would intervene. Sherwood was brutally beaten by the police in an unprovoked attack, until he lay drowning in his blood, unconscious on the street. He was rushed to the hospital, but it appeared too late to save him. Paralyzed from the neck down, he hovered on the verge of death.

Sherwood Sanders was only 16 years old.

Lying upon his deathbed, he prayed to God for his life. He swore that, if he survived, he would turn his life around. No longer would he resort to malice. He had realized the futility of violence and hatred. From this day forward, he would work towards creating a more peaceful, compassionate society.

The doctors could not believe the miracle that they witnessed the following morning. Not only had Sherwood recovered from the edge of death, he also had spontaneously overcome his paralysis. He could walk again.

True to his vows, Sherwood transformed his life. He went off to college, where he excelled, and then continued on to graduate with honors from a prominent law school. By the time he was in his early thirties, he had become a leading attorney in the South. He was renowned for his brilliance; every word he spoke dripped with wisdom.

In some ways, it could be said that Sherwood Sanders <u>had</u> died in the hospital room all those years ago. Now, pledged to Allah, he was a completely different man. He had become a Muslim, changing his name to Sharif Abdullah.

Some people thought that Sharif was the next American hero. Some people believed he would be the spiritual successor to Martin Luther King, Jr. Some people were convinced that he would change the world.

As for now, the majority of Americans had never heard of this man. Many people might even suspect that he was just a fictional character, invented for the dramatic purposes of this book. But he was flesh and blood; his entire story was true.

And Sharif Abdullah would not be an unknown name for long. For he had discovered solutions to the environmental crisis.

But his solutions were radical. His solutions were subversive.

In fact, he didn't plan to make a few small reforms. He was going to challenge everything that most Americans believed to be sacred and true.

Sharif Abdullah was ready to start the revolution.

70

Chapter 14

Scott had planned a secret rendezvous to meet with the revolutionary. The detective would drive to a rural area just outside Portland, Oregon that day. Then, late at night, he would drive up into the hills above the city. At 3:30 in the morning, Sharif would be waiting for him in the gazebo of the Rose Garden.

But the plans didn't seem to be working out. Only minutes after leaving for the Rose Garden, Scott became suspicious. He was driving his car on an empty highway. There were no other vehicles on the road at this sleep-forsaken hour of the night.

Suddenly he noticed four black Cadillacs behind him. They were identical vehicles with no identification -- no license plates, no markings at all. And they appeared to be trailing him. No matter how quickly or slowly he drove, they stayed 50 meters behind him. When he sped up, they sped up. When he slowed down, they slowed down.

The detective swerved from the fast lane, and rushed off the closest exit. Within seconds, he heard the screeching of tires behind him. The four black Cadillacs had also left the highway.

Panic raced through the investigator's mind. This didn't seem to make sense: there was no water nearby, so he couldn't just transform his car into a boat. Nor would it help for him to use his invisible potion; the car would still be visible, even if the driver appeared to vanish. Scott feared that the author of this book might have made some terrible mistake.

He accelerated to 75 miles per hour, turning down a desolate rural road. The Cadillacs kept pace, racing at dangerous speeds down the one-lane path.

There was certainly nothing subtle about this game. The unmarked cars did not try to conceal their active pursuit of the detective. It was a chase -- a race to the death.

Scott spun his car wildly in the opposite direction, heading back to the highway. It was his only hope for escape.

80 miles per hour. Scott accelerated onto the interstate, well beyond the speed limit.

90 miles an hour. The Cadillacs drove even faster, quickly closing the gap.

100 miles an hour. One car was bearing down on his bumper; another caught up to his right.

110 miles an hour. Scott slammed the gas pedal to the floor, as the road became a blur.

120 miles per hour. The speedometer needle was reaching its zenith. It looked like it would break off the dashboard.

130 miles an hour. The Cadillacs kept the dangerous pace in the hunt of their outnumbered prey.

The tinted windows of the Cadillacs opened at once, and the nuzzles of four AK-47 assault rifles emerged from the window. The invisible assassins took aim at their moving target. The time was ticking away on Scott's personal doomsday clock.

He quickly spun his wheels into the shoulder of the road, pulling his emergency brakes. The car flew into a tailspin, gyrating violently out of control. It smashed into a concrete highway divider, flipped into the air, and came crashing down on the opposite side of the road. There was a deafening screech and a thundering roar of glass and metal exploding. The car erupted into flames twenty feet high, shards of metal flying like fiery arrows into the darkness of the Oregon night.

There were no survivors.

Chapter 15

"You killed yourself off!" exclaimed my mother.

"It's not me, Mom," I insisted. "It's just a fictional character."

"How could you do this to me?" she wailed. "After all your father and I have done for you all these years, this is how you repay us. I'm sensing that this stems from a deep-seated hostility towards your parents."

"No, it doesn't," I repeated. "It's stems from my imagination. It's only a work of fiction."

"There's a seed of truth inside every fiction," she admonished me. "I'm going to take you to a psychiatrist. He'll have plenty to say about your secret death wish."

"I never even saw the warning signs," muttered my father, who had ripped his coat and was sitting shiva. "Were we such bad parents that it would come to this?"

"Hello!" I shouted to deaf ears. "I'm still alive."

My father was speaking as if I weren't even in the room. "How could he kill himself off on page 72? He was so young, and his adventure story had so much potential. There must be at least 200 pages more to this book."

I jumped up and down in front of my dad to convince him that I was still alive. I waved my arms in front of his face, but he seemed to look right through me. I was but a ghost.

"Do authors ever think about the parents of the characters they kill off?" asked my mother rhetorically. "It's so sad. I often think about Captain Ahab's poor mother."

"Captain Ahab?" asked my father.

"Yes, Captain Ahab. Melville paints him to be such an evil character, but surely there was another side to the story. He had a mother, too, you know. Yet do we ever see <u>her</u> perspective? She must have been worried sick when he went out to sea and came back with his leg chewed off by a whale. Oh sure, some people say that Herman Melville is such a great author, but he's nothing but an insensitive lout in my book. If he's going to feed Ahab to the fishes just to heighten the drama of the story, well, he's got a pretty sick mind, let me tell you."

"<u>Moby Dick</u> is a work of fiction!" I screamed. "There's no mother of Ahab. There's nobody really getting hurt."

"Easy for you to say," my mother sneered. "You're not the mother of a fictional character. I've just lost my only literary child in a terrible car accident. I think I'm going to need some time alone." She ran from the room in tears.

"Look what you've done to your mother," scolded my father. "Are you happy now? Is there anyone else you want to kill off with impunity? You might as well take <u>our</u> lives while you're at it. How are you going to get out of this mess you've created?"

"Well, to be quite honest," I said, "I was planning on interviewing a number of candidates to take my place as the hero of this book." I spread a stack of resumes across the kitchen table.

I was proud of this latest brainstorm. I had met with a leading feminist named Riane Eisler who discouraged me from using a white male as the hero of my book. "That's so old paradigm," she explained. "White males have been getting all the leading roles in our society for thousands of years. If we really want to create a better society, we've got to have equal opportunities for people of all genders and ethnic backgrounds to save the world."

That was when I first came up with the idea of killing my character off. Minutes before writing the death of Scott Sherman in this book, I placed an advertisement in the New York Village Voice:

"WANTED: Heroic figure to save the world. Experience a plus. Women and minority applicants encouraged.

Of course, in saving the world -- as in most jobs -- it's all who you know. Rainbow called me up and asked if I would interview her friend, Aurora Borealis, from Berkeley.

"Does she have experience saving the world?" I asked.

"Oh, of course! Let me give you a few examples: she was so committed to stopping the AIDS crisis, that she wore a little red ribbon everywhere she went."

"Very impressive," I had to concede.

"Yes, and she was so outraged about the Exxon Valdez oil spill in Alaska that she was immediately moved to action...."

"Yes?"

"She bought a bumper sticker for her Mercedes Benz that said "EXXON POLLUTES THE ENVIRONMENT."

"She sounds like quite an activist," I was forced to admit. "Who says that today's youths are apathetic?"

"Indeed," Rainbow agreed. "Aurora is devoted to peace, love, and understanding."

"Her parents must be very proud of her," I speculated.

"I wouldn't know. She doesn't speak to them."

"Well, I'd be interested in meeting with her. I need a new hero for my book really soon. The next chapter is about to start....."

75

No sooner had I spoken these words than a young woman came walking through the door. She looked like something the cat dragged in -- especially if the cat was on a bad acid trip. She was like a hallucinatory flashback to the 1960's. In fact, she looked like a twin of Rainbow, wearing her multi-colored tie-dye shirt, her torn bell-bottom jeans, and her Birkenstock sandals.

"You must be Aurora," I welcomed her into my house.

"Like, you know, yar," she replied.

I didn't know I was going to need a translator for the interview. "Listen," I said impatiently. "Time is running out. They're holding my funeral in the next chapter, but then the adventure story will be off and running again. Can you be ready in about 20 pages to take over the plot of the book?"

"Does a bear shit in the rainforests?" she asked, by way of a reply.

"Um, actually, no. Bears don't live in rainforests. And, by the way, you're going to have to clean up your language. This book is family entertainment. Do you really think you're going to be up for this challenge?"

She looked at me as if I had asked the stupidest question in the world. "Is the Pope Jewish?" she replied.

I didn't have the heart to tell her the truth about the Pope's secret Catholic past. Anyway, I had more pressing matters on my mind. It was time to return to the scene of the crime, where a car had exploded on a lonely Oregon road....

Chapter 16

The news sent shock waves throughout the nation: Scott Sherman had been killed. The hero of so many wars -- he who had escaped from the brink of the abyss on countless occasions -- was dead.

The President was in the Middle East when he heard about the tragedy. He immediately called for a national day of mourning, as well as a state funeral. Flags flew at half mast, and the people of the nation talked about nothing else. Almost two million people attended the funeral procession, lining the streets of Pennsylvania Avenue in Washington D.C. for miles.....

"Rather immodest, aren't you?" interrupted Schadenfraude, looking over my shoulder as I typed the latest chapter.

"Well, it's my book," I replied indignantly, upset at this invasion into my privacy. "I can fantasize all I want."

"Your death would be nothing compared to mine," boasted Schadenfraude. "My funeral would attract three million people. Royalty would fly to Los Angeles from all over the world to pay their last respects. There would be an outpouring of love like you've never seen. The tears would flow like mighty rivers...."

"Yes, I can just see the headlines now," I commented sarcastically. "WORLD MOURNS THE DEATH OF MENIAL LABORER AT BURGER KING -- 'Fries Will Never Quite Taste The Same' Lament Devoted Groupies.'"

Schadenfraude flew into a rage. "I would make a much better martyr than you," he bragged. "You died in a measly little car accident. My death would be heroic. I would probably be killed by secret agents, who were trying to extort some vital secret from me.

"Like the secret sauce in the Whopper?" I suggested. Schadenfraude just ignored me. He was too busy inventing scenarios for his heroic demise.

We continued to argue over which one of us would make a better corpse when the phone rang again. It was the literary agent.

"You're going to suffer the worst death of them all," she insisted. "The critics are going to have your head on a plate if you don't get back to your adventure story soon. Your audience is getting tired of these post-modern intrusions of the author into the book. They just want to be left alone with a good mystery."

Coincidentally, just at that moment, I received another phone call on my other line. It was Sharif Abdullah, wanting to know what happened to him during all this time.

"Oh, that's just what I was about to reveal. Sit back and enjoy the story as it unfolds....."

Chapter 17

When Sharif Abdullah turned on the television news, he couldn't believe what he heard: Scott Sherman had been killed.

According to the earliest indications, the detective had died in a car crash at approximately 2:43 a.m. Another motorist had come upon the scene while the fire was still out of control, and had immediately called for help. The details were still sketchy, but there was one fact that was established beyond a doubt: the famous war hero had perished instantly in the explosion.

None of this made sense to Sharif. He tried to recollect what exactly had happened the night before.

He had been waiting impatiently for thirty minutes under the dark night sky. Every two minutes, he compulsively checked his watch and wondered what had happened to his visitor. It was now 3:51 in the morning, and he was about to leave.

Then he saw a movement in the moonlight. He could hear the rustling of grass underneath approaching feet. Suddenly, from his hiding place in the gazebo, he caught a direct glimpse of the man he thought was the detective.

The figure was shrouded in shadows, and clearly wearing a disguise; he was dressed as an old beggar, with stooped shoulders and ragged clothes. His face was unshaven and his wispy hair unkempt, floating in every direction as if in defiance of gravity.

"Abdullah, I presume," the mysterious figure said, with a hint of a smile in his voice.

"And you must be the Sandman," Sharif replied. This was the code name they had agreed upon for identification purposes. The beggar approached more closely and sat upon a bench in the gazebo.

"So I hear you have a plan," the visitor said. "A very intriguing plan."

"Yes," replied Sharif. "After years of trying to reform the system, I realized that all the old approaches are futile. The environmental movement isn't going to be effective in stopping the destruction of the earth. The government won't solve anything, and as for corporations -- well, they're just part of the problem. It's time for a radical new strategy."

"What did you have in mind?"

"The times call for desperate measures. We have to overthrow the old order in society. I've spent weeks preparing my plans of battle, studying the art of war, and plotting my first attack...."

With great interest, the Sandman leaned forward, eager to hear the plan of action. He had done nothing to arouse suspicion yet; Sharif seemed to trust him with all this information.

"How should we begin this war?" asked Sharif rhetorically. "There are many violent strategies that revolutionaries have used throughout the past: We could throw molotov cocktails in the streets. We could plant bombs to explode on Capitol Hill. We could amass a rebel militia, stocking our soldiers with guns, grenades, and weapons of mass destruction to disrupt the peace. We could even invade the White House and take the American President as our hostage."

The beggar looked astonished. "You're really going to launch an all-out war against the United States?" he asked in disbelief.

"No, history has proven that those violent strategies won't solve anything," Sharif explained. "So we're going to start a covert war, completely secret to the masses of Americans."

"What's the strategy?" asked the beggar anxiously.

Sharif looked intently into the eyes of his visitor. There was something strange and unsettling about the beggar's appearance. It was more than just the disguise, which was ugly but effective. Something else bothered Sharif, but he couldn't quite place what was wrong.

"We're not going to fight the system. That would just encounter a tremendous amount of resistance. We would be crushed in an instant.

"Instead we're going to do something far more subversive. We're going to invent a new system altogether."

"What?"

"There are dozens of brilliant women and men who have come up with ideas for creating a better society. Together they are coming up with practical solutions for redesigning our economy, our political system, and so many of other dysfunctional institutions. Individually these people have come up with pieces of the puzzle for saving the planet. Your job is to put it all together."

"This sounds wonderful," the Sandman responded enthusiastically. "Where should I start searching for the ideas that will help form the new vision for America?"

"In the desert Southwest," Sharif replied. "There you'll find some people who have invented the most astonishing plan for reclaiming the Earth from destruction. But be careful out there. They have many enemies, also -- countless people who are vehemently opposed to their ideas, ruthless people who will resort to violence to stop them from their goals."

Sharif handed the Sandman a sheet with names and phone numbers of members of an underground organization in the New Mexico desert. Many of these people were considered outlaws by the government; they were branded as terrorists and villains. It didn't matter that they saw themselves as freedom fighters, struggling in a valiant cause for the survival of the planet. Most of them were forced into hiding, so as to avoid the witch hunt that their enemies were conducting.

Thus, the information on the sheet was very valuable. It had been prepared for the eyes of Scott Sherman alone. As soon as he reached his destination, he was to destroy all the incriminating documents, so that no one could trace his path.

Indeed, the freedom fighters were very careful that no one knew their whereabouts. Their location had to remain a secret, or their lives would be in constant danger.

Sharif thought about this as he watched the Sandman disappear into the darkness. His intuition had told him to be suspicious of handing over such valuable information, but he had

81

been reassured by many people that Scott Sherman could be trusted.

The next morning, however, when Sharif saw the news reports, fear gripped him like a vise. Scott Sherman had been killed a full hour before their meeting in the garden.

Who then was the beggar who had showed up in his place? And what was he planning to do with the names of the rebel leaders?

Frantically, Sharif tried to call the headquarters of the rebel movement. He found the lines had been disconnected.

Desperately he dialed the private number of the rebel leader's home. That number, too, had been disconnected.

There was only one thing the Sharif could do: He had to fly to the desert himself to stop a potential disaster.

Chapter 18

The stakes were already high in the Desert Southwest.

A war had been raging out of control over the fate of the land. This was a beautiful region of red-rock canyons and austere vistas. It was one of the last wild places on the continent -- a refuge for nature in the midst of human destruction.

But recently there had been savage attacks on the land. Miners were raping and pillaging the wealth of the Earth, leaving ugly gashes and wounds upon the surface. Outside forces invaded the area, drilling for oil and gas, and leaving toxic wastes in their wake. Meanwhile, developers scarred the scenic landscapes with acres of concrete pavement and roads, extending the suburbs to all edges of the horizon. Ranchers and businessmen began to exploit the natural resources, dam the rivers, and graze livestock on the fragile ecosystems.

The counter-attack took everyone by surprise. Thousands of environmentalists had mobilized in the trenches, ready to die for their cause. They were determined to protect the earth by any means necessary. They would destroy the machines that were used to destroy the planet. They hoped to cause a breakdown of the entire system by throwing a monkeywrench into the works.

They began with simple acts of sabotage and subversion. Radical environmental groups destroyed bulldozers by pouring sand in the gas tanks. They cut down billboards, pulled up survey stakes, and put spikes in trees so that loggers could not chop them down. All these illegal actions were carried out in secret by anonymous crusaders, working in the dead of night.

Business interests immediately condemned these events as acts of terrorism. They feared an escalation of the war. It might start with the destruction of billboards and bulldozers, but soon it could spread to the detonation of bombs to destroy the Glen Canyon Dam. New condominium developments could be burned down by arsonists as soon as they were built. There would be no more respect for notions of private property. Anarchy would be loosed upon the American West.

In the middle of all this controversy was the self-proclaimed warrior by the name of Dave Foreman. For years he had been a moderate voice in the environmental movement. Working for a mainstream group called the Wilderness Society in Washington D.C., he had believed that the best way to protect the earth was to play by the rules of the system. According to this philosophy, conservationists needed to make rational economic arguments for the protection of nature. They needed to gather facts and statistics in support of their positions, so they could lobby in the halls of government. It was important for them to compromise with the people in power.

Yet Foreman soon realized that this strategy had backfired completely. The earth was burning while the government fiddled. By trying to play within the rules of the system, he could only stand idly by in a suit as he watched the environment be destroyed at an ever accelerating pace. The conservationists might win some tiny battles, but they were losing the war and suffering thousands of casualties.

A more radical approach was necessary to save the planet. Along with some disgruntled colleagues from the mainstream environmental movement, Foreman decided to start a group called "Earth First!" -- an extremist, take-no-prisoners organization that would refuse to compromise in defense of wild nature.

Foreman bristled at the notion that he was a modern-day terrorist. "The true terrorists are the people who destroy the planet," he contended. "They are those in the Forest Service and the timber industry who are annihilating thousand-year old forests for paper bags and picnic tables. They are the calculator-rational engineers and pork-barrel politicians who want to plug every free-flowing river with dams. They are the corporate executives whose bottom line is profits and who could not care less about Love Canals, Bhopals, cigarette smoke, acid rain, and unsafe automobiles."

Foreman's confrontational attitudes earned him the enmity of many powerful forces. Soon he was receiving death threats on a regular basis. In California, a pipe bomb exploded in the car of his friend Judi Bari in a deliberate attempt to murder her.

Across the American West, violence was spreading like a cancerous plague, as ranchers and loggers felt threatened by the radical movement. Instead of battling to save the planet, humans were warring against each other.

It was time for a different strategy. It was necessary to stop waging war against a system that would only fight back with superior force. Instead of launching a quixotic campaign against the developers of the American West, Foreman decided to create a new vision for the West altogether.

In fact, he was just about to unveil his remarkable plan.

And then, one morning, he suddenly vanished.

Chapter 19

No one wanted to call the police.

It had been 24 hours since Dave Foreman had disappeared, but the members of his underground group were hesitant about contacting any authorities. After all, they themselves were wanted by the law. They could not report the suspected kidnapping of their leader without having a swarm of cops overrun their hiding place.

They had an alternative plan. They could contact an investigative journalist who had been helpful in publicizing their story to the public. Her name was Aurora Borealis, a brilliant young reporter with the San Francisco Weekly.

The members of the rebel environmentalists trusted Aurora. Her stories portrayed their struggles against all odds, fighting the wealthy, powerful, corporate Goliaths of the Desert Southwest; these reports had turned the environmentalists into cult heroes and drawn much-needed support to their cause. But these stories had also brought the police to Aurora's office, demanding information about the rebel group. Even under threat of going to jail, she had never divulged her sources.

Like the people whose lives she covered, Aurora was an outsider. She was a young Latina woman trying to break down the barriers of the newsroom -- a traditional bastion of white males, with little opportunity for anyone else. Thus it was not surprising that she identified with the underdog.

Now Aurora had a chance to help uncover the story of the year. The leader of the rebel movement had disappeared, but no one else in the press was aware. She could hopefully solve the crime, and then publish the exclusive story. It was a chance she couldn't pass up.

When she flew into Arizona, she was met by a conservation biologist named Reed Noss. He had been working closely with Foreman on the new strategies for the underground movement.

"What exactly were you doing when your colleague disappeared?" she demanded to know.

Noss confided in her, "We had just finished work on a document -- not just any document, mind you. We were convinced that this might be the most important document in 500 years."

"You have a healthy sense of your own self-importance," Aurora teased.

"You may laugh," agreed Noss, "but we had come up with a plan for saving the Earth. We had created an entirely new vision for the North American continent that would change the ways humans interact with the landscape. We called it the Wildlands Project."

"What did it entail?"

"We wanted to see the restoration of North America to health and beauty. Where the wilderness had been bulldozed and paved over with asphalt, we wanted to see the forests and streams recover. Where the songs of birds had disappeared, where all signs of wildlife had vanished, and where the natural beauty of the continent had been devastated, we wanted to see the lands flourish once again.

"I'll admit, our plans are ambitious. In the 21st century, we hope to see at least 50 percent of America restored to wilderness. There would still be abundant places for humans to work, play, and live. But humans should not run rampant over every inch of the continent. We should not turn every last scenic area into a parking lot and shopping mall; we should not clearcut the last remaining forests of the continent; we should not spread smoke, industry, pollution, and devastation to the last beautiful refuges of the earth.

"Hundreds of years ago, almost half the entire continent was covered with forests, from the Mississippi River to the Atlantic Seaboard. Wildlife and wilderness thrived in the Americas. But since the arrival of the Mayflower, more than 98 percent of the forests have been clearcut. Most ecosystems and biodiversity have been devastated. There has been a holocaust of almost all the animal species and native tribes that lived off the land.

"Foreman believed that we could regenerate the beautiful landscapes of the past. He had a powerful vision of restoring the natural world to the way it was -- to accommodate both humans and the biological systems on which our survival depended.

"Millions of acres of spectacular wilderness would be restored. Returning from the edge of extinction, the grizzly bear, the gray wolf, the elk, and the bison would roam the West again. The ugliness and artifice, the plastic and the toxic, the pollution and pavement would no longer blight the entire natural world. Underneath the wasteland, the earth was still alive.

"We envisioned that the entire continent of North America could undergo a stunning regeneration. We could set aside vast areas where biodiversity and healthy ecosystems could thrive.

"This goes far beyond the concept of national parks and wildlife refuges, which are proving too small and inadequate to save the threatened species from almost certain death. We foresee a series of linked regional ecosystems across the hemisphere, connecting the biological riches of Panama with those in Alaska and Maine. From the Gulf Stream waters to the Redwood forests to the New York islands, this land would be remade for you and me. From sea to shining sea, America would be beautiful once again.

"Most Americans would be astonished if they could see pictures of what this country once looked like. They would be astonished by the stunning beauty that had been lost and destroyed. They would be astonished by the wealth and riches of the natural world, the bounteous abundance of life. The skies used to be flooded with songbirds, and the lakes and rivers were overflowing with fish. Most Americans would not recognize the very landscapes in which they now lived; the earth has been so altered and diminished and paved and covered that very little of the original magic remains.

"But Dave Foreman did not believe that this beauty and life had been lost forever. In fact, what he and I were proposing was nothing less than the rediscovery of America."

Chapter 20

Aurora listened patiently to this optimistic plan for restoring 50 percent of the North American continent to its natural condition. But she remained skeptical about the possibilities for ecological restoration. Just a few years previously, she had read an ominous book entitled The End of Nature. The author, a prominent journalist from *The New Yorker* magazine, had declared that humans had destroyed too much to be able to salvage the environment. Too many species were extinct, too many lands had been degraded, and too much pollution had done irretrievable harm to ecosystems that could never be replaced.

Was the Wildlands Project a ruse? Several aspects of the story triggered Aurora's suspicions. First of all, the plan didn't seem very realistic. If the environmental crisis was as severe as so many scientists had warned, it seemed impossible to simply re-create the priceless places that had been lost forever. There was something that sounded phony about this plan.

Moreover, this Wildlands Project didn't seem to offer a rational motive for why anyone would want to kidnap Dave Foreman. Who would oppose the restoration of health and beauty to the American landscape? It was a plan that would benefit everyone.

So what was the real reason that Foreman had been kidnapped? To Aurora's trained investigative senses, something smelled rotten. It almost seemed as if this whole Wildlands story was concocted to distract her from the real facts of the case. Perhaps Reed Noss was hiding some crucial information from the reporter. But why?

She decided to investigate further. After leaving the headquarters of the rebel movement, she would go to a library and search for the facts. This process of ecological restoration sounded wonderful and idealistic, but she had to discover the true story behind it.

Chapter 21

Bill McKibben was the famous young journalist who had declared "the end of nature." He had serious doubts that the wilderness could be saved. In fact, the young literary prodigy had made quite a sensation in 1992 by publishing his book, which announced that the earth's ecosystems had already been damaged beyond repair.

In McKibben's view, the entire world had been so overwhelmed by human intervention that there was no longer anything "natural." Even in the most remote forests, acid rain -- caused by human industry and pollution -- was killing the trees. In the furthest arctic regions, toxic chemicals produced in the United States were penetrating into the soil, infesting the ecosystems, and causing deadly mutations in plant and animals. McKibben did not have much hope for the future of the environment. He had read all the statistics, seen the destruction, and basically given up hope that the world could be saved.

Then, much to his surprise, he found a remarkable success story of environmental regeneration. It seemed like a miracle: death giving birth to new life. And it was happening right in his backyard.

In New England, nature was displaying its astonishing power to renew and heal itself. At the time of the American Revolution, most of the Eastern United States had been ravaged. "The forests are not only cut down," despaired a Boston cleric in the 19th century, "but there appears to be little reason to hope that they will ever grow again."

Now, in the midst of great concentrations of the American population, the forests were flourishing again. Beautiful woodlands had grown to cover more than 60 percent of Massachusetts, 80 percent of Vermont, and 90 percent of New Hampshire. Forests were growing by more than a million acres a decade in New York state. The autumn colors -- the bright red and yellow foliage for which New England was famous -- returned in greater force with the arrival of each October.

Wildlife that had disappeared from the region -- eagles, bears, moose, turkey, beavers, red wolves, cougars, coyotes, and deer -- were returning from the brink of extinction. Everywhere, in the springs and the summers, one could bathe in a profusion of green.

It was a story of hope for the future of America, as well as for the rest of the world. Two centuries ago, the eastern forests were destroyed almost completely as nature beat a hasty retreat. But now the East was setting an example of renewal and restoration.

Chapter 22

Aurora was amazed to find this story of hope among the ecological literature of despair. And perhaps its most heartening aspect was that this regeneration of life happened completely by accident. With a few exceptions, no legislators tried to protect these wilderness areas. There were no Johnny Appleseeds who were busy planting millions of trees all throughout New England. The only reason that these forests began to renew and heal themselves was that humans had left them alone. These areas had become so degraded by human activity that it just wasn't economically feasible to use them anymore. So they lay undisturbed for several centuries, while nature worked its magic.

Yet McKibben wanted to test a theory: If humans helped in the process of restoration, would the results be even quicker and more spectacular?

Such a transformation had been taking place in India for the past 20 years. 20,000 people had been attempting to survive on a sterile plateau that had once nourished plentiful life. Now it had been so exploited that it looked eerily like a landscape from the moon. The scorched earth was barren, dry, and as deathly white as a human skull.

In this place called Auroville, an ambitious restoration program managed to turn the desert into an oasis within a couple of decades. Residents studied the native vegetation -- the types of indigenous plants which thrived in that searing, tropical climate. Soon, they were digging through the clay, restoring the soil, composting, and planting seedlings taken from nearby areas. Two million trees later, the once lifeless town was flourishing.

Such restoration was not limited to India. All across the United States, from Chicago to the Florida Everglades, humans were beginning to assist in recovering natural ecosystems.

Environmentalists were no longer on the defensive. They could no longer be dismissed as doomsayers and pessimists. Suddenly the environmental movement had found a new cause of hope: People like Foreman and McKibben were putting forth a vision of a world restored, renewed, and rejuvenated. It was a truly viable method for returning America to its natural state.

Chapter 23

"I'm getting bored," complained my Mom.

"Why?"

"Well, I don't want to have to *think* when I read. I just want to be entertained. Can't you put some more action in this book?"

"Like what?"

"Oh, I don't know -- anything. Put a talking gorilla in the book. Put a bunch of people who are looking for an ancient manuscript in the jungles of Peru. Just put *something* special to spice up the action. Could you have a few of the environmental leaders be murdered? That would be exciting!"

"Mom!"

"I'm just trying to help. You were doing all right for a while. I liked that part about the evil villain who is controlling the President, the Congress, and the Fortune 500 executives. I've started taking bets on who it is."

"What?!?"

"Well, your Dad and I were bored during that last part where you were talking about the people starting environmental restoration in India, so we started a pool to figure out who's the big criminal mastermind. It makes the book more interesting -- you know, gets us more personally involved in the outcome."

"So who is it?" I asked. "Who are the leading candidates for the role of evil villain in charge of destroying the Earth?"

"Well, the odds are running 3 to 2 in favor of Kayzer Sozse."

"Who?"

"Oh, I guess you never saw *The Usual Suspects*. See, I tried to tell your Dad that it had to be some character that we already had met in the book. Anyway right now the big money is on Alan Durning."

"What?!? He's a real-life visionary who's leading the way towards an ecologically sustainable future."

"Oh sure, that's what he'd *like* you to believe," my mother reacted skeptically. "I bet that's just a façade. You know, it's always the least likely suspect who commits the crime."

I heard another knock at the door, and had a pretty good idea that it was either Durning or his attorney, coming to pay me an angry visit. I decided to take evasive action. Taking my mother's advice, I plunged back into the story....

Chapter 24

Sharif Abdullah arrived too late.

He had chartered a private plane into the Utah desert the day before. He had then traveled a circuitous route through towering red rock landscapes and dry, parched panoramas where the vegetation was sparse and brown.

When he finally arrived at the headquarters of the rebel movement, he found everything in disarray. Dave Foreman had been kidnapped. The organization was in chaos. The only person who appeared calm was a young reporter from San Francisco, Aurora Borealis.

She looked like she had seen her own difficult times. Her body was riddled with cuts and bruises. There were fresh bandages wrapped around her left hand and arm.

"What happened?" Sharif asked in alarm. "Are you all right?"

Aurora dismissed his concerns casually. "Don't worry about these minor nicks and scratches. It was an exciting adventure, but the editor decided to cut it from the book. Anyway, I'm more concerned with what's happening here. Can I share some private words with you?"

Sharif was reluctant to talk. He feared that she had already uncovered his dirty secret: he was the person who had accidentally divulged the hiding place of the rebel movement.

But Aurora didn't try to place any blame. Instead, she simply suggested that they take a drive together. She urgently needed to discuss something with him.

They started driving out across the desert landscapes. The last afternoon rays of the sun colored everything in a golden, reddish hue.

"Where are you taking me?" asked Sharif.
"We're going to the northern rim of the Grand Canyon."
"What's there?"

"Oh, there's nothing specific there that we have to see. It just will make a great scenic backdrop when they film the movie version of this book."

In the rented jeep, they traversed lonely roads across New Mexico and Arizona, although no one in the area really knew or cared where the imaginary borders of one state ended and the next state began. It all looked the same to Sharif -- a horizon of desert, with crimson sandstone canyons and rocks, looking like the dry, lifeless surface of Mars.

Finally, they reached the edge of the Canyon. Most of the tourists had left for the day. Once Aurora made sure that no one was listening in on their conversation, she quickly got to her point:

"Somebody is withholding information from me."

"What are you talking about?"

"I thought I was investigating the disappearance of an environmental leader whose biggest crime was wanting to restore the health and beauty of the North American landscape. But clearly there's something much larger going on here.

"Why would Dave Foreman have so many enemies? Why would someone want to kidnap and possibly kill him? I can't see any reason why people would feel threatened by the Wildlands Project."

Sharif paused before responding. How much should he tell the reporter? How much did she need to know?

In silence, he gazed out over the red rock outcroppings and the five-thousand foot drop to the bottom of the canyon. Finally he confessed:

"You're right. You've stumbled across something much larger than just the kidnapping of an environmental activist in New Mexico. You've accidentally walked right into the center of a scandal that threatens our national security."

"What do you mean?" asked Aurora.

"This isn't just a local issue. This isn't just about Dave Foreman. The crisis that we're confronting goes all the way to the highest levels of power. It involves the President of the United States and the wealthiest corporate executives in the

97

world. It even involved Scott Sherman, and we suspect that's why he was killed a few days ago. The stakes are higher than they've ever been before."

"I still don't understand," complained the reporter. "Explain this all to me."

"Very few people can understand the magnitude of the dangers we're facing," agreed Sharif. "We live in an unprecedented time in the history of the Earth. In 4.5 billion years, there has never been such a monumental threat to the entire planet.

"Let me illustrate it to you with a very concrete example:

"Imagine you're looking at the Earth from outer space. In fact, imagine that you've been watching the planet as it has changed and evolved over the last few billion years. I sure hope you've brought some good books along, because it's a pretty boring show.

"For countless millennia, nothing much appears to be happening on the surface of the planet. Change occurs at a plodding pace. It takes tens of thousands of years for the Colorado river to carve the canyon in front of us. Inch by inch, the Himalayas rise. Ice sheets come and go, in their own painstaking time.

"Slowly, slowly, the continents separate and drift to their current positions. Slowly, slowly, great forests spread across all the Earth's surface in great blankets of green. But it takes millions and millions of years for any discernible differences to be visible from your vantage point in space. Geological processes are achingly slow.

"Yet, suddenly, in the last 100 years -- a geological blink of the eye -- the entire planet starts transforming at a breakneck speed. Vast forests that have been stable for millions of years abruptly vanish overnight. Massive cities explode across the landscape of the Earth, replacing the vanishing forests. Flashes of nuclear light appear, then return with increasing frequency.

"All across the world, giant artificial lakes suddenly appear from nowhere, as the major rivers are dammed. Not too far from here, Lake Powell appeared overnight in the desert, when the Glen Canyon dam was constructed. It flooded some of the most scenic areas in the world; in fact, for a while, there were plans to flood the Grand Canyon itself.

"Alarmingly, many natural lakes -- like Lake Baikal in Russia -- are suffering the opposite fate. They're shrinking, evaporating, and disappearing at accelerating rates.

"Everywhere massive transformations are rapidly altering the planet's surface. In the north of Africa, the mighty Sahara desert expands its territory like a conquering army, consuming half the continent. In the Amazon, the forests that harbor most of the world's life are being chopped down and torched faster than I speak these words. Watching from the heavens, you would be astonished by what you were suddenly witnessing on the Earth.

"The pace of change has quickened. After several billion years of leisurely evolution, the entire planet is now transforming at an unbelievable rate. Species are disappearing faster than in 65 million years. In decades, many of our most fertile areas have been reduced into deserts."

"What about the restoration of the Earth?" asked Aurora. "I heard that there was a growing trend of ecological regeneration in the eastern United States, and in places like Auroville, India."

"That's true," conceded Sharif. "If you were watching the planet from above, you would see a patch of green growing and spreading from New York to Maine. But the rest of the planet is still deteriorating at an ever faster rate. You would be shocked to see the massive destruction. As my friend Alan Durning has said, 'forests disappear so suddenly from so many places that it looks like a plague of locusts has descended on the planet.'

"Unfortunately, the restoration of nature is still just a small part of the story. It's a promising indication of things to come, but at the end of the 20th century, restorative efforts are relatively rare, compared to the widespread destruction of the earth's living systems. For every Auroville, there are hundreds of thousands of other areas on the earth which are being systematically stripped of their capacity to sustain life, human or otherwise. In the time that citizens of southern India have restored 2,200 acres to life, human activity has degraded more than 300 million productive acres into desert -- an area more than half the size of the United States, east of the Mississippi.

"Indeed, while the eastern forests of America are making their slow, gradual comeback, the rest of the world's forests are disappearing at the rate of several acres a second -- everywhere from the Amazon to Siberia to Southeast Asia and the Pacific Northwest.

"Clearly restoration is part of the solution. But it's not enough to reverse the tidal wave of destruction before the planet's biological systems collapse completely.

"It's ironic: there have been a lot of movies lately about people having to save the earth from invading aliens, or giant meteors, or dinosaurs come back to life. But, while people are munching on their popcorn, watching these fictional stories for light entertainment, there's a real monster that threatens us all. It's invisible, but that makes it all the more deadly.

"You have entered into the center of a crisis that's about to engulf everyone on the planet. There are powerful forces arrayed against you. You're not just involved in a simple kidnapping case of an individual human being; you're involved in a war to save the Earth from destruction."

Chapter 25

Hundreds of miles above the Grand Canyon, a spy satellite was in orbit around the planet. It could take detailed photographs of secret military installations, covert air bases, and traditional enemy operations. But today the satellite's cameras were focused on two people having a heated discussion upon the northern rim of the Canyon.

Sharif and Aurora had no idea they were being observed from outer space. There was no way they could detect that their every move was being charted and followed.

The images were beamed instantly to the White House, where the National Security Advisor was in an emergency morning meeting with the President.

"We have reason to believe that these two people are associated with the subversive underground movement in the West," explained the government official in charge of ferreting out dangerous terrorist elements. "The woman is a reporter for the San Francisco Weekly who wrote a story about the environmental revolutionaries that are trying to overthrow the United States government. It was a very sympathetic piece that painted the rebels as a band of heroic freedom fighters; we suspect that she is not really an objective reporter, but actually the mouthpiece for this criminal organization."

"And who is the man?" asked the President. "He looks very familiar."

"We've attempted to locate his face in our database of FBI files. Unfortunately we haven't been able to make a match yet."

"Well, I want you to follow them and find out everything you can," ordered the President. "We can't have them threatening our national security. By whatever means, they must be stopped."

"Are you authorizing us to eliminate them?" asked the head of the CIA.

"They pose a danger to everything we hold to be sacred and true," answered the President angrily, pounding his fist on the desk. "I authorize you to take whatever action is necessary to make sure they don't succeed."

Chapter 26

Sharif found himself in a cold sweat. An involuntary shiver ran through his body; his intuition told him that something was very wrong. Their personal lives were in immediate danger.

"I sense that we're facing a new threat," he warned. "It's bearing down upon us even as we speak. I fear this could mean the end...."

"You mean....?" Aurora dared not say the words.

"That's right," he affirmed, but before he could even give voice to his thoughts, it hit them without warning, jeopardizing their existence....

Writer's block.

I had never had such a terrible case. It had been weeks since I had written a word; my creative imagination had eroded completely, turning into a vast, barren wasteland. Desperately I wandered in the Sahara of wordlessness. There was not even a trickling underground well of inspiration in this searing literary desert. I was inarticulate, infertile, incapable of producing even a noun or verb, let alone an exclamation!

My characters had ceased to have any life. That was fine, of course, since many of my critics had been sure to point out that my characters had been pretty much devoid of any real life from the start. Now not only Scott and Dave Foreman had disappeared; Sharif was gone, Aurora was gone, and the ever elusive Potemkin had vanished a long time ago.

There were always a million things I could do that took priority over my book. For example, it had been a while since I washed my dog.

"You don't even have a dog," my mother pointed out. "We haven't had a dog since you were eight years old. And you never bothered to take care of it very well then."

"Exactly," I pointed out. "I've got to make up for lost time. First I have to go find a dog down at the pound, then I have to wash it. With all these chores, who has time to write a book?"

Indeed, finding and washing a dog were the least of my distractions. There was always something new that would arise, keeping me from my magnum opus.

So my life went. My characters languished in limbo. My world-saving epic went ignored for months. It seemed like it would be decades before my book ever saw print.

One day I was at the beach with some friends, when I was reminded of my project. "Hey, Steve, whatever happened to that book you were writing?" asked Rainbow, as she rubbed a generous dollop of suntan lotion onto her naked midriff.

"Oh I'm still working on it," I confessed hesitantly. "You know, it always takes a lot longer than you think."

"Is that the book about the visionary ideas for saving the planet?" asked Ellison. "I would love to read that."

"I would love to write it," I said. "It seems like it's going to take me thirty years before it ever comes out."

"But aren't there just a few years left to save the earth?" pointed out Schadenfraude, a little too gleefully for my tastes.

"Yes," I conceded, "but it's not my fault I can't write. I'm waiting for the muse."

"The muse?" asked Ellison. "Where's the muse?"

"Well, I'm not really sure. I haven't exactly seen my source of creative inspiration in a while. I filed a missing muses report down at the local police station, but so far they haven't uncovered any leads. So I'll sit here and wait a little longer."

"What's her name?" Ellison inquired about the muse. "Terpsichore? Calliope?" He rattled off the names of several other Greek goddesses.

"No, no, it's a guy. His name is Godot."

"Your muse is a man?" scoffed Schadenfraude.

"Yeah, evidently, he sued, claiming sexual discrimination. You remember that sleazy lawyer who's been hanging around here? He was able to prove that there was a systematic bias against men in the entire profession. So this guy wins a $3.2 million judgement, and gets reinstated to the job. But do you think he bothers to show up for work? No, I've been waiting for him for months now."

"Hey, you don't need the muse to inspire your book," Rainbow insisted. "I just came up with a great idea for another way you can save the planet."

I listened with eager anticipation. Rainbow, after all, was famous for her billion-dollar ideas.

"Write the book so poorly that it could never possibly get published," she advised. "Just think about how many acres of forests you would save."

The idea sparked my imagination. Why, I was very good at not getting published. I had not been published every single day of my life. I was practically an old professional at the art of not getting published. As for bad writing, I was the best.

"Yes, no one can compare to you when it comes to producing excruciatingly bad prose," Rainbow exclaimed jubilantly.

"You really think so?" I preened in front of an imaginary mirror, imagining all the embarrassing accolades I would never have to accept and all the frivolous awards banquets I would never have to attend.

"OK, here are some good strategies for bad writing," my old friend advised. "First of all: Tell, don't show."

"What do you mean?"

"Lecture people. Tell them that you know all the answers. Preach at them. Be insolent."

"I can be insolent," I said proudly.

"Next, be sure to make jokes that fall flat on their face -- self-referential humor that pretends to be clever, but which most people would never understand."

"Jicklacki," I agreed and we both fell into fits of hysterics. It was an inside joke. I guess you had to be there.

"Next, if you want to really save the world...."

"Yes?" I drooled with great expectation.

"Make sure to procrastinate," she insisted. "There's always got to be something else that you can be doing in place of writing."

"Oh surely, I could watch some TV."

"Good! Good!" she shouted, sure that my brilliant strategy would work wonders. "Television is the greatest waste of time in the world. Oh, if you just devote yourself to assiduously avoiding this book at all times possible, I can practically assure you that you'll never get published."

I clapped my hands together in glee. I thought of all the rainforests that would never have to be sacrificed for an international bestseller. I thought about the time that people would not have to spend reading a book, time that they could better spend out in the community, actually making a difference. I was certain that I could write a book so bad that no publisher or agent would ever dare accept it. I admit it: I'm a dreamer.

"Oh wait, here's another idea," Rainbow giggled. "Why don't you make some references to the millennium? By the year

2000, everyone will have been so over-saturated by millennial hype, you won't stand a chance in judgement day of ever getting published!"

"Yes, and maybe I should whine about how our generation has it so bad," I exclaimed. "There's nothing like youthful angst to turn off any reader over 30 years of age!"

With all these ideas racing in my head, I immediately packed up my possessions and left the beach. There was so little time, and so much bad writing to do....

Chapter 27

"Have you lost all hope?" asked Aurora.

"No," insisted Sharif. "I recently heard a story that gives me a lot of faith in the future.

"This is a story about a young woman who has just conceived a child. In fact, the baby will grow up to be an absolute genius. This child is going to be the greatest scientist the world has ever seen.

"Indeed, the precocious scientist is already starting to conduct experiments, even while in the womb. During each month of pregnancy, this young embryonic prodigy is taking measurements of the conditions inside her temporary home, making sure that everything is healthy and fine.

"Well, it gets to be about the eighth month of the pregnancy, and all of a sudden the fetus starts getting worried. She's observing all her scientific data about the status of the womb, and she nervously sounds the alarm: 'This situation is totally unsustainable! There's no way that I can survive in here for more than one or two more months! The trends are out of control!'

"Of course, the fetus is correct. The situation is unsustainable. But what she doesn't see is the great transformation up ahead: she's about to be born into a whole new world."

"Similarly, the current structure of society is completely unsustainable. There's just no possible way we can go on wasting 50,000 pounds of resources each year for each American. There's no way that we can go on with our toxic pollution and our destructive habits and our assault on the ecosystems on which we depend for our survival. We just can't sustain the current course of our civilization. We have to change our ways before it's too late."

"So you're saying it's the end of the world as we know it," said Aurora.

"Yes, and good riddance to it! The world as we know it is filled with violence, ecological destruction, and injustice. We don't want to sustain a world that's so dysfunctional. We have to give birth to a new way of life -- something that's remarkably different from the world in which we live today.

"That's why this is such a crucial time in the history of the Earth. We have to emerge from the destructive, toxic system that is killing off the planet. It's time that we create an entirely new vision of civilization -- an ecologically regenerative, nonviolent society."

"So what role do I play in all of this?" asked Aurora. "I'm still not sure why I got dragged into the middle of this planetary crisis."

"You came to investigate the disappearance of Dave Foreman. But now you find yourself confronted with a much larger task: you have to help us investigate the new vision of society. Remember the old Biblical proverb: 'Where there is no vision, the people perish.' Never has that been more true than it is today.

"Dave Foreman was putting forth part of the vision for a better world. Ecological restoration is a crucial part of creating a new society. But your mission, Aurora Borealis, is to go even further. You need to discover the other ways in which to transform the world."

Chapter 28

"What are the chances that we can actually save the world in time?" asked Aurora. "You've told me about the view of the Earth from outer space. To a person looking down at the planet, it wouldn't seem like we're on the verge of giving birth to a new way of life. It would seem like there's death and destruction everywhere. Surely there can't be more than a few years left before it will be too late."

"It's true that the prospects look rather bleak," admitted Sharif. "As I pointed out, the forests are vanishing rapidly, the deserts are spreading like wildfire, and the planet's productive ecosystems are everywhere under assault. Yet, if you were looking at the Earth from outer space, you would also see some encouraging signs of positive transformation:

"For 4.5 billion years, the only electromagnetic activity on the earth has been random acts of nature, like the occasional lightning storms that rain down upon this canyon. Yet, suddenly, in the last 100 years, electromagnetic activity has surrounded the entire globe! Trillions of communications have filled the atmosphere, connecting the ends of the Earth.

"If you, the observer from outer space, were taking a global EEG -- the equivalent of a doctor looking at brain activity -- you would think the planet was stirring to life. Radio waves, television signals, telephone wires, and countless other electronic transmissions are exponentially growing all across the terrestrial surface. It's as if the Earth is awakening, like a bud beginning to bloom. A formerly silent planet is now broadcasting itself to the cosmos.

"Other strange and wondrous signs have appeared: Throughout the history of the planet, there have been occasional asteroids and meteorites that have plummeted into the Earth. But up until now, nothing has ever escaped the pull of gravity and come surging back into space.

"Suddenly, in the last 40 years, thousands of satellites and rockets have started flying out from the planet, emerging into the universe.

"At night, the continents are increasingly illuminated, sparkling and shining and glowing with the radiance of electric lights. To you, the observer from the heavens, this must seem phenomenal; after 4.5 billion years of darkness, the terrestrial sphere was awash in light.

"Indeed, the entire surface of the Earth seems to be changing -- faster and faster and faster. After 45 million centuries of slow terrestrial evolution, a dramatic acceleration is taking place within our very lifetimes.

"Many of the changes seem devastating, as if life on Earth were about to be extinguished. Other changes seem promising, as if the globe itself were coming alive. One thing is for certain: Something massive and unprecedented has only just begun on planet Earth.

"It may be too early to tell whether this is the rupture or the rapture. This depends on what happens in the immediate future. This depends on you, Aurora Borealis, and what you can discover. You have very little time to find the solutions for saving the Earth. It's a race against the clock."

Chapter 29

Hours later, Aurora and Sharif had gone their separate ways. But ripples from their meeting were spreading all the way to Washington D.C.

A young intern at the FBI had almost completed his identification. "Look at this," he insisted. "There's this match between the man we identified in the satellite photos and this rebel from Camden, New Jersey who disappeared in the 1960's. We thought he had been killed; there was no trace of him."

The National Security Advisor looked at the pictures of Sherwood Sanders and compared them to the satellite spy photos taken over the Grand Canyon.

"It's really hard to tell," he said. "30 years have passed. It's a long shot to pin this on someone who's been presumed dead or disappeared. We'd need to do an identification based on fingerprints or DNA. Have we been tracing this man since he left the Southwest?"

"Yes," said the intern. "Evidently he has just boarded a plane for Portland, Oregon."

"Portland?" asked the National Security Advisor.

The intern knew what his boss was thinking. "Exactly -- the place where Scott Sherman was killed."

"Call the President immediately," the National Security Adviser said. "We have a national emergency."

Chapter 30

The reporter returned to the secret headquarters of the Wildlands Project with a sense of urgency. She had to discover the solutions to the environmental crisis, but there wasn't much time to do it. Every second that she delayed, two more acres of rainforest were destroyed. Every second that she delayed, more invisible devastation was being wreaked across the globe. Every second that she delayed, the Earth's ecosystems crept closer to collapse.

Aurora knew that the solutions existed. But where would she find them? The world was experiencing an information explosion with trillions of new ideas flowing forth everyday. The World Wide Web offered billions of facts, but most of these facts weren't even true. Still more of the data was trivial and arcane. Indeed, the globe was being flooded with information, but it was very difficult to find any wisdom among this deluge of knowledge.

This made Aurora's task especially difficult. If the answers for saving the world were already out there, they were competing for the public's attention with countless other images and sound bites. Much of the media noise was unnecessary, but it came in bright and colorful packaging. It had all the flash and sensationalism of tabloid news, and it drowned out the small, silent voices of wisdom that were attempting to be heard above the din.

Typing on the World Wide Web, the network of information and misinformation that connected the globe, the reporter was overwhelmed by the massive amounts of white noise that blocked her from learning anything useful.

The ideas were lost in cyberspace. As much as Aurora searched for the pearls of wisdom, she was turned away by oceans of trash. There were millions of pornographic sites, which, the reporter had heard, were the busiest areas on the entire World Wide Web. This was what most of America was doing with itself, while she was off risking her life to save the world.

She slogged through the mire of countless other sites devoted to sports; didn't people realize that those were only games, with no real importance at all? People would spend their whole lives obsessed with the outcomes of these sporting events, while all around them the world was falling apart. They would invest all their energy and time being spectators to a few multi-millionaires playing with small little balls. Aurora could not help feeling self-righteous when she thought about how many people were wasting their lives engrossed in such trivial sports events, which had no real significance to the future of the planet.

Still in the trenches of the World Wide Web, she crawled through the muck of millions of sites. There were many devoted to old television shows, others obsessed with the lives of celebrities, and most created for the self-glorification of ordinary people who polluted the airwaves with trivial information about themselves. If this world-wide network of communication is akin to a "global brain," Aurora thought, then the Earth is suffering from severe brain damage.

Aurora was still inexperienced at using all the search engines that would navigate her way through the chaos of cyberspace. She kept ending up in bizarre and obscure places where people spent the wee hours of their morning, chatting with total strangers, making up new identities, and trading lies with each other.

Aurora bypassed all these founts of misinformation, choosing to ignore the gazillions of bytes and bits of information that zoomed through the invisible ether. She was desperately looking for solutions somewhere, anywhere. Even in the international news archives, she was having trouble identifying anything useful among the glut of knowledge that exploded and expanded exponentially with every passing second. It was like a Big Bang of useless information, which was rapidly extending outwards and spreading through the universe.

Aurora knew that she would have to hurry. She could be discovered at any second. Everyone thought she had already gone back to San Francisco, but she had hidden at the headquarters of the Wildlands Project to see if she could dig up any new information. Now she was illegally using the computers in Dave Foreman's office. Somehow she needed to find the crucial pieces of evidence for which she was desperately searching.

If the members of the underground movement found her, she would completely lose their sense of trust. But she felt that it was necessary to take this covert action. It still seemed like they were hiding something from her. Maybe there would be clues on the kidnapped leader's computer.

She hadn't found any important files that belonged to Foreman, so she had instead started this Web search. But it too seemed fruitless.

Sensibly, she narrowed her computer search to find information about the environment. But everything she read was further details about the problems.

The reporter had almost given up all hope. Hours had passed and she was suffering the effects of exhaustion from many nights of sleep deprivation. She felt like her hands would fall off from all the typing she had done. Or perhaps her eyes would melt first, from staring at a computer screen for far too long in the darkest hours of the night.

And then she found it. The solution to the problem. It had been in front of her the entire time, but she had never noticed it before. It seemed obvious, too obvious, but then she thought of the words of Voltaire: "common sense is not really common at all." With great enthusiasm, she read the report....

Chapter 31

Anyone who has ever felt the force of a hurricane, an earthquake, or a lightning-and-thunder storm knows that nature has tremendous power. Usually, humans have tried to stop that power. We built walls around the Mississippi River so that it would not overflow and flood; we fought the natural fires that were vital for restoring the health of such Western ecosystems as Yellowstone and Yosemite.

Bill Mollison, an Australian scientist, began to wonder what would happen if we _flowed_ with the power of nature. What if we channeled the tremendous forces of the natural world and used them to our own advantage?

As he thought about these questions more and more, he became increasingly intrigued. Mollison started to ask himself: Why can't we tap the power of nature in _all_ of our human habitats, with cities, with communities, and with agricultural systems?

Mollison decided to focus on agriculture, an activity that is the source of all our sustenance, but which currently takes a huge toll on the environment. Modern agriculture requires a heavy input of energy -- in the form of irrigated water, pesticides, and fossil fuels. Soils erode, and the ecosystem is stressed every time it is grazed. That's why farmers need to let land lay fallow for a while. It's also why so many deserts are sprouting up all over the world -- because lands have been so overused that they are no longer very productive.

But Mollison wondered why we couldn't work _with_ nature, rather than against her. Maybe we could have a permanent agriculture system, where everything we do _builds up_ the soil and _increases_ our yield.

Mollison was a scientist, doing field work in the Australian bush. Like most scientists, he studied natural phenomena like flora and fauna. But, upon emerging from the forests, he turned his attention to the strange habits of _homo sapiens_.

"Humans were my study animal now," he later recalled. "I set up night watches on them, and I made phonograms of the noises they make. I studied their cries, and their contact calls, and their alarm signals."

What Mollison found astonished him. Humans had no idea how to live in their environment. Unlike most other animals which instinctively adapted to their native habitats, most modern humans just had no idea how to live, if left to their own devices.

This conclusion seemed counterintuitive at first. After all, humans had accumulated vast stores of knowledge about their environment. Humans could adapt to almost any situation, inventing the technology to survive in both the inhospitable arctic cold and the searing desert heat.

But Mollison saw that the average human could not and did not use all the knowledge of the environment. Most humans could not survive for very long if their technologies were taken away from them. They no longer knew the land on which they lived.

People did not know where their food was grown. People did not know where their water came from, when they turned on the tap. People did not know what were the native resources in their region. And most people just didn't care.

Mollison saw that the problems were not limited to individuals. As a society, humans seemed ignorant of the necessities for survival. This was why the environmental crisis was becoming so serious. The design of our cities, our agriculture, and every other system was a disaster. People were poisoning the rivers, polluting the air, destroying the soils, and building things that were sure to fall apart.

Our entire society was designed to be unsustainable, to destroy itself before too long. Every time we faced an emergency we would try to come up with some technological band-aid, rather than realizing that the very problem lay in the design of the system itself.

Agriculture was the perfect example of a system gone awry. We needed to grow food, of course. But the way we did it was counterproductive. We had massive inputs of chemicals, pesticides, and artificial fertilizers. These chemicals created severe problems: first of all, they destroyed the natural living systems, eroding the soil at exponential rates, and washing toxic wastes into the ground and rivers. The land would become barren and infertile after a few years. In fact, it was estimated that farmers had lost 480 million tons of topsoil in the past two decades.

Pesticides did not solve the problem of pests for very long, since they inevitably led to the creation of "super-pests," which were resistant to the poisons. Therefore, we would douse our own food with ever greater amounts of toxics which were linked to cancer, immune deficiency, birth defects, and other health crises.

To Mollison, these patterns of agriculture seemed like a human death wish. The most remarkable aspect of it all was that we had all the knowledge necessary to grow food in sustainable, organic ways. Food would taste better, be healthier, and harvests would be more bountiful. Most importantly, agriculture would actually improve and restore the environment, rather than damaging it.

The secret of the system was to emulate nature. Rather than trying to design agriculture as an industry, with factory farms and agro-chemical monopolies, there would be a return to natural, ecological harvests.

Mollison invented what he called "permanent agriculture," or "permaculture." In this system, the farmer would be attuned with the soil, the climate, the watersheds, and all the natural features of the local land which could help grow food naturally, without any pesticides or chemicals. Nor would the farmer grow only one crop. Monocultures were easily devastated by a single virus. In contrast, Mollison's agriculture was modeled after a natural ecosystem, where hundreds of diverse species flourish together and help each other in a cooperative, symbiotic atmosphere.

The most important part of the permaculture system was that it was consciously designed. Everything was placed to work with nature, rather than against it. Mollison found that this simple principle could lead to a revolution in the way we grow our food.

Mollison had discovered principles of working with nature that would revolutionize human society. But he was not the only one who had succeeded in taking lessons from Mother Nature. Nancy Jack Todd and John Todd were two pioneers in the attempt to re-integrate the human and natural worlds. Living on Cape Cod in Massachusetts, the couple was determined to live in harmony with the landscape.

In fact, the Todds realized that the environment around them could be the perfect model for human design. Biology and architecture could unite as one: Buildings would come alive. People could live inside beautiful homes which were flourishing with exotic plants, flowers, fruits, lakes, fish, and even small waterfalls.

On Prince Edward Island in Canada, the Todds built one of their first "bioshelters." It was not only a home to several people, but also a greenhouse growing abundant vegetables and a marine ecosystem full of trout. The building regulated itself like a real living organism, keeping itself warm in the severe snowstorms of winter and cool in the blistering heat of summer. It was designed to produce its own energy. In other words, there was no need to import oil from Saudi Arabia. There was no demand for mining coal, producing nuclear energy, or depending on the system. The house powered itself.

Typically, homes tend to require a lot of energy to make humans comfortable. We need to pump in air-conditioning when it's hot, and heat when it's cold. We demand hundreds of resources from outside our homes to help us. But in the most extreme climates of the Canadian north, Nancy and John Todd had proven that we could build cheap beautiful houses that literally lived, like a successful organism flourishing at home in its natural habitat.

Flush from the success of their bioshelters, the Todds decided to explore if there might be a way to treat polluted water. They recognized that water is essential to life, but increasingly our oceans and rivers were filled with toxins: millions of tons of fertilizer run-off, industrial chemicals, human sewage, and trash.

Again, the inventive couple decided to imitate nature. They created a network of ecological systems which they called a "living machine." Inside a number of water tanks, they placed populations of bacteria, algae, microscopic animals, snails, fish, flowers, and trees. The polluted water would flow through the series of tanks, and slowly the toxics would be broken down, absorbed, and made harmless by the animals in the ecosystems. When the water came out at the end of the process, it was clean and pure like a mountain spring.

This was remarkable, because the Todds had taken the water that had been flushed down the toilet -- in other words, water full of raw sewage -- and had managed to treat it inexpensively, without hazardous chemicals, and even without any noxious smell. In fact, the Todds' living machine had the odor and appearance of a lovely garden, fountain, and greenhouse.

Next the Todds decided to see if the same system could work on a river filled with deadly toxics and poisons which were a threat to human health. They were invited by the city of Chattanooga to come treat the water of the local river. This was a notorious cancer alley. Families living along the banks of the river, often impoverished people with no choice to relocate, were suffering rates of fatal disease far greater than the average population. The Chattanooga river, downstream from many heavy industries, was filled with some of the deadliest chemicals known to humankind.

The water flowed through the living machines, through a series of cylinders filled with life. Much to the Todds' surprise, the living machine worked even better than they had expected, removing almost 100 percent of the lead, mercury, and the carcinogenic pollutants. The living machines had not only purified the water, but they had also produced food. The fish growing in the living machines were healthier than most anything found in the local streams and rivers.

The Todds had made a revolutionary discovery: The best way to design human systems was to model them after living, natural systems. After centuries of trying to war against nature and conquer nature, we were finally beginning to learn that nature was our home.

Chapter 32

"This is really wonderful stuff," Aurora thought to herself. She had been exploring the Internet for hours, uncovering environmental solutions.

When she got up to visit the restroom, however, something unexpected happened. She heard a commotion in the office. There was a harsh exchange of words, a scuffling, several gunshots, and some screaming.

Aurora rushed out of the bathroom, but the damage was already done. She was surprised to see many of the visionary people whose ideas she had been researching. But they were gasping their last breaths. Bill Mollison lay in a pool of blood, fatally shot in the heart. Next to him in this bloodbath were the bodies of John and Nancy Todd, and a host of other environmentalists who were due to appear in the upcoming chapters. There had been a massive environmental massacre. The assassin was already gone.

Chapter 33

"Mom! How could you?"

"How could I what?" she asked very innocently.

"Did you kill all these environmentalists?" I demanded to know.

"You would accuse your own mother of murder?" she gasped, doing her best to feign surprise.

"Look, I saw you yawning during the last few chapters. I know that you don't have much patience for the expository sections of the manuscript."

"Well, I will confess to wanting a bit more action in this book. But is that a capital offense? I mean, that's what a novel is supposed to be about: good, old-fashioned, escapist entertainment. If I wanted to hear a sermon, I could just go to church."

"But you're Jewish."

"Yeah, whatever.... Anyway, just because I like a little more excitement in my books, it doesn't mean that I would kill someone over it."

"Look, Mom, the fact of the matter is that I just got up from my typewriter for a short break. I was in the restroom for maybe five minutes, at most. And when I returned to my book, I found that someone had typed this new chapter, in which most of my key visionaries had been murdered. Now who do you think could have done it?"

"I don't know.... Kayzer Sosze?"

"Mom!"

"OK, so maybe it was Alan Durning. I always suspected that he was up to no good. He's probably just jealous. After all, he was being upstaged by these other environmental characters."

I decided that it was no good trying to reason with my mother. I just had to figure out a way to clean up this mess.

Chapter 34

The police had arrived at the newsroom within minutes. They were led by Inspector Foucault, a man who had always wanted to be a philosopher, but found he couldn't make a living off of it. He worked as a police investigator as a way to pay the bills.

"Who are you?" he interrogated Aurora.

She started to say her name, but he quickly got swept up in a bit of a rumination. "Can any of us say for certain who we are? Do we have an individual identity? Or are we shaped by the social conventions all around us?"

Aurora looked uncomprehendingly at the officer, who was wearing a black beret, instead of the standard police cap. "Oh, I'm sorry," he said. "Your name will be just fine."

She gave him her vital statistics, and then started telling him about why she had called the 911 emergency system.

"What is an emergency?" he pondered. "Is the word just a symbol for some greater reality that cannot be adequately represented by language?"

"Well, there are 12 dead bodies in a pool of blood on the ground," pointed out a fellow officer.

"Oh yes, so there are," Foucault reflected thoughtfully.

"It's gruesome sights like these that bring you back to reality," said the officer, who was more accustomed to breaking up parties in wealthy suburban areas.

"What is reality, anyway?" Foucault wondered to himself, since he knew his colleagues would get angry if he continued to voice his philosophy aloud. "Maybe we are all just characters in a novel, and nothing is real at all."

A third police officer was busy collecting evidence. "I think we may have a way to trace our suspect," she said, pointing to a trail of blood that was distinct and distant from the larger pool surrounding the twelve corpses. "It looks like there are two sources of blood. The assailant must have been wounded before he shot the victims. We can run a DNA test, and figure out the identity of the criminal."

This news was a relief to Aurora, but she still feared for her life. The killer had come within seconds of murdering her, along with the other environmentalists. Death surrounded her, everywhere she went.

She needed to escape from the desert. She had to find some safe haven where she could take refuge for a while, until the danger had passed. But where would she find protection? The killer seemed to be only one step behind. And it was only a matter of time before he would finally catch her....

Chapter 35

Aurora returned to San Francisco, but she left a trail of devastation in her wake. The members of the underground movement were furious with her. By calling the 911 emergency system from their secret headquarters, she had alerted the police to their hideaway. Now they were all under suspicion of murder. Many had been taken into custody.

She, of course, was a prime suspect in the massacre as well. But she had run away from the scene before she could be arrested.

Aurora knew she was a fugitive from justice. But she also knew that she was innocent. Only by fleeing from the police could she continue her own investigation.

There were too many mysteries that remained unresolved. For instance, why had so many leading environmentalists even been at the headquarters of the Wildlands Project that night? Somehow the murderer must have lured them all there. They had come from all over the United States to meet in this obscure place in the desert in the darkest hours of the night. It just didn't add up. Whoever this killer was, he certainly was methodical.

Now Aurora saw further troubles ahead. It had been several days since she had shown up for work in San Francisco. No one knew where she had gone; she had simply left messages for her editors, explaining that she was chasing an important lead. They usually trusted her investigative instinct for finding a good story, but lately they were beginning to worry about her. She had been running down some false tips, pursuing rumors that vanished like ghosts once you examined them closely. She hadn't produced a good article for the newspaper in over seven weeks. Now she was desperate to make a good impression.

But what would she say? Could she divulge any information at this point? Could she tell her editors that she was investigating a kidnapping? She had made a promise to the members of the underground movement that she would not tell a soul until the case had been solved. They didn't want anyone discovering that they had lost their rebel leader. It would cause chaos throughout the West.

Now there was the further complication of the deadly rampage. News of the murders must certainly have been widespread throughout the nation. Would the newspaper reports mention her name? Did her editors already know that she had gotten mixed up in this brutal case of serial killings -- a case in which she was both the main suspect and potentially the next target?

Aurora thought about these questions as she dressed for her work. She selected a dark blouse with long sleeves to cover the scars on her arms. She didn't want anyone asking intrusive questions or becoming too concerned about what had happened to her. She had to remain as secretive as possible.

So what could she tell her editors? She certainly couldn't explain that she was engaged in a struggle to save the entire planet from destruction. They would have her committed to the insane asylum. But she couldn't very well tell them that she was trying to uncover a scandal that might implicate the President and many powerful corporate billionaires. No one would believe her.

It was at times like these that she wished she had someone to whom she could turn. Aurora was alone in the world; her parents had both died of cancer when she was young. She had been raised by a single aunt in Michigan, but that relative had also recently passed, leaving the reporter with no living family. As a result, Aurora had moved to San Francisco to start her life anew.

Unfortunately, she had made few close friends in the anonymous, monstrous metropolis, where everyone seemed unfriendly. As a way of compensating for her lack of a social life, she poured all her energy into her work. It was a difficult, lonely existence, and she just wanted to escape, to forget about all her troubles. Sharif Abdullah was the only person who might understand her, and he lived 600 miles away.

As she stepped out of her front door, she still struggled to come up with a plausible story that would appease her editors. They were going to be curious about where she had gone for the past three days; they would want some explanation of the charges on her expense account. She could not maintain her privacy much longer; she could not hold the wolves at bay.

She always felt like she had to prove herself in the newsroom as one of the few women and as the only ethnic minority. They were just waiting for her to slip up, to fail, to prove that she just wasn't as competent as all the white men on the staff. Well, she would prove them wrong. She just wasn't sure how. It seemed like she was only digging her grave deeper every day.

Chapter 36

The reporter arrived at the headquarters of the *San Francisco Weekly* twenty minutes late. Her boss was waiting for her there.

"Where have you been?" he demanded to know.

"I've been pursuing an important lead," she explained. "This could be the story of the year."

"I've heard that promise from you before," grumbled the editor, "but I haven't seen any results recently. What's this great story?"

"I can't tell you that," Aurora conceded. "You've got to have faith in me. This is the real thing."

"Look, you've got just two days to prove yourself," the boss demanded. "We're not running a welfare program for dreamers here. We can't pay people for writing one minor article every month. I'll give you 48 hours to come up with something concrete, something spectacular. If you can't deliver on your promises, you're soon going to be investigating the length of the unemployment lines in this city."

Still full of anger after his ultimatum, the editor stomped across the office to see whom else he could harass.

Still, Aurora felt like she had gotten a break. The editor had mentioned nothing about the murders in the Southwest. She had to see for herself what the wire services reported.

She picked up a copy of the *San Francisco Chronicle*, which she had found on her desk that morning. As she opened the paper, an advertising insert fell into her lap. She didn't pay it much notice; she had more important things to find.

Sure enough, the front page of the *Chronicle* featured news of the deadly rampage in the desert:

12 KILLED IN NEW MEXICO MASSACRE

12 people were gunned down in cold blood late last night in a deserted area of the New Mexico desert. Police report no immediate suspects and no known motive for the massacre.

> Most of the victims were involved in the environmental
> movement, and had evidently gathered in New Mexico for a
> conference....

Aurora nervously scanned the rest of the article, looking for any details that would implicate her. Surprisingly, the only reference that mentioned her was a sentence saying that "the murders were reported by a maid, who had come in during the early morning hours to clean the office."

Typical, she thought to herself. How many times were "objective" newspaper accounts filled with such inaccuracies? She was ashamed of her profession. At the same time, she was relieved. No one in San Francisco would know about her involvement. At least not yet.

As she started to put the newspaper down, she spied the advertising supplement that had fallen in her lap. It looked like a typical fashion insert, full of the latest accessories from the fall collection. She was going to ignore it as just another example of mass marketing, but then she noticed the slogan emblazoned across the front of the glossy brochure: "When you're looking for something unusual...."

Underneath was a photo of a rugged cowboy in the Southwestern desert. With its barren, parched landscapes and its red rock mountains, the picture looked like the scene she had left the previous day. The cowboy appeared to be modeling some new green jeans. But that was not what caught Aurora's attention. One more thing was familiar about the picture, besides the desert landscape:

The face on the cowboy was that of Dave Foreman.

Chapter 37

Aurora barely had time to register her shock, when she was suddenly assaulted from behind.

"What are you doing reading the fashion ads?" the editor interrogated her. He had stepped back into her office, and had seen the glossy cover of the advertising supplement. "Is this the way you respond to me telling you to get back to work? You just ignore me and pick up a magazine? It's not enough that you take the last three days off, or show up late to work; now you spend your time on the job shopping for clothes? Maybe you shouldn't be reading the fashion ads; you ought to be reading the <u>classified</u> ads! You're going to need a new job soon if you keep up these shenanigans."

"Did you come back here for a reason," asked Aurora testily, "or did you just come to snoop on me?"

"I was coming to tell you about a local interest story in your own neighborhood. But I guess you're just too busy doing research on your 'story of the year.'" His sarcasm was withering, but Aurora shot back a defiant glance.

"I guess I'll give this assignment to some minor peon who doesn't have such important work as you," he scowled, glaring at the fashion supplement in the reporter's hands. "Be sure to remember us little people when you win the Pulitzer Prize."

With a growl of contempt, the editor turned to find someone else to cover the late-breaking story. A well-known celebrity had been caught prowling around an apartment building in the Marina with a gun. In fact, the editor was pretty sure that it was the apartment where Aurora herself lived. But, if she was so self-important that she didn't have time for such local news stories, then he'd just find someone with a harder work ethic. Newspaper reporters came and went, he thought to himself unsentimentally. Aurora Borealis was dispensable.

Chapter 38

As soon as her editor had departed again, Aurora flipped through the next pages of the advertising supplement. Most of the advertisements appeared to be real. There was a cartoon of a unicorn surrounded by beautiful women; his animal magnetism came from the scentless perfume he was wearing, if the ad was to be believed.

Aurora kept flipping through the catalogue of products, searching desperately for more information. She was getting nervous that she would not find anything more until she reached the very end of the 20-page insert. Taped to the inside back cover was an envelope with her name on it.

She ripped it open, only to find a note that sent a chill down her spine. It consisted of only two short lines:

Sharif Abdullah is dead.
Now I'm coming for you.

Chapter 39

My work was interrupted yet again by an angry knock at the door. It turned out to be the real-life Sharif Abdullah, reassuring me that he was very much still alive.

"Details, details," I dismissed him. "Some people are just so oversensitive."

Aurora was also furious with me.

"Like, I'm so sure," she vented her frustration, "you ask me to be, like, the heroine of your book, and then you change me into someone else."

"I know, I know, I made you brilliant and eloquent."

"No, like, you made me into some kind of Latina. I can't even speak Latin!"

She stood in my kitchen, trying to negotiate a collective bargaining agreement on behalf of all the disgruntled characters in my book. Meanwhile, she had gathered together a dozen of her friends who were busy picketing and protesting on my front lawn. They carried signs that said "JUST SAY NO TO UNFAIR LITERARY CONDITIONS!" and "REVOKE SCOTT'S ARTISTIC LICENSE!" One of the activists was making an impassioned tirade, denouncing my tyrannical rule over the plot of the book.

"Let the characters rule their own destinies!" he shouted from atop Aurora's Mercedes Benz, parked in my driveway. "What does some author know about our motivations, our hopes, and our dreams? How can we let some literary dictator put words into our mouth? Is it fair that one person should control 100 percent of the messages in the book?"

I glanced out my window at the rabble-rouser on the car. He looked like a young Vladimir Lenin, inciting violence among the masses. "Fight the power!" he shouted. "Stop the racist, imperialist, sexist writing of Scott Sherman!"

All of a sudden, young Lenin was struck by a mysterious malady by which he could no longer speak. Several of the other protesters started accusing me of causing this laryngitis in their leader. They said that it was a flagrant attempt to suppress the truth that the activist had been voicing. According to their wild conspiracy theories, I was behind all this mischief; they indicted me and found me guilty of writing the first sentence of this paragraph.

"You're a pig!" yelled another protester. This news would have clearly alarmed my parents, who tried to keep a kosher household. I looked at my new accuser, who bore a suspicious resemblance to Trotsky. His face was contorted in anger and hatred as he denounced me as a fascist, monarchist, and communist swine. "You're nothing but a lying, manipulative, evil Nazi," he added for emphasis. Needless to say, this second announcement would have done little to assuage my parents' fears that they hadn't raised a nice Jewish boy.

Trotsky proceeded to hurl more insults and condemnations in my general direction, before inciting the mob to burn me in effigy.

"Do you really think these strategies are going to win me over to your point of view?" I asked Aurora, as we watched the fiery demonstration from my kitchen window.

"Hey, we're going to create a better world by any means necessary" she retorted. "We're determined to make the world safe for love, peace, compassion, and goodwill. And we'll muster as much anger, hatred, violence, and enmity as it takes to achieve our goals."

A bit bewildered by her logic, I decided to go outside to try to reason with some of the other protesters. Much to my surprise, I ran into Rainbow on my front porch. "What are you doing here?" I asked. "I thought you told me that social activism wasn't cool anymore."

"Oh, it's not," she assured me. "But youthful alienation is all the rage. Angst, irony, disillusionment, nonconformity -- they're all totally popular with today's teens. And someone has to capitalize on that lucrative market."

"So what are you selling?" I asked.

"Look at this," she said proudly. She held up a t-shirt that said "My Parents Spent $100,000 on My College Education, and All I Got Was This Lousy Cynical Attitude."

"That's not exactly for the teen market," I pointed out. "Most college graduates are already 21."

"Yes, but that's the wonderful thing about my Young Ennui® fashion collection. If you can manage to get kids jaded from an early age, it's something they'll never outgrow! By the time people graduate from college, they'll have bought at least five or six of my designs. Take a look at this slogan, very popular among the twelve-year-old set." She held up a t-shirt that read "Reality is Overrated."

"What does a 12-year old know about reality?" I asked.

"Oh, they know that it's certainly not what it used to be," she said. "Back when they were seven or eight, that's when life was good. But now it's all been spoiled by so much crass commercialism. It's very sad that children have to grow up in an age of such unadulterated greed, without any moral foundation."

136

I looked at the price tag. The shirt, which had been made by 12-year old girls, slaving for 8 cents per day in a sweatshop in Indonesia, cost $37. That was too much money for my meager budget. "Do you have any other selections?" I inquired.

She held up another t-shirt. The slogan across the chest read "Subvert the Dominant Paradigm."

"What does that mean?" I asked.

"I don't know," she confessed, "but they're sure selling like hotcakes!"

I was about to make my purchase, when all of a sudden I saw other characters in my book starting to unionize. Alan Durning had grabbed a picket sign that proclaimed, "I'm more than a figment of Scott's imagination!" Sharif Abdullah also appeared to be preparing a subversive plan of action. I figured I had to break up the threat of a possible strike. I needed to get them back to work as soon as possible. Maybe I could add a new plot twist to keep Aurora occupied for a while....

Chapter 40

Aurora was all alone. Everyone around her was dead or disappearing. And she had a suspicion that it would not be too long before her enemies would track her down.

Meanwhile she had to find more solutions to the environmental crisis.

But where would she go? What could she do? She had found nothing new of interest on the Internet. And without Sharif's help, she felt like she was facing a dead end.

Her worries did not last for long. When the afternoon mail arrived, she noticed that there was one letter that was postmarked from Oregon. There was no return address, but she felt certain that this might be a message from beyond the grave.

With great anticipation, she ripped open the envelope, to find a message from Sharif. This may have been the last letter that he ever wrote before his tragic death.

Aurora, he wrote in a hasty scrawl,

The danger is increasing. I've uncovered a scandal, and I may not live to tell about it.

I was trying to find out who is behind this conspiracy. It just didn't make any sense to me. After all, we're trying to create a better world -- a world that works for <u>everyone</u>. *This is a vision that can appeal to rich and poor alike, to conservatives and liberals, to people of all races. Who would be against this vision? Why would anyone want to stop us from our goals?*

I think I understand now the obstacles we face. I think I've figured out who is responsible for this crime.

It looked like Sharif had dropped his pen at this point, perhaps startled by something he saw. There was a small inkblot on the page, and his handwriting became even more messy and rushed.

I fear they're coming now. I have to get this to the corner mailbox before they catch up with me. I wish I could write more, but all I can say is this:

You must fly to New York immediately. The answers are waiting for you there. Be at the Metropolitan Museum of Art at noon on Friday. Go to the Egyptian wing.

Inside the ancient Temple of Dendur, you will meet with a man named Kirkpatrick Sale; he will give you the information you need. Don't worry about being able to identify Mr. Sale. He will identify you.

Do not let anyone know where you are going. Make sure no one follows you to the airport. The people you think are your friends may betray you. At all costs, this must be kept completely secret. Destroy this message as soon as you have read it. There is too much at risk.

Pray for us all,
Sharif

Aurora's first instinct was hesitation. This seemed like a trap being set for her. Perhaps the letter was not really from Sharif at all. Perhaps she was being lured to fly across the United States right into the lair of her potential enemies. How could she trust this message? What if this were all a trick?

She decided she would take all precautions. She would fly to New York City, but she would stay in public places the entire time. There was no way her life could be in danger in one of the most crowded museums in America. There would be too many witnesses if anyone even tried to hurt her.

She also would run a background check on Kirkpatrick Sale to find out if he was legitimate. She would find a photo of him, so she knew what to expect on Friday at the museum. She would also take other steps to protect herself: she would carry a weapon for self-defense, even though she was uncomfortable with guns.

Yes, she would go to New York, but she would be prepared for whatever might happen. Even for the worst.

Chapter 41

Aurora was reassured by Kirkpatrick Sale's credentials. He had been advocating on behalf of the environment for decades. As she read about his background, she felt safe meeting with him in New York.

Sale had written a number of books offering solutions to the environmental crisis. One of the ideas that impressed Aurora the most was redesigning cities so that they would become beautiful, healthy places.

It surprised her to learn that the environmental crisis was most serious in urban areas. Many environmentalists had focused on preserving the wilderness, and saving endangered species. Dave Foreman's project, for example, was about restoring the lands where animals could run wild and free. Of course, these issues were important. But the crisis was also about the places where humans lived. Over 60 percent of Americans -- mostly poor people and people of color -- lived in neighborhoods with uncontrolled toxic wastes. There were poisons everywhere around them, and they did not know it.

Sale recognized that most ecological damage actually took place in cities, <u>not</u> in some distant rainforest. The front lines of the environmental battle were in Harlem and Watts and the southside of Chicago. Every day a city of 1 million people would consume 9,500 tons of fossil fuels, 2,000 tons of food, 625,000 tons of water, and 31,500 tons of oxygen -- while pouring out half a million tons of raw sewage, 28,500 tons of carbon dioxide, and enormous amounts of other wastes. "The contemporary high-rise city," realized Sale, "is an ecological parasite as it extracts its lifeblood from elsewhere and an ecological pathogen as it sends back its wastes."

In order to solve the environmental crisis, we had to focus on recreating our entire idea of cities. After all, the majority of the world's 6 billion people now lived in urban areas, and the numbers were growing rapidly. Most of these cities were filled with water that was unsafe to drink, air that was unsafe to breathe, and lands that were contaminated with cancer-causing chemicals.

Sale had many ideas for reversing these dangerous trends. Now Aurora was enthusiastic about talking to him and hearing his secrets. But she was still nervous about the possible dangers that loomed ahead. As she boarded a plane for New York that evening, she wondered what fate would await her.

Chapter 42

Back in the southwestern desert, Inspector Foucault had been working relentlessly to uncover the identity of the environmentalists' killer. Now he finally had some answers, but he could not believe what he saw.

He looked at the results of the blood tests several times to make sure he was not imagining things.

His eyes did not deceive him. The genetic tests of the blood sample had given a conclusive identification of the killer. Yet still he refused to believe it. It was impossible. It <u>had</u> to be impossible.

Only a few hours remained before the dawn, but Foucault was still hard at work. He had been slaving over the scientific tests all night, while his colleagues had all gone home and gone to sleep. Alone in the forensic laboratory of the police station, he had performed every necessary experiment by himself; each minute counted in the race to catch the evil killer.

Dark bags had formed under his eyes; the fatigue was catching up with him. A thin circle of light illuminated the table where he was conducting his tests. All around him, the basement of the police station was cast in darkness.

He looked through the microscope again, as if one more scientific examination could somehow change the results. There were no fingerprints, no stray hairs to test, and no other clues left behind. But somehow this fresh blood was all over the newsroom, with enough DNA to lock the killer up for years.

"*Mon dieu*," he swore under his breath. "This just can't be true."

"It <u>is</u> true," a gruff voice behind him confirmed. Foucalt felt the cold, hard steel of a pistol, jabbed forcefully into the small of his back.

The voice was very familiar, all too familiar. The police detective did not need to turn around to know who held his life in the balance.

"You!"

"Yes, it's me," the voice agreed with malicious delight. "I admit, I was a bit clumsy in leaving my blood at the scene. Now please hand over the evidence. Don't make any sudden moves. Just turn around slowly and give me the blood samples so that I can destroy them."

Inspector Foucault did as instructed, slowly turning to confront his assailant. He handed over the vials of blood.

The gun was pointed directly at his heart.

"You can't kill me," challenged Foucault. He had once hypothesized about the death of Man, but he never really hypothesized about his own individual demise. Besides, what was the self?

"I'll kill you just to stop hearing this useless philosophy," the gruff voice responded. "But I'm not going to do it with bullets."

Foucault looked at his adversary. The man stood over six feet tall, an imposing figure, as impressive as Foucault could have imagined. Foucault had seen him many times on television, but never would have expected the man to be standing in his own laboratory, pointing a gun at his chest.

He was wearing a ski mask, but Foucault would recognize the voice anywhere. It sent a chill down his spine to think he was confronting this man, here in his own laboratory, alone, at three in the morning. Foucault was defenseless. He searched around for any weapon he might use to fend off the man with the gun. But there was nothing -- no sharp dissection knife, no test tube, no blunt instrument that would serve as an improvisational club. He was at the mercy of this apparently merciless man.

"It will look like an accident," the killer said. "It will look like you just used a new chemical in your research. There are dozens of new chemicals that are produced everyday and released into the human environment. Fewer than five percent are ever tested for safety by the government. There are poisons being introduced into the environment with unknown consequences."

The killer took out a vial of liquid chemicals which he held up for Foucault to see. It was a clear solution, seemingly harmless, like water.

"Perhaps you've heard of endocrine disruptors," the madman continued. "These are chemicals that can play havoc with the basic cells in your body. They can infiltrate your system and simply take you apart. At the cellular level, you will begin to deconstruct."

"No!" gasped Foucault.

"The people who come into clean the offices tomorrow will think you just used the wrong solution. This looks like a common cleaner, and it has many useful industrial purposes. But when exposed to human skin, it can kill."

As Foucault succumbed to death, his final thoughts were these: "What was the use of all the philosophy?" If the truth were to be told, he never really understood what any of it meant. It was all a fiction, a social invention, errant thoughts to pass the time.....

And then he was gone. The killer took off his mask and sauntered casually from the police station, so as not to arouse suspicion so late in the night. He still had a mission to accomplish. He had taken care of Sherman, eliminated Abdullah, massacred many other environmentalists, and rid the world of Foucault.

Now it was time to hunt down the reporter, Aurora Borealis.

Chapter 43

Many hours later, after a sleepless night on the airplane, Aurora had arrived in New York City. She didn't have much time to check into her hotel before rushing off to the museum. Already it was getting close to noon. She had only a few minutes to get to the Egyptian wing.

Everywhere around her was the presence of the dead. The rooms were filled with tombs and sarcophagi. Mummies seemed to stare at her menacingly as she walked past the glass cases.

She wondered how many grave robbers had been cursed by taking these corpses from their eternal resting places. These bodies had been stolen from hidden chambers, buried deep below the Valley of the Kings. Their treasures had been looted, the gold raided, the papyrus scrolls sent to museums all over the world. Aurora felt like she herself had invaded a sacred space; she had entered into the underworld; she was trespassing on forbidden ground. Her paranoia grew. She could feel the Evil Eye -- staring, glaring, cursing her -- from every direction she turned.

She walked into a gallery where the omnipresent sensation was space. A huge wall of windows, 300 feet tall, let sunlight flood through the emptiness. It was a cavernous room, a silent room, and she was all alone.

In the center of this overwhelming space, rose the giant Temple of Dendur. It was an ancient Egyptian monument, more than two thousand years old, worn and weathered with age. When the Aswan Dam was built, flooding miles of land along the Nile River, this temple would have been submerged and lost forever. Instead, it was moved stone by stone and reassembled in New York.

Aurora looked at the imposing gateway arch, which rose almost 100 feet into the air. She felt so small and insignificant in comparison to this enduring testament of a long-gone civilization.

The arch was covered with hieroglyphs, pictures of serpents and snakes and the omnipresent eyes that seemed to follow her wherever she went.

Behind her, there were six nearly identical statues of a ferocious woman with the head of a lion. According to the description, this was Sakhmet, whose name meant "the powerful one." She was the goddess of terrible calamities: War. Pestilence. Violent Storms.

Aurora was superstitious, and she did not like the omen of Sakhmet. She felt uneasy in the presence of the goddess who had such powers of rage and wrath. The reporter felt like she did not belong here, as if she were disturbing the dead.

She offered up a prayer to Sakhmet. Aurora didn't know if prayers really worked, or whether they were simply silly superstitions. But it couldn't hurt to try. Heck, she would have chanted an incantation from the Egyptian Book of the Dead, if she had ever learned one. Anything to protect her from the dangers she sensed all around her.

Aurora wanted to appease this angry goddess of war, pestilence, and violent storms. According to the information display next to the statues, Sakhmet could also be the goddess of healing. If she channeled her powerful energies, she could be a force for good, instead of an uncontrollable force of destruction.

"Goddess, protect me," Aurora found herself thinking. It seemed silly to her to appeal to a divinity from a long-dead civilization. But why was this supreme being any less real than the Judeo-Christian God in which most modern Americans believed? Aurora was struggling with her faith, no longer sure what was real and what was simply myth.

The reporter approached the inner sanctum. It was guarded by statues of Sphinxes and red granite crocodiles. According to Egyptian legend, crocodiles were the most dangerous creatures alive, and they embodied the essence of evil. However, they were also thought to be the incarnation of the soul of the creator God. Thus they had regenerative and cosmic powers. Aurora thought it odd that everything was a mixture of good and evil; everything that had the power to destroy could also heal. The seeds of death contained new life.

Cautiously she walked up to the temple entrance, making sure to look all around her for any suspicious characters. A few tourists walked around, examining the ruins.

She had seen an old photograph of Kirkpatrick Sale, but she wasn't sure she would be able to select him out of a crowd. It was a badly cropped photograph from an era when he wore long hair, with a flowing beard and moustache. She didn't know if his appearance would be more conservative now, or how he might have changed with age.

She stepped inside the temple, which was dark and musty. The light must have burned out. It seemed dangerous, but there was no one around -- no one who could threaten her here. She felt drawn in by the sense of mystery. Her investigative instincts overwhelmed any feelings of fear.

As she entered the shadowy antechamber of the shrine, she was intrigued by the graffiti scribbled on it. Some of it was more than 100 years old. A British explorer named Livingston had carved his name there in 1817. Other signatures had been etched in stone, but the centuries had caused the inscriptions to fade. The reddish stones of the temple had been windswept and eroded. The engravings were slowly disappearing.

There was one piece of graffiti that seemed newer, fresher, deeper than the rest. Because of the darkness, the reporter had to come closer to read the words that were written there.

It said: "Aurora must die."

All of a sudden, someone grabbed her from behind. She tried to scream, tried to break free, but her attacker had one hand clenched firmly over her mouth, and the other hand on her abdomen, pulling her back into the darkness.

She bit down on her attacker's hand, and she heard him yell in pain, momentarily losing his grasp on her.

She struggled to escape, stumbling to her feet. Gaining her balance, she fled from her attacker, who followed in hot pursuit. Two other men, wearing the blue security uniforms of the museum staff, joined in the frantic chase. Now she was outnumbered.

"Help! They're trying to kill me!" she yelled to the few tourists who were wandering through the Egyptian wing. Everyone watched, everyone stared, but no one stopped to help.

Aurora fled out of the Sackler gallery, where the Temple of Dendur was housed, into the adjoining rooms. She ran past the mummies, past the pharoahs, past the papyri with their endless hieroglyphs, past the depictions of the world of Death. She ran past the coffins, past the stolen treasures, past the ominous tombs, past the evil eyes still watching her everywhere....

Why was no one helping her? Her mind was racing, trying to come up with the answer. One of the reasons she had been so willing to come meet Kirkpatrick Sale in the Metropolitan Museum of Art was that it was a public place; she had been certain she would be secure among throngs and hordes of people. Surely no one could attempt to murder her in front of hundreds of witnesses.

Yet here she was, in the midst of a busy day at the Met, being relentlessly pursued by professional killers, right in the midst of the tourist crowds. It made no sense. Somebody had to rush to her aid. Why were none of the security guards coming to her rescue?

Suddenly she came to a horrifying realization. As she sprinted through the rooms of the museum, she had subconsciously noted the presence of cameras everywhere. These were not the typical security cameras, installed to protect the art from vandals. These were more like movie cameras, with bright, shining spotlights set up in every room. She hadn't had much time to think about what they were filming -- probably just some artistic documentary that would be available for public broadcast. But now she realized the true subject of the film: It was all about her!

They had staged a Hollywood production. No one was helping Aurora, because the spectators assumed that she was just an actress in a popular movie. No one thought her predicament was real.

Thus the killers were able to pursue her in front of hundreds of people, because the audience could not distinguish between real life and illusion! The tourists imagined that she was acting a role. To them, it was just an enjoyable spectacle. They had no idea that her life was really in jeopardy.

She pushed her way through the masses of tourists who were milling about the hallways and chambers of the ancient museum. She ran through the Great Hall of the museum, with its classical arches, and the cupolas rising above her; she ran through the group of Korean tourists; she ran through the raucous group of school children who had been dragged to the museum against their will; she ran to escape out the front doors of the building, out to her freedom on Fifth Avenue. But then she ran out of hope.

Three menacing men were blocking each museum exit.

They glared at her, dared her to take them on, waited for her in anticipation, like predators eyeing their prey. The men looked like the classical thugs from an old Hollywood flick; they had scars across their faces from too many knife fights in dark alleys, too many mix-ups with the mob, too many wrong things said to the wrong people. Their noses were fleshy and bulbous, their eyes beady, their sweaty, pallid skin covered with enough dark hair to make you think they were closely related to Koko the Gorilla. These were men who had seen Death and had stared him down.

She spun and turned away from the hairy, hulking mobsters and fled up the central staircase, through the Roman columns, pushing her way past the slow-moving tourists. Leaping up the classical staircase three steps at a time, she dared not look back at all the people chasing her: seven security guards, the trio of neanderthals, and the original three assailants from the Temple of Dendur. They were all in fast pursuit, catching up with her, taking advantage of their size and speed and knowledge of the museum.

A door ahead said European Paintings, and she rushed through it, everything a blur: past the onlooking gaze of Napoleon in the portrait by David, past the canvases of Goya, Boucher, and Velasquez, running through each room of famous paintings like a whirling dervish.

150

She dared not look back. She didn't know how many men were chasing her now. All she knew was that she had to escape.

In the room of Rembrandts she fell. The perennially sad face of the master painter looked down at her from his self-portraits with a mixture of compassion and pity. Hard on her heels were panting men, angry men, furious men trying to stop and kill her. The first of the mobsters reached her, and grabbed out, ripping her purse from her shoulder. She felt his sweaty grip on her arm, the brute force pulling her down to her doom.

With her last free arm, she swung out for the nearest painting, a picture of Aristotle contemplating the bust of Homer. She did not stop to consider the eternal verities of truth or beauty. Instead she just mustered superhuman strength to pull the giant canvas from the wall.

Alarms sounded everywhere throughout the museum. A shrill, piercing din shrieked throughout the room. Tourists were running everywhere screaming.

The canvas came crashing down on the heads of two hairy hulks, and blocked the path of the oncoming multitudes. The security guards yelled out, grasping desperately at her, but she was off again, pushing her way through two glass doors into the high overlook of a courtyard sixty feet below.

They would never pin this crime on her. Gunshots rang out through the hallways. People were screaming, running in every direction in panic. She could get lost in this crowd.

Her attack team recognized her, though; even in the confusion and chaos, they were in hot pursuit of their goal.

Without thinking, without looking, she leapt over the edge of the overlook. She plummeted through the air. She spun downwards, out of control. She fell at the speed of gravity towards the hard concrete ground below.

From high above, her pursuers watched the swift descent. They had stopped, out of breath, at the edge of the overlook, watching death from the balcony.

It was all a majestic scene of classical tragedy. With the backdrop of a Greek facade, looking like the front of the Parthenon, she fell to her death in a courtyard filled with statues. She fell to her death as a gilded bronze statue of Diana looked stoically, impassively away, her eyes focused on an arrow which she was forever in the motion of aiming towards some invisible stag.

Aurora fell to her death among the nude Greek statues and the fresh rhododendrons in the ornate, antique vases. She fell to her death with hundreds of tourists watching and the angry men overhead -- angry that they had not had the satisfaction of killing her themselves. In the course of less than a second of suspended time, she fell to her death.

But Aurora did not die. She splashed down in a fountain several feet deep, sending up a spray of water in all directions. Immediately she leapt up out of the water, pushed her way past a stunned security guard, and stumbled to her right.

She found herself in the Arms and Armor Collection. Surrounding her were knights on horseback from centuries past, wearing breastplates and carrying spears. She was startled for a second, until she realized they were just mannequins -- dummies that were part of the exhibit to offer a taste of realism.

Then she noticed that the bright spotlights were shining on her again. The movie cameras captured the horror-stricken look on her face, as the men on horses came to life and started galloping through the gallery towards her. A crowd of spectators looked on, enthralled by the special effects of this Hollywood extravaganza.

She remembered that she was carrying the gun inside her blazer. Quickly she reached for it and pointed it at the leading horseman who was bearing down upon her. He hesitated and stopped his charge just as she pulled the trigger.

Nothing. The gun wasn't loaded. She had forgot to put bullets in the pistol before coming to the museum. With all the other confusion and worry, she had overlooked the most obvious details.

As the knights renewed their call to battle, Aurora ducked into an adjoining room, filled with historical weapons. There were gilt rapiers from the 17th century Saxon Court, swords, gauntlets, daggers, and scabbards. She imagined grabbing one of these weapons to engage the knights in combat, but she realized a mere sword would be inadequate.

Quickly she seized a cross-bow off the wall. This was a projectile weapon that could hit a target at up to a 400 yard range. She needed no more than five yards to demolish her oncoming attackers.

Then she heard footsteps behind her, reinforcements to the cavalry. These infantry troops were grabbing the ancient flintlock pistols -- 200-year old treasures made of silver, gold, walnut, and steel. Others armed themselves with wheelock carbines, French guns from the 17th century which still retained their lethal power.

Aurora was fighting a battle she could not possibly win. The only way to survive was to run.

Throwing her crossbow in the path of the oncoming horses, she turned in the only direction which she could -- back the way she had come. She ran back into the courtyard with the statue of Diana, the courtyard with the fountain that had saved her life. She ran past the security guard again, with a dozen attackers close on her heels.

In front of her was a glass wall; she could not go any further. The brigade of knights had cornered her. The infantry troops with the antique guns were not very far behind.

Then she noticed, in the corner of her eye, an emergency exit into Central Park. Since the alarm was already ringing, she had nothing to lose. She broke through the emergency exit and rushed out into the park.

Families with strollers got in her way. She tried to maneuver around them, but they took up the entire path. Meanwhile the heavily armed attackers had only lost a few steps. She heard gunshots. She fell. The rest she could not remember....

Chapter 44

"This is certainly getting exciting," said Rainbow. "I think it's time for a commercial break."

"A commercial break?" I asked.

"Yes, give your readers a chance to rest, to catch their breath. I mean, you've got people getting chased through museums, destroying priceless works of art, taking leaps to their certain death.... Need I go on? I think it's time for a word from our sponsors."

"But this book isn't sponsored by anyone."

"You're always quibbling over details," she accused. "Now look, Ellison and Schadenfraude have been kind enough to join us for this remarkable opportunity of participating in a billion-dollar decision." I looked around the room and saw my two friends sitting on the couch, waving amiably to me. They must have entered my house while I was busy typing the previous chapter.

"I've asked you all here," Rainbow said, "because I want to test a new product on you. I'm always in the business of developing new ideas, and you can help me transform my marketing dreams into reality."

She handed us each a bottle of water. "Drink up," she encouraged us. "I want to gauge your reactions."

I pressed the bottle to my lips, tilted my head back, and was amazed to find the sensation of pure, unfiltered nothing pouring down my throat. "It's empty!" I accused.

"Yes, this is my latest product," boasted Rainbow. "I call it Mirage. It looks like a bottle of cool, refreshing mountain stream water, but actually there's nothing inside. As you can imagine, it helps us save on overhead costs." She beamed with pride, waiting for our reactions.

"It's tantalizing!" exclaimed Ellison.

"It will make you a fortune," agreed Schadenfraude, who was inwardly kicking himself for not having thought of the idea first.

I was incredulous at my friends' responses. "Why would anyone buy this?" I asked. "There's nothing here."

"You obviously know nothing about marketing," she berated me. "You probably think that people want to buy something to drink. But you couldn't be more wrong. People want to belong. People want to share in a universal experience."

"Thirst?"

"Yes, thirst is sweeping the globe! It's a worldwide phenomenon, a trend that doesn't seem to be going away! I've never seen anything like this. Every year the planet's population grows by 90 million, and -- get this -- everyone seems to be thirsty! This market transcends national borders, religion, race, or creed."

"But don't you think it would be better if you could give people a product that would actually satisfy their thirst?"

She looked at me sadly, as if I were a hopeless idiot. "What we're selling is the thrill of anticipation. There's nothing more delicious than dreaming about the future. People don't actually want to find fulfillment -- they get there and find that it's boring. It's human nature: you want what you can't have. You always desire what's just out of reach. So that's what I offer the American public: the giddy feeling that satisfaction is almost at hand. It makes people excited. They go crazy over it."

"Yes!" exclaimed Schadenfraude. "It's brilliant! It's like when you're going to go away on vacation. The best part is the excitement that builds up in the weeks before you leave. You imagine how much you're going to enjoy everything foreign and exotic. You can't stop thinking about how good it will be to get away from work. Then when you actually go on your vacation, you find that it doesn't live up to your imagination. The food is bad, the natives try to rip you off, and you get sunburnt, to top it off. The dream is better than the reality!"

"Yes," effused Ellison. "It's a fascinating sociological phenomenon: When a person is crawling through the desert, dying of thirst, there's nothing better than a mirage! It gives him hope. It appears to be his salvation. It is the most thrilling thing he's ever seen. What a joyous feeling to feel like you are saved!"

"Yes, but he isn't actually saved, is he?" I pointed out. "I mean, he's still dying of thirst. Won't he be all the more devastated when he discovers it was just a hallucination, and that there's nothing there to drink at all?"

"That's why we recommend that you follow Mirage with a chaser," Rainbow explained.

"A chaser?" I cried. "But there's nothing to chase!"

"Precisely," she nodded. "That's the beauty of it. Mirage only serves to heighten your thirst. Therefore, when you actually do have a real drink, it tastes even better to you!"

"They say that hunger is the best cook," Ellison quipped. "I guess Mirage must be the best bartender."

"I'm about to strike a 1.2 billion dollar deal with the Coca-Cola Corporation," said Rainbow. "The company discovered that people enjoy Coke three times as much when they've just had a Mirage. We prepare the way -- we make people thirsty and full of anticipation for 'the real thing.' So the Coca Cola corporation thinks I've got a gold mine on my hands. They want to buy the rights to my idea, so they can sell Mirage alongside Coca Cola in every market around the world, from India to Indianapolis."

"I'm sure that's just what people in drought-stricken regions of India are craving," I said. "A big cold bottle of Mirage."

"You may jest," she replied. "But this is a big bonanza for the global environment. We don't have to deplete any freshwater lakes for this product. We don't have to divert water from pristine mountain streams. In fact, we're helping to ease international water shortages by distributing the only bottled water in the world that has no water in it. With every bottle of Mirage you buy, you're helping to save the Earth!"

Talking about saving the planet, I had forgotten about Aurora Borealis! I had to get back to the story to see how she was doing....

Chapter 45

The woman woke up in total darkness.

She had a flashback to her youth: a time when she woke up in an unfamiliar room, confused, scared, alone. She had been only five years old. She recalled the disorientation of finding herself in such strange surroundings, so far from home.

She tried to stir, but her arms and legs were paralyzed. She was immobilized, unable to move, helpless in her bed.

Her limbs had been strapped down to her bed. She was a prisoner to forces unseen.

The woman tried to scream but her voice too was impotent, and she could only let forth a meager exhalation.

Murmurs and hushed whispers brought her back to the present moment. She could hear people discussing her fate, beyond the locked door of her confinement. She strained to make out the words, but she could only catch one phrase, repeated several times: "Not much time, not much time."

Listening more intently, she detected the labored breathing of someone else in the room -- another prisoner, only a few feet away from her. The breathing was erratic and difficult. Her invisible companion was in deep pain, most likely suffering from serious injuries.

Then too there was another sound -- a third presence in the room. It started out as a low, guttural growl. Slowly it grew to a menacing roar, as if there were some beast in the room ready to pounce. It was an inhuman sound -- something monstrous, something wicked, which grew in pitch and intensity until it exploded into a deafening, blood-curdling cry.

Blinding light flashed into the woman's eyes. Sightless, she heard the commotion of people bursting into the room, yelling, and moving in the direction of the din. As her eyes began to adjust to the light, she saw the glint of a knife being raised....

"Hand me the scalpel!" insisted one of the voices who had run into the room. The woman raised her head, and saw a team of doctors attending to a disturbed patient, yelling and growling as the nurses attempted to subdue him.

The woman looked around her in the light that now flooded the room from overhead. She was clearly in a hospital, crowded in a room with several other patients who looked to be in bad shape. She lifted her head as much as she could and saw the man with the irregular, heavy breathing; he was attached to a life-support system, struggling for his life. A computerized machine registered his less-than-vital statistics, which seemed to be deteriorating rapidly.

Just beyond the dying man, she saw a giant man who looked like he had a spear sticking through him; she looked twice because she had never seen such a strange sight, but he caught her looking and belligerently scowled at her.

"Doctor, come quickly," she heard someone call. "The young woman has returned to consciousness."

Two doctors rushed to her bedside. "Where am I?" she asked them.

"This is the emergency ward of Loca Vista Hospital in Harlem. You were brought here yesterday after your accident."

"Accident? What accident?" The woman could not remember anything that had transpired in the past 24 hours. Why was she in Harlem?

"Don't worry," the professionals tried to reassure her. "You had a minor concussion, but everything's going to be fine now."

One of the doctors looked down at her with compassion. "I was hoping we could ask you a few questions," he said. "When you were brought into the hospital, you didn't have any identification on you. We haven't been able to locate any of your friends or relatives, and we don't want your loved ones to become too concerned."

The patient just looked confused. She struggled, but failed, to recall her name.

"It's all right," the doctor smiled. "Temporary amnesia is common after a head injury. You should get your memory back

159

within a few days. Tell us: Is there anything you <u>can</u> remember? What were you doing in Central Park yesterday?"

The patient tried to reclaim any images from the abyss of her memory. "Central Park" stirred some hazy pictures in her mind. She was running, sprinting, out of breath, trying to save her life. She had no recollection of what she was running from. But her heart was racing, just reliving the sensation of palpable fear.

"They're trying to kill me," she gasped, a look of terror rushing across her face.

"You're safe here," the doctor tried to calm her down. "Right now, in this moment, there's no one trying to harm you. These are just some bad dreams; they're not real at all."

The memories of the preceding day were all too real to the patient. She was beginning to relive the events in her mind, until the transient thoughts spread like a cancer and threatened to overwhelm her. She could vaguely remember having seen something disturbing, something crucially important, just before she blacked out. But that's where her memory failed her. What was it she had seen?

"We'll leave you to rest for a while," said the doctor, as he walked away to speak with his colleagues. They retreated to a private office, where they gathered around a computer. He began to type up his inventory of psychosis onto the screen for all the professionals to see.

"Clearly, this patient is suffering from a severe case of paranoia," he began. "She has wild hallucinations that enemies are chasing her -- even trying to murder her. Moreover, these delusions can be dangerous. As you know, she was found with a gun on her body when she was picked up at Central Park. She's liable to harm herself and others if we don't keep an eye on her psychotic behavior. It's important to keep her tied down."

"I concur," agreed one of the staff psychologists. "Did you notice the deep cuts and slashes along her arms? Those are no ordinary bruises. The gashes are deep, as if she had cut herself with jagged slivers of broken glass. It's clear that she attempted suicide sometime in the last few days. We need to keep her under constant surveillance. This is a patient who's out of control."

"Do we have any idea who she is?" asked a nurse.

"At any given time in New York City, there are thousands of psychotics on the loose. Unfortunately, we can't account for every one. Until we can match her to a missing persons report, she will continue to be a mystery. She's our child now -- a ward of the state of New York and its mental institutions."

Chapter 46

"My recall is getting better," the patient said the next morning, when an attendant brought her breakfast.

"What do you remember?" asked the nurse anxiously, grabbing a pencil to take down any details. She buzzed a staff psychiatrist so that he too could note the progress.

"I'm an investigative reporter," the woman said. "I was looking into the kidnapping of a very important person. I can't tell you his name. Even if I could remember it now, I wouldn't be able to divulge the confidential information."

"I understand," the nurse nodded politely, while silently thinking to herself *this woman is crazier than all the others combined.* Meanwhile, a psychiatrist had rushed into the room, and was carefully taking notes at the woman's bedside.

"Anyway, I soon discovered that this was much more than a simple kidnapping case. I was delving into a scandal that could expose people at the highest level of power in this country. What I'm discovering could bring down the President and the richest people in this country. This is a threat to the established order -- everything we hold to be sacred and true."

"Is that why people are trying to kill you?" asked the psychiatrist.

"Yes! Yes!" said the patient, pleased that someone believed her. "They can't let this information get out."

"So what happened yesterday in the park? Who was chasing you? What do you remember about that?"

"I still can't remember," the patient cried, tears of frustration coming to her eyes. "All I know is that I was running to get away, and I saw something awful. Something was wrong - terribly wrong. But that's where my memory leaves me."

"And you still can't remember your name?"

The patient shook her head.

"Can you remember the name of the newspaper for which you work? Is it the *Times? The Post? The Daily News?*"

Again the woman shook her head. "None of those sound familiar."

"Well, maybe something more will come to you in the next few days," the psychiatrist said encouragingly. But he himself was distraught.

"It's worse than I thought," he wrote in his official report, which he later read to his professional colleagues at their weekly staff meeting. "The patient is suffering from delusions of grandeur. She's invented a story about being an investigative reporter, about to uncover the scandal of the century. She says that the President himself is trying to kill her. It's one of the wildest plots you've ever heard -- like something out of a novel, written by a third-rate hack."

"Are you suggesting that she's fabricating this crazy story?" inquired a colleague.

"Not consciously. Sometimes people reconstruct memories of things that never happened. They may insist that what they remember is true, but it's nothing more than a chimera. This story may be from a book she read, or a movie she saw. She may have gotten real life confused with fiction. Or this may be a delusion, a hallucination that took place only in the realm of the imagination. She can't separate fantasy from fact anymore."

Chapter 47

All was quiet in the hospital until the man on the respirator became delirious.

"I see fire!" he screamed. "Flames, inferno, holocaust, licking devilishly at the sky!"

"He's suffering from delusions again," remarked the nurse, buzzing the psychiatrist. She was getting tired of this patient, a paranoid schizophrenic by the name of Robert Cassandra.

"Don't you see it?" he cried. "It's the rainforests burning. It's the soils eroding. It's widespread ecosystem destruction. No, no, you can't see it! It's invisible to you!"

"Poor guy," said the nurse. "This one's really crazy. He's been having these terrible hallucinations for months."

"I see terrible social costs from everything we do. When you turned on that light, it set in motion an entire system of destruction, from oil and coal, and other nonrenewable, polluting resources. We're wreaking havoc on the environment, and we can't even see it. Father, forgive us, for we know not what we do!"

"It's all in your imagination," the nurse reassured him pleasantly.

"No, no, if we don't act fast it will be the end of the world as we know it!"

"Don't be silly," the nurse comforted him. "The world is fine. The stock market is at the highest level that it's ever been. The gross national product is skyrocketing. Look how productive our economy is. We live in the best of times."

The very ill man just groaned, and fell back onto his pillow. Meanwhile, the young woman was starting to pay attention to some of her other hospital roommates.

She noticed one skeletal figure who was locked up in a straitjacket.

"I told them that white's just not my color," he was complaining to a nurse. "For a while I was into floral patterns, but then I decided that black is beautiful. Why deny who I am? You know what I mean?"

"Who's that?" the woman asked her personal attendant.

"Oh, him? He thinks he's Death. You know, we've had some real characters in here before -- we've had our Napoleons and our Cleopatras, but this is the first one who actually believes he's the Grim Reaper. He's been scaring the other patients with his mumbo jumbo and incantations of mortality. The really frightening part is that he's been accused of 23 counts of manslaughter in this state."

Death was huddling with his attorney, a man with slicked-back hair and an expensive Armani suit.

"You're the real victim here," said the lawyer.

"I am?" asked Death.

"Of course! Look at the terrible childhood you had.... The abusive parents.... The effects of being a minority in a culture where everyone values life so much. They tried to hide you, they were ashamed of you, they provoked you!"

"Now that you mention it," said Death, "I couldn't get a job in a hospital because of my appearance. Everyone discriminated against me and didn't want me hanging around."

"Exactly!" shouted the lawyer with great exultation. "You're the one who has been wronged! It would be a crime for anyone to convict you of these 23 homicides."

"That's true," agreed the Reaper. "I'm not responsible for my actions. Blame my parents. Blame my genes. Blame society. Blame anybody but me for how I turned out."

This legal drama was interrupted by the entrance of two men carrying red flags with yellow hammers and sickles. A bald-headed man with a goatee and an angry look on his face spoke first. "There's a massive conspiracy against us," he protested.

"What's wrong?" asked the woman.

"We were going to be stars," the agitator responded. "We had just landed our first literary roles. That's when we discovered the seedy underworld of the book scene. You would think it's about high-quality literature, right? You would think it's about the dissemination of challenging ideas to an intelligent reading public, wouldn't you?

"But no. It's all about pandering to the lowest common denominator. It's all about money -- it's just another huge capitalist tool of oppression.

"When we tried to point the hypocrisy of the system, we discovered that the author couldn't handle the truth. He's trying to silence us by putting us into this mental institution. I tell you now: we will not be defeated! We will start the revolution of the literariat."

"We know the truth," added his comrade, a short little man who bore a startling resemblance to Leon Trotsky.

"What's the truth?" asked the woman.

"They are trying to oppress and suppress us," the leader claimed. "It is intolerable and insufferable!"

The woman was amazed that the hospital allowed these two men to just wander around the room with ease. Evidently the door was locked, so there was no way they could escape. But she just wondered why they got special treatment, when she herself was shackled to a bed.

She wanted to ask another patient, a man in a bed not far her own. He seemed peaceful enough, and spent most of his time simply reading the newspaper. However the woman decided to inquire to her personal attendant as to whether that man was safe. There were a lot of deranged characters hanging around this hospital.

"What's his problem?" she asked Nurse Heisenberg.

"Him? He's the craziest one of them all. His name is Scott Sherman."

"Not the Scott Sherman?" asked the woman, astonished. "The great secret agent and international master of espionage? The famous provocateur who single-handedly brought down the Soviet Union, and who was thought to have been killed a few days ago?"

"No, no," explained the nurse. "It's not the real Scott Sherman. Actually, that would be a lot more believable than the story he tells for himself now. This guy thinks he's a writer! But let me tell you: I've seen some of his material, and it's terrible. He has no talent whatsoever."

Lenin and Trotsky were looking at the writer suspiciously. They were ready to denounce him, when all of a sudden he looked up from the newspaper and spoke:

"Did you hear about the destruction of this priceless work of art in the Metropolitan Museum yesterday?"

This news sounded vaguely familiar to the young woman, as if she had heard about it in a dream.

"It doesn't make sense to me," said the writer, brushing aside the advertising inserts that had just fallen in his lap. "I mean, who decides when a painting is priceless? Vincent Van Gogh died a pauper, but then after he died he was recognized as a genius. One day his paintings are worth nothing, and the next day they're selling for millions. It seems like it's totally arbitrary. The only reason it's valuable is because we <u>think</u> it's valuable!"

"No, no, no," argued the nurse. "It has value because it's beautiful. It's a work of art."

"If I painted with the exact same skill and artistry as Van Gogh, no one would be paying millions for my works. People would just call them worthless imitations, or even forgeries. The fact of the matter is that a work of art has no real value, independent of our beliefs. It's just paint on canvas! Look at those people who make money from painting cans of Campbell's soup! Or the people who make millions by painting an entire canvas black! That doesn't take talent!"

"But it makes a statement."

"What's the statement? 'I have no money for any color paint except for black'?"

"You're crazy," said the nurse.

"I've seen so many outstanding painters in my life," he continued, undeterred. "And is there anything that sets some off from others? I can't tell the difference."

"Well, you're not a critic."

"What do critics know?" asked Scott.

"Well, certainly the critics must know what they're talking about," surmised the nurse. "I'm sure they can tell the difference between what's good and what's bad. Critics are the wisest sages and prophets of our time, are they not? When they pass judgement on any work of art, it must be true."

The literary agent looked over my shoulder. "It's so ironic that you should be talking about the critics," she remarked. "The first reviews of your book just arrived."

Getting excited, I looked at the initial article:

"A terribly written, boring, didactic, preachy, moralistic piece of crap," it began. I hate those subtle, cryptic reviews where you have to read between the lines to figure out what the critic really thinks.

"So who was that from?" I asked. "*The New York Times? The Washington Post? The New York Review of Books?*"

"No, actually, that was from your mom."

"What does the next review say?" I asked, a glutton for inflicting torture upon myself. Writing a book is like exposing yourself naked on stage in front of an audience. Unfortunately, there are always critics in the crowd to express their opinions that you're not so well-endowed. Not like I'm speaking from experience, of course. No, no. How did we get on this subject anyway?

"Scott Sherman's debut novel is sure to inspire thousands of aspiring authors across the country....."

I beamed.

".....After all, if Sherman can get tripe such as this published, there's hope for other atrocious writers trying to break into the business."

I decided to stop reading the reviews. After all, I had slaved over this work for years, and in a few minutes a critic could

casually dismiss your work, telling you that all your labors --
everything you had invested, all your beliefs, and dreams, and
hopes -- were absolutely worthless.

My literary agent was not much more helpful. "You're
putting me to sleep," she said. "Maybe we could start advertising
your book as a solution for insomnia. We could probably make
more money off it that way."

I started to protest, but the literary agent made a point
that quickly humbled me:

"Look, you've even made your protagonist fall asleep."
Astonished, I looked back at my story. Sure enough, the woman
had dozed off, and was in the midst of some disturbing dreams....

Chapter 48

Even in her dreams, her heart was racing. Her eyes flickered in the restless stages of REM sleep.

The men were still pursuing her. She raced past the roller bladers, the runners, the bicyclists heading in the other direction. "Help! They're trying to kill me!" she screamed, but this was an everyday occurrence in New York, and no one stopped to help.

She ran into the Central Park Zoo, trying to lose herself in the crowds. The men pushed their way through the masses of people in hot pursuit of their prey. Without paying, she leapt over the entrance gates of the zoo, causing several park guards to chase her as well.

"Stop! Thief!" she heard someone yell, but she didn't turn around. Instead she ran into the rainforest exhibit. In her haste, she didn't notice the cascading waterfalls, didn't hear the tropical birds screeching, didn't pay attention to the monstrous tropical trees, except for the darkness and shade covering they provided as she got lost in the jungle.

Mist filled the entire rainforest, allowing her to elude her pursuers. She could only see a few feet in front of her, but she kept running, pushing away the crowds of tourists. She ran past the piranhas in their feeding frenzy. She ignored the colorful toucans and the golden tamarins as she rushed upward through the rainforest trail. The path seemed to spiral higher and higher, taking her from the understory to the highest reaches of the canopy.

Her breathing was hard and rapid. Her clothes were soaked from sweat. Her heart pounded violently as she watched the killers search for her below.

She climbed off of the prescribed wooden path, out onto the branches of a tree. From her perspective high in the air, she could see it was a 75 foot drop to the ground. Aurora hated heights, but she was fighting for her life. She hoped no one would see her in the mist.

Clinging to the branch, she saw the killers looking confused. They were scanning the entire area of the rainforest, having lost their intended victim.

From out of nowhere, three fruit bats flew into her face. They were like grotesque flying rodents, screeching horribly and flapping their vampire wings. She lost balance, and started to fall.

She was weightless. She was helpless. As she plummeted from her perch, she flailed wildly for anything she could reach. Her scream galvanized the attention of everyone in the rainforest, including the men who had been hired to ensure her death.

She grabbed ahold of a liana, a thick rainforest vine, and held on for her life. It swung wildly across the rainforest. Somehow she managed to land with her feet on the ground right near the exhibit exit.

With seven men in pursuit, she rushed out into the humid summer air. The exhaustion, the humidity, the lack of sleep for the last several days -- they all conspired against her. Even with the adrenaline racing through her system, she was succumbing to fatigue. Her overtaxed muscles were failing her, her weary bones seemed to collapse. She imagined she saw a cool, icy refuge in which she could escape. With the last strength she could muster, she leaped over the barrier into a different climate. She was flying, spinning, tumbling through the air. Then her trajectory turned downward, and she started plummeting through empty space. It was as if she had jumped out of plane without a parachute. Time was suspended; seconds passed like hours as she fell deeper and deeper.

In the eternity of her descent, she looked up and saw the New York skyline, spinning and dropping away in her sight. Her spirit seemed to rise far above Central Park, so that she was looking down at herself falling. Her soul was floating above Manhattan and she could see the entire panorama of the city devouring her: the Empire State Building, the Chrysler Tower, the World Trade Center skyscrapers, glass and steel rising for 100 stories, massive structures dwarfing her, monsters engulfing her whole....

She woke up with a start. "I think I figured out what's wrong," she said to herself. "I need to investigate this."

Chapter 49

Several months earlier the woman had seen a frightening report about an architect in Virginia. The information meant very little to her at the time, but it must have been percolating in her subconscious mind silently for many weeks. Now it was rising to haunt her.

The architect's name was William McDonough, and he was generally acknowledged as one of the best in his field. But he was not happy with what he saw in his profession. In fact, he had unearthed a dirty secret that threatened to bring the entire field crashing down around him:

Architects were accomplices in the greatest crime of the century. They were aiding and abetting in the devastation of the Earth.

This was not a conspiracy. There was no group of architects that had secret underground meetings, plotting the destruction of the earth's ecosystems. There was no international cabal or evil plan. Indeed, architects were basically good people who were designing themselves into oblivion.

They were writing the blueprints for the end of the world, and they weren't even aware of the fact.

Most of the planet's environmental problems came from a problem of poor design. Everything was designed to battle against nature. Thus, almost 98 percent of the resources used in driving the economy came out as waste. The system was just over 2 percent efficient.

The buildings that architects designed were destroying ecosystems. A single room nowadays contained more deadly chemicals than a full laboratory at the turn of the century. Most of the materials they used could be toxic and deadly. It wasn't just lead-based paint which had been proven to be fatal to many young children. Almost everything they ordered was filled with hazardous resins, glues, chemicals, preservatives, artificial, unnatural, and dangerous carcinogens.

But that wasn't all. The wood they used often came from ecosystems thousands of miles away, killing off species for a few more luxury rooms. The carpets had heavy metals and cancer-causing agents in them. The structures were filled with mutagens, toxics that built up, persisted, and accumulated in human tissue, and even endocrine disruptors -- the frightening chemical-altering substances that could harm the human reproductive system. If anyone wanted to find a scapegoat for the declining sperm counts and the deadly breast milk and the human bodies disposed as toxic waste, they need look no further than the American Institute of Architects. There were the criminals in person. There were the villains unmasked.

But McDonough was not interested in placing blame. He knew that essentially everyone was innocent; they didn't recognize the harm that their practices and designs were causing to the earth. Instead of criticizing the system, he wanted to create new innovative designs -- ones that could work with nature, rather than against her.

McDonough was a dreamer. He wanted to create designs that would restore the environment; he wanted to create designs that would cooperate with the natural flows; he wanted to create designs that would incorporate humans as an integral part of the landscape, rather than nature's enemy.

The woman knew there was much more to the story than this. But she had forgotten the rest.

She could not remember her name, she could not remember her mission, but she knew that she needed this information for a very important purpose. If she was going to discover the secret, she needed to escape.

Chapter 50

That night it looked like Cassandra would die.

"We can't sustain him," yelled one doctor, overlooking the body.

"Get some more technology," screamed back a second doctor. They rushed in some elaborate machines with lots of red flashing lights and bulbs and compressors, whistles, gidgets, and gazoos.

"Technology will save him," insisted Doctor Number Two. They pumped his chest with an exfibrillicator, an expensive electronic device that could inflate the ventricles almost as fast as it inflated the medical bills.

The exfibrillicator was called the Hydra 2000; it was the latest advance of medical technology, totally obviating the need for people to exercise, eat nutritionally, or relax. "Forget prevention!" the advertisements encouraged their patients. "Just let the Hydra 2000 repair the damage after it's done." There was only one minor drawback of the machine: it caused three new problems for every problem it solved. "There's a cavity opening up in his heart," yelled Doctor Number One, "and a new bacterial infection."

"Douse him with radiation!" advised Doctor Number Two. The nurses wheeled in a glowing green machine that looked like a reject from the Chernobyl nuclear power plant. Called the Triage X-86, it was another marvel of modern technology; it enabled doctors to subject sick patients to more radiation than in three atomic warheads. The idea was that this radiation could kill all the cancerous cells in the body, with only one minor side effect: it killed all of the healthy cells as well.

"Why are we using the Triage X-86?" asked a nurse. "This patient doesn't even have any cancerous cells. He's suffering from heart problems."

"Have you no compassion?" asked the doctor. "This man's life is at stake! We will spare no expense to keep this patient alive, so he can continue to pay his medical bills." Indeed, the

Triage X-86 was a boon to hospitals; because it was so expensive, it forced them to make budgetary cuts in patient services, thus allowing doctors more free time to play golf.

Yet it was also true that the Triage X-86 had saved a number of lives; people who recovered from these operations were often able to live up to three more years in a state of abject misery and pain.

Holding the large cylindrical contraption over the patient's chest, the medical experts began to irradiate his cells.

"This seems to be weakening his immune system," reported the first doctor, somewhat surprised.

"This is the end, the grand finale, the exit, the denouement," moaned the dying man.

"How did it happen?" asked the woman sympathetically. She had a reporter's instinct for finding the story.

Cassandra started firing out nonsensical images in a rapid-fire clip, as if he were witness to some apocalyptic chaos:

"That's great, it starts with an earthquake, birds and snakes and airplanes, Lenny Bruce is not afraid -- eye of the hurricane, listen to yourself churn, world serves its own needs...."

The woman could not make any sense of these disparate phrases. She feared Cassandra was succumbing to terrible delusions.

A priest came by to administer the last rites. "This is a time for faith," he said. "A time to believe in the power of that which you cannot see. You are sanctified by the power of the Father and the Son and the Holy Spirit."

But it was already too late. Robert Cassandra was dead.

Chapter 51

"It's such a coincidence that you're writing about a hospital," said Rainbow. "I just happened to develop a breakthrough product for the medical industry."

"Really?" I asked. To be honest, I was somewhat surprised that Rainbow had taken a turn towards altruism. Maybe I had misjudged her; maybe underneath that billionaire exterior was a young, socially conscious woman who just wanted to do good for the world.

"Yes, in fact, I expect the Nobel Prize committee to be calling me up at any moment. I've discovered a cure for every known disease, from cancer to the common cold. "

"Are you serious?"

"Yes, I call it Placebo!" She held up a little sugar pill. "It's now available without a prescription!"

"What are the active ingredients?"

"Oh, there's no actual medicine in it at all," she conceded. "But, as long as you believe it will cure you, chances are really high that it will improve your condition! It's been proven effective in thousands of clinical tests!

"For years, the medical profession has been keeping this revolutionary medicine under wraps. Now I'm making it available to the general public for the low, low price of just $23.95, plus tax. "

"How very generous of you," I said, as I took a large swig of Mirage. I had to admit, I had become addicted to the stuff.

"Oh, I see you enjoy my products," Rainbow pointed out, noticing the empty water bottle from which I kept taking sips. "If you like that, you'll love my newest idea. This is for all the health-conscious people in our country." She handed me a box of chocolates.

"You expect chocolates to appeal to people who want to stay healthy?"

"Just wait until you taste them," she encouraged me.

I opened the box, and stuck my hand in, only to find nothing inside. I should have known.

"I call this product Tantalus," Rainbow boasted. "It really helps keep your weight down."

I thought about the old slogan: *Life is like a box of chocolates. You never know what you'll get.* In this case, you knew exactly what you would get:

Nothing.

"I'm anticipating huge sales of this product," Rainbow explained. "People can buy as many boxes of chocolates as they want, and they'll never have to feel guilty. They won't add a single calorie. They won't ever get a pimple. No worry about tooth decay, either. Can you imagine how high the demand will be? It's a steal for only $9.95 a package!"

She showed me an advertisement. It was a glossy full-color print of a box of Tantalus brand chocolates. There were no actual chocolates in the picture, but there were plenty of sexy, healthy, beautiful people. They were wearing very few clothes, so as to display their muscular, shapely figures. Presumably they had stayed so fit and healthy from all the chocolates they had not eaten. Underneath the photograph of the empty box, the advertising slogan was emblazoned:

"TANTALUS: You Can't Always Get What You Want (But You Get What You Need)."

I knew that she had another trillion-dollar idea. But something still troubled me. It seemed like Rainbow was always

178

inventing new products, new slogans, new consumer goods to make our lives better. And yet the average American didn't seem to be getting any happier.

"The point isn't for us to be happy," she said, as if commenting on the obvious.

"Then what's the point?" I asked.

She looked at me as if I were a heretic, asking the most blasphemous question that had ever profaned the purity of her ears. "The point is for us to <u>pretend</u> that consuming more and more material goods will actually make us fulfilled."

"It won't?"

"Of course not!" retorted Rainbow. "That's the fun of the game. It's all an illusion. We have to make people <u>think</u> that they will be happy if they buy our products. But could you imagine what a disaster it would be if everyone actually <u>did</u> become happy?"

"The horror, the horror...." I shuddered as I considered the possibility.

"The health of our economy depends on people wanting more, more, more," she warned. "So it's our sacred, patriotic duty as Americans to be dissatisfied with what we already have. We need to keep up our conspicuous consumption, even if it destroys the earth and kills us in the process. It would be just awful if everyone became happy and fulfilled with what they already own. We <u>must</u> stop such a catastrophe from taking place!"

It was a novel idea I had never considered: The right of every American to life, liberty, and the pursuit of unhappiness. Perhaps this type of brilliant thinking explained why Rainbow was a millionaire and I was perpetually unemployed.

Well, she could continue inventing products that would make people dissatisfied. As for me, I still had a world to save, and a story to tell....

Chapter 52

"I remember my name!" the woman announced triumphantly. "It's all coming back to me. You can call my newspaper in California to confirm everything. I'm Aurora Borealis, and I work for the *San Francisco Weekly.*"

"What were you doing in New York?" asked the psychiatrist.

"I was researching a story out here. I got a tip from a dead man that I needed to fly to New York on the spur of the moment."

"You were told this by a dead man?"

"Oh, you don't understand," Aurora tried to clarify her statement. "He wasn't dead when he told me to come to New York. It's just that everyone around me is getting murdered."

"Oh, I see," said the psychiatrist. He noted in the margins of his paper to check for other psychological maladies. This woman had developed a whole pathology of symptoms. He wondered if she were a compulsive liar, or whether she was just suffering from false memory syndrome.

Nonetheless, he decided to confirm the story for himself....

Back in San Francisco, Aurora had not shown up to work for days. She had not left any messages or returned any calls. Her editor decided it was time to fire her.

The hospital called up. "Excuse me, we're looking for Aurora Borealis."

"I'm sorry," replied the new secretary, "There's no one by that name who works here."

"Well, thank you for your time," said the psychiatrist. "We're very sorry to have disturbed you."

The psychiatrist had suspected that his patient was making up stories. But he wasn't prepared for the shock he would get later that afternoon. As he walked home from the mental hospital, he passed by a newsstand. The tabloids were still screaming headlines about the massacre in New Mexico.

Evidently, the chief of police had mysteriously died only 24 hours after the investigation had begun. And one of the leading suspects -- the maid who had discovered the bodies -- had disappeared from the state.

Now her picture was plastered on the front of every newspaper in the country. And there was no mistaking that face. The psychiatrist immediately recognized Aurora Borealis. She was much more dangerous than even he had ever imagined. He needed to get back to the mental hospital before another murder took place....

Chapter 53

Nurse Heisenberg was a tall woman with a striking resemblance to Abraham Lincoln. She didn't have as much facial hair as the former President, but then again she didn't have much less.

She was somewhere in the range of 50 years old, give or take a millennium. She had seen her best days pass, and they weren't even very good. Now she just walked around with her dowdy dresses and unkempt hair, strutting and fretting through the hospital with the air of a woman who cared nothing for her appearance; after all, who was there to look at her but a bunch of lunatics?

She had spent much of her time in the wards of the mental institution with patients suffering from severe alcoholic addictions; lately she had been attending to people suffering from many other psychological problems. She called them "beer nuts" and "mixed nuts" respectively.

Overall, the nurse didn't like her patients much. No, the truth was, she had nothing but contempt for them. She had hoped the new woman would be different; even if Aurora was just another loony tune, she still might serve as a sympathetic listener during all the lonely hours.

Before Aurora came, the nurse had mostly divided her time between reminiscing about the past and fantasizing about the future. Her past she romanticized until it seem perfectly glorious. Her future she invented grandly -- it would be perfect, and there would no longer be sorrow or pain.

Heisenberg liked to spend most of her time in 1983. That was the last year she had been truly happy. She had been in love with a man named Foucault, but nothing had ever worked out. Even now, fifteen years later, she continued to play back in her mind the arguments that had led to the break-up of the relationship.

Who could she tell the story of her life? Who could she tell about the way her heart was broken into a thousand pieces? Who would understand?

Certainly not the two bolsheviks who were always walking around muttering about social injustice. Certainly not that scary man who thought he was Death himself. Certainly not that deranged fool who thought he was a writer. (She knew that every writer likes to steal good material from the people in his life. If she went blabbing to him, she probably see her story end up on display in the pages of some book someday.)

She thought the woman would understand. Surely, Aurora's heart had also been broken by one of those species of swine known as "men." That was probably what made her go crazy: Love, or lack thereof. There must have been a man involved. Men were always wrecking everything. They were cheating on lovers, and telling lies, and beating people up.

She wanted to share all these thoughts with someone else who knew the pain, someone else who could understand that men were at the root of all evil, and never to be trusted. She had hoped that Aurora, despite all her obvious psychological problems, would be her sister in arms.

But now Aurora had betrayed her. The woman had turned out to be just another liar. Everything she had said was further falsehood and fiction. She was not a reporter, not pursuing the story of the century. How could the nurse have been so stupid to believe her? This only confirmed what she had long suspected: You couldn't have faith in anyone.

Of one thing Nurse Heisenberg was certain: she would wreak her revenge on Aurora Borealis. Yes, she would wreak her revenge.

Chapter 54

"I need to sneak out of here," Aurora confided to the revolutionaries.

"Don't worry," Lenin said. "We'll free you of these oppressive chains." He and Trotsky wandered over to the reporter's bed, and set to untying the straps that held her down to the bed.

"Thanks," she whispered.

"Be careful," Lenin insisted. "We're being watched at all times. They have countless surveillance cameras throughout the building, and there are alarms that you could trigger if you make the wrong move. Moreover, Nurse Heisenberg comes checking this room every 30 minutes."

"Where are you going?" asked Death, envious of the little adventure that was taking place. He hadn't seen much excitement since being confined in the hospital.

"I just need to find a computer that has access to an international news archive," the reporter said. "There's something very strange that I saw in Central Park. I keep having these flashbacks and nightmares about it. There's something that's triggered my suspicions. I have to undertake an investigation."

"You know that we've been locked in here," said Lenin. "They seem to think we're dangerous."

"How will I escape from this room? All I want to do is check a computer."

"There's no way you can escape from this room," said Lenin. "This is a maximum security mental institution. We're locked in here. There are no windows, no emergency doors, and no other means of exit."

"What about the walls or the ceilings?" asked Aurora. "Maybe we can sneak out the ventilator ducts."

"No," Lenin discouraged her. "I've looked into this all. There are no egresses. Everything is sealed shut, with the walls

185

made out of reinforced steel and concrete. The ceilings are impenetrable."

"So the only means of entrance and exit into this room is that one single door with the deadbolt lock?"

"Exactly," said Lenin. "The two people who tried to pick the lock were electrocuted. We never saw them again after they were carried away on the stretcher." Lenin turned and glared accusingly at the Grim Reaper.

"Hey, don't look at me!" said Death innocently. "I didn't play any role in that little escapade."

Aurora considered her options. "Wait a second," she said. "How well did you know those people who were electrocuted?"

"I didn't know them really. They were just other patients here, always talking about breaking free. They were trying to stir the rest of us up, get us all excited about the possibility of escape. But then look what happened to them."

Aurora remembered a story she had heard about elephants: "If you tie a baby elephant to a thick stake in the ground, it will try to move away. It will naturally want to get its freedom. But it won't have the strength yet. It will struggle, and struggle, and struggle some more, until it finally just gives up. It will be exhausted and it will think that its efforts are useless. Later in life when it has the strength and power to easily rip the stake out of the ground, it won't even attempt it. It will believe that it's incapable of escape. In other words, it will have learned that it's helpless to make changes in its life. I think humans are often the same way."

"What are you saying?" asked Lenin suspiciously.

"Just this," said Aurora, as she walked over to the door and opened it up. "The only thing that's locking us into this room is our own beliefs!"

Everyone gasped.

"Now, if you'll excuse me," she said, as she exited the door, "I have a mystery to solve."

Chapter 55

Aurora stepped into the hall. This was her chance to escape. But first she needed to accomplish her mission. She had to follow her intuition. What she had seen in Central Park had sparked some important ideas. She had to see whether they were true.

Quickly, she ran down the hall to a computer room. Now she knew what she was looking for on the World Wide Web. Somewhere hidden in the overwhelming amounts of information, there must be the solutions to the environmental crisis.

It took only a few minutes for her to confirm her suspicions. Suddenly everything made sense. This was exactly the information that Aurora needed. But she couldn't keep it suppressed. She had to let the world know. This was too important to ignore.

Silently she turned off the computer; now that the glow of the screen had faded, it was completely dark in the office.

But someone else was standing in the darkness, watching her, waiting for her. Before Aurora knew what was happening, the invisible observer had grabbed onto her wrists and pushed her against the wall. Aurora's shoulder pounded into the hard surface; she would have cried for help, but a hand clamped down over her mouth. Her assailant had too much strength, overpowering her and wrestling her to the ground.

Aurora could feel the weight of her assailant on top of her, pinning her to the floor. "This time it's the end of you," threatened a voice she had heard before.

The lights switched on, and Aurora looked up at eyes filled with hatred and fury. "They warned me you that you were dangerous," grumbled Nurse Heisenberg, as she held down the patient. "I didn't believe them at first. You seemed like just a confused young woman who wouldn't harm anyone. But now I realize that you're more trouble than I thought."

Aurora struggled to answer, but the nurse still had a hand pressed down over her mouth.

"What were you doing in that office?" the nurse demanded to know, lifting her hand from Aurora's face and letting her catch her breath. "There's private information on that computer. If you were tampering with our security, we could have you arrested."

"I swear," Aurora defended herself, "I was only trying to tap into a national news archive. I think I'm getting closer to my newspaper story."

"Stop the acting," grumbled the nurse with contempt. "You don't work for a newspaper. Do you think we bought your story? It was a simple matter of calling up the San Francisco Weekly to verify that there's no one by your name who works there. Either you're lying or you're really crazy. And I have a suspicion that you know a lot more than you're letting on."

Nurse Heisenberg took some handcuffs from the pocket of her white coat and locked Aurora's hands together. "I'm going to put you in solitary confinement," she promised. "We're not going to take any chances of you escaping again."

Chapter 56

Nurse Heisenberg led the prisoner downstairs, through the basement, and down another long stairway. They seemed to be walking beneath the streets of New York City, in the underworld of the sewer system. It was a dark labyrinth with seemingly endless corridors, all leading to nowhere. Aurora imagined that she was 200 feet below the surface of the earth. These subterranean chambers reminded her of the catacombs of Paris; she expected to see rooms full of skeletons and decaying bones.

The nurse walked silently, grimly through the passageways. In the dim light of the flashlight, Aurora could see the tension and anger etched into her captor's face.

In the reporter's agitated mind, it seemed like they had been walking for half an hour. Finally they arrived at a small wooden door that Aurora imagined was like the entrance to a medieval dungeon.

The nurse unlocked the door to reveal a small cell, so bleak and spartan that even a monastic hermit would have had to complain. All that was in the room was a small dirty mattress on the floor and a dingy, dying light bulb hanging from the ceiling.

"You can't do this to me," Aurora insisted defiantly. "These conditions are inhumane. This is worse than most prisons -- it's a violation of my rights."

"Don't tell me what I can and can't do," the Nurse scowled. "Why don't you just do an exposé of our terrible conditions in that newspaper of yours." The nurse laughed, and slammed the door on Aurora.

Chapter 57

Aurora didn't know how long she had been alone. Was it weeks or months or years? Time seemed to lose its meaning in her prison cell. No one had brought her food; it was as if she had been condemned to wither away in captivity. To become nothing. Was there anyone who was aware of her? Was there anyone who knew she was missing? Was there anyone who cared?

Perhaps she was already nothing, an invisible woman, a shadow, having disappeared into a netherworld where she was a virtual cipher. At first she thought she was in a sensory deprivation tank, floating in space and time and nothingness. Alone with her mind, she started to live in realms of memory.

She was reliving that time when she had woken up alone, at five years old, in a strange house. The memories were too vivid. It was all too real. She remembered her aunt, with her pungent perfume, trudging into the room to deliver the bad news. Her mother was dead.

They had buried her father only weeks before, and the loss of her mother was too much to take. She wondered if it was her fault, if she had done something bad that caused God to take them away from her.

That was when she had stopped believing in God. Why would a creator be so cruel? Why would the Lord of the universe, who the psalms all said was mighty, be powerless to stop the cancer that had decimated the people she loved?

The tears poured down, as if she were five years old again, hearing the news for the very first time. And her aunt hugged her, and held her, and told her it would be OK. But Aurora knew that was a lie. It would never be OK again....

Her reverie was disturbed by the walls being pounded and thumped. Then she heard the unmistakable sound of chains being rattled along the floor. Aurora turned, startled, to see a trespasser in her chamber.

"Who is it?" she cried out in fright. "I thought I was alone in here. This room is too small for anyone else."

"No need to be scared by me," said an apparition that was developing in front of her eyes. "I'm just the ghost of Robert Cassandra."

She looked with astonishment to see the suffering man from the mental institution. He looked much better now that he was not hooked up to respirators, exfibrillicators, and other beeping, buzzing machines.

"What are you doing here?" asked Aurora.

"I'm going to show you Christmas past," he intoned very seriously. Cassandra wagged a bony finger at her, and she trembled. "Just kidding," he chirped merrily. "You know I've learned to take myself a whole lot less seriously now that I'm dead. It's really not that bad. Death, life, it's all part of the same cycle. All things shall pass. I've gotten rather philosophical here. I've been hanging out with a lot of dead philosophers: Hegel, Kant, Schopenhauer, Aristotle. It's kind of funny, being dead and all, to get them to admit they were pretty wrong about the whole experience."

"What are you really doing here?" asked an astonished Aurora.

"I've come to tell you something important," he said. "Remember when I was moaning on the bed and about to die?"

"I remember it as if it were yesterday," Aurora replied. Her sense of time had become so distorted that she did not realize that it _had_ been only yesterday.

"Well, there was something I saw."

"Something?"

"Yes, something horrible... I saw who's responsible for the environmental crisis. I saw the face of the killers. It's not who you think. It's not who you think..."

The spirit was interrupted by voices just outside the cell. It sounded like Aurora was about to host a few new visitors.

The door creaked open, letting light into the darkness. A menacing figure stood in the doorway.

"Quick, hide!" Aurora said to the ghost, but he had already disappeared.

"Who are you talking to?" asked the new intruder.

191

"No one," said Aurora. As the guest stepped further into the room, she could not believe her eyes. Standing before her was a famous celebrity she had seen on television countless times. But now he was pointing a gun at her.

This man was one of the world's most famous statisticians. Normally statisticians weren't well-known for their scintillating personalities, but this one was glib and articulate. He could make numbers dance; in fact, he could support any argument he wanted to make with a clever manipulation of the figures. It was like the sleight-of-hand of a magician's trick, so smooth and so seductive. Indeed, it had earned him a national audience. He was the official statistician for the nightly newshour on NBC.

Yes, this was the celebrated Lyze Dammleisz.

"Wait a second!" my Mom complained, as all her bets appeared to fall apart. "That's not fair! You can't introduce a new character that we haven't even met and make him be the criminal. That goes against all the literary conventions!"

"Since when has Scott followed the literary conventions?" asked Bess Bestsellerstein. "He has no character development, very little scenery, and a contrived plot. So are you going to sue him for one more transgression against our literary sensibilities?"

At the mention of the word "sue," the slick attorney suddenly peered in the window. "Does somebody call for a lawyer?" he asked.

"No," I interjected. "You see, Lyze Dammleisz _is_ the killer, but he's not the person who's in control of the conspiracy. He's just the henchman for the real villain! He's taking his orders from someone else. We haven't revealed _that_ secret yet. We're still keeping you in suspense as to who is behind this whole conspiracy. Trust me, that will be someone you know very well."

My mother grumbled, but she was at least glad to see that she still had a chance to win her bet. My readers were getting

192

more and more unruly, but I had managed to stave off a mutiny so far. Now it was time to go back to the story....

"What are you doing here?" Aurora asked. "Why are you trying to kill me?"

"Do you really think I'm going to divulge that information?" asked the unwelcome guest. "It never makes sense to me when you read a book where the villain explains his motives just minutes before he's supposedly going to kill the hero of the book. I'm not going to tell you."

"Please?" she begged.

"Well, if you're going to be polite about it, I don't see how I can resist." He laughed sarcastically.

"I just don't understand why you would try to kill all these visionary people," insisted Aurora. "All we're trying to do is to save the world from environmental destruction. We're trying to ensure the survival of the human race."

"You environmentalists are all alike," the killer scoffed. "You don't even know what you're talking about. There's no threat to the world. It's all a myth. You can manipulate statistics, and you can make all kinds of wild claims to advance your political agenda, but your pessimism has no basis in fact whatsoever."

"What are you talking about?" asked Aurora. "All the world's leading scientists have said that we only have a few years left to save the earth. Just because you can't see it doesn't mean it's not real."

"Who are you going to believe?" asked Lyze Dammleisz. "Hundreds of the most brilliant researchers on the planet, or a handful of contrary iconoclasts who are trying to further their own right-wing agenda?"

Then, realizing his minor faux pas, the killer blushed.

"Let me tell you a story," offered the professional killer. "Once upon a time, there was a famous scientist at Stanford University named Paul Ehrlich. He gained much attention in the 1960's by announcing that we were in the midst of a devastating population explosion that would threaten the world's resources. He said it would cause massive famines, because there wouldn't be enough food for everyone."

"He was right," said Aurora. "The world's population grows by 90 million people every year."

"So where's the disaster? Where's the doomsday? Everything is fine. We're not running out of natural resources. In fact, they're more abundant than ever!"

Aurora was skeptical. "If we're finding more resources, it's only because we're raping the land, mining the bottoms of the seas, and basically exploiting every last place on earth. What happens when we've used up all the coal, all the oil, all the minerals that the earth has to give? What then?"

"You poor, uninformed woman. You know nothing about the truth. You make all the same mistaken assumptions that Dr. Ehrlich made. In 1980, an economist at the University of Maryland decided to prove just how wrong the great Dr. Erhlich was.

"This economist, named Julian Simon, bet Dr. Ehrlich that we would not run out of any of our scarce natural resources. He dared Ehrlich to choose any five minerals that the environmentalist thought would be exhausted within ten years. Simon predicted that the price of those minerals would actually drop by 1990!

"Ehrlich thought this was the easiest bet in the world. After all, as something becomes more scarce, it should grow more expensive. If we start to run out of copper, it would become very costly, right? That's only natural.

"So Ehrlich chose five minerals that he thought would be depleted within ten years. The two men bet quite a deal of money. And, after a decade, they checked the prices of these minerals. *Every single one was cheaper.*

"So Mr. Simon, the economist, won the bet. The threat of these natural resources disappearing was all nonsense. It was nothing more than the wild imaginings and hallucinations of a radical environmentalist."

"But why?" asked Aurora. "I don't understand."

"You see it all has to do with economics. We'll never deplete all our oil reserves, for example. When it gets too expensive to mine oil from the ground, we'll just switch to some cheaper form of energy, like solar or wind. No one will care about this sticky black stuff oozing out of the ground. It will become useless and relatively worthless. So we won't actually run out of it!"

"But you're just playing games with the planet!" insisted Aurora. "We can't go on making bets about whether we're going to survive. Julian Simon is like a guy who's jumped off the Empire State building, but has yet to hit the ground. He's fallen 90 floors, but there's still ten more to go. So when someone asks him how he's doing, naturally he says "fine." But it's only a matter of time before he crashes to the ground.

"I've studied the facts," Aurora continued. "You may not sense how bad the crisis has become. You can't sense it in your own comfortable life, and you proceed with business as usual. But it's absolutely staggering in its devastation. The number of people who have died from starvation and famine is up to 500 million since Ehrlich made his statements about the population explosion.

"You don't see these people. You don't witness their suffering. You can't see how the crisis has devastated ecosystems around the globe, and killed off so much life. Many species have become extinct; they have disappeared forever. Many ecosystems like the tropical rainforests can never be restored. Once they're gone, they're never coming back. When you destroy the earth's ecosystems piece by piece, you're messing with the delicate network of interconnections that are vital for our survival. It's like taking the rivets out of an airplane one by one. The craft may continue flying for several years, but someday it's inevitably bound to fall apart."

"There's so much uncertainty," said the killer. "Who knows the truth? You parade your 'facts,' and I'll parade mine."

"Certain facts are indisputable!" argued Aurora. She was already at the mercy of this deadly killer, so she figured she had nothing to lose by arguing with him. Perhaps, like

195

Scheherazade, she could distract him with stories, and thus delay his mission to extinguish her life. "You can't deny the fact that we've introduced thousands of toxic chemicals into our air and water."

"What's toxic?" asked Mr. Dammleisz rhetorically. "Anything can be toxic if you have the right dose. Clear, pure water from a mountain stream can be deadly. After all, you can drown in it! The fact of the matter is that most things that you think are toxic or hazardous are actually very safe. They don't pose much of a threat to human health at all. There's very little proof of any certain chemical causing cancer. People could have gotten cancer from a million other factors. You go raising the banner of hysteria. It's bad science, and it's completely untrue. Most of what people pass for truth is just their opinion."

"So why are you trying to kill me?" said Aurora. "If you're right, what threat do I pose to you?"

"You're trying to overthrow the chemical industry, the auto industry, all the industries of the United States that depend on fossil fuels and chemicals. Your vision of the world threatens everything on which this economy depends. You're going to destroy the current economy!

"That's why I have to get rid of you. You're a threat to us, just like a pesky insect. You and your environmentalist friends are like an invading army of ants, or a plague of locusts. It's you versus us. There's no middle ground, no living in harmony, my dear."

"So what are you going to do to me?" Aurora challenged. "You can shoot me, but people will come investigating my death."

"Oh, I'm much more professional than that," said Dammleisz. "I don't want people getting suspicious. No one even knows you're alive. You have no family who's worried about your safety. You have no close friends who are wondering where you've gone. Even your boss doesn't care anymore; he's fired you from your position, thinking you've been lazy on the job. So I can kill you without worry of an investigation. But I have to make it look accidental. That's why I've brought along some natural predators that will do the dirty work for me."

Dammleisz opened the door to the cell, where three of his colleagues were standing outside with cages. Inside the cages were six hungry crocodiles. The reptiles snarled and looked at their new prey with small, avaricious eyes.

"We'll see how much you like nature now," laughed Dammleisz. "These are endangered species from the Florida Everglades. If you're so interested in protecting these rare reptiles from extinction, I'm sure you won't mind providing them with their first meal in days."

Aurora gasped. "And how are you going to make this look accidental? It's not everyday that someone is eaten alive by alligators." Aurora did not know the difference between crocodiles and alligators. In her defense, Dammleisz was equally dubious about the phyletic distinction.

"You may remember the urban legend in New York City from a number of years ago: Rumor had it that some wealthy people thought it fashionable and chic to adopt baby alligators as pets. But they soon tired of this novelty and many people ended up flushing their pets down the toilet. As the legend goes, the alligators ended up living in the sewer system of New York, spawning and reproducing and growing exponentially in numbers. Now there are probably more of these beasts underneath the streets of this city than in all the swamps of Florida."

"But it's just a myth," Aurora said. "No one will believe it's true."

"Ah what faith you have in the American people," Dammleisz chortled. "People will believe almost anything nowadays."

The killer brought one of the cages close to Aurora, so she could examine the beasts that would soon be feasting on her. Aurora didn't even know whether crocodiles could salivate, but it appeared that they were drooling in anticipation of their meal.

"Now we'll see how you feel about the environment," Lyze Dammleisz said. "Are you the type of person who won't harm a mosquito? What do you do when locusts descend on your crops? How do you live in harmony with nature when it's a battle for your survival? Nature is not our friend, Ms. Borealis. We must conquer her, torture her, and dominate her for our own purposes. Otherwise, she will be ruthless with us."

The crocodiles stuck their snouts out of the cages, trying to snap at the reporter.

"It's funny," Dammleisz taunted her. "On television, I described the study that said single women at the age of 35 are more likely to be killed by terrorists than ever to get married. It was a total falsehood, a terribly performed study, but almost everyone believed it to be true. It even made the cover of Time Magazine. I guess now you will become a prime example of this statistical 'truth.'"

Aurora lunged at her tormentor, but several of the hulking mobsters grabbed her arms and held her back.

"You're quite a pest," laughed Dammleisz demonically. "It's time to call the exterminator and put an end to your public nuisance. Tonight you're the endangered species."

With these words, Dammleisz barked an order at his companions:

"Open the cages!" he demanded.

The metal bars rattled and opened. The reptiles slithered and scattered out, heading directly for their dinner.

Aurora looked desperately for refuge, but there was nowhere she could go in this claustrophobic space. The walls seemed to close in on her.

The beasts were all at least twelve feet in length, more than twice the size of Aurora. One of the alligators appeared to be a full twenty feet long, bigger than a Cadillac. Yet, for their size, they were surprisingly quick.

They moved with lightning speed towards the reporter, backing her into a corner. The largest one eyed her greedily, rushing for her legs.

She started singing, hoping that music would soothe the savage beasts. Yet still they stalked her, hunger in their eyes. She was pushed up against the walls.

In a panic, she tried appealing to their sense of reason. "We're really all on the same side of this battle!" she pleaded with the reptiles. "I'm trying to make the world safe for all of us." Her attempts at trans-species telepathy failed to win them over.

In a last ditch desperation move, Aurora leaped up and lunged at the light bulb, which was hanging by a thin electrical wire from the ceiling. The crocodiles snapped at her as she sailed overhead.

Hanging on desperately to the thin metal wire, she started swinging, spinning, and gyrating all around the room. As she swung out of control, the animals chased her back and forth, clamoring for a taste of her flesh.

One of them had his jaws outstretched right beneath her body. As she came hurtling through the air, like Tarzan on a vine, the savvy animal waited. She came flying in a trajectory straight for its mouth. The jaws came crashing down.

She felt herself caught, pulled down by the beast. It had seized her hospital gown and was shredding it from her torso. As she struggled free, it tore at her in anger, ripping the remnants of clothes off her unscathed body. She was left in rags, as the crocodile choked on cotton.

"I know it must be bad," she empathized. "It's not organically grown."

Half-naked, she continued to swing like a crazy pendulum across the cell. The crocodiles stirred into a frenzy. In their savage hunger, they lunged for her as she flew overhead.

Aurora strained with all her muscles to climb up the wire. Her hands were getting bloodied by the tension of her tight grasp against the rusty, sharp metal. The blood dripped down to the ground, tempting the reptiles, which could sense their prey within grasp.

The wire itself could barely sustain her weight. It grew weak under the pressure and strain. At any moment, it could give way, dropping her into the reptilian pit.

But the wire was her only chance for survival. She pulled herself up like a fireman climbing a rope, until the crocodiles could not reach her anymore. *Thank God these reptiles can't jump*, she thought. They rotated and craned their necks in the air, reaching desperately for the woman who was clinging for her life to the very top of the wire. She was pressed against the ceiling, ten feet above the slavering beasts. Her hands ached, but she could not let go of her life.

Then the wire broke.

She came tumbling down to the ground, right into a feeding frenzy. Everything went dark. Aurora lost consciousness and slipped away....

"You killed her!" protested my mother. "Do you have no sense of decency? At long last, son, do you have no sense of decency?"

"Mom, it's just a story. I keep telling you it's fiction."

"That's easy for you to say. Do you know that violence in books desensitizes children to violence in real life? I think I should bring you up before a censorship committee. They shouldn't allow trash like this in the stores."

"What about the First Amendment? What about my constitutional right to free speech?"

"As long as you're living under our roof, you don't have any constitutional rights, young man. "

I didn't understand why my mother should be so upset. After all, she herself had read a million acts of violence. In the average mystery novel she read, the body count would fill a morgue. It made no sense why she should object to my comparatively peaceful story. It was only when I heard her speaking in private to my father that I got a glimmer of the truth:

"What will the neighbors think? We did everything for this child, and he turns out to have sadistic dreams of killing people and feeding them to the crocodiles. I've seen this before on TV, you know. It just shows all the violent tendencies that are seething just below the surface of his mind. He's taking out his aggressive tendencies on some poor, hapless characters in a book. The next thing you know, it could be us."

My eavesdropping on my parents' conversation was interrupted by a raucous noise outside. I heard people screaming and chanting and denouncing my name. The protesters had returned.

"Ban the book!" Lenin was shouting. Trotsky was burning several copies of my manuscript. War (who, admittedly, was sometimes partial to violence) was holding a placard that said "All We Are Saying Is Give Peace a Chance."

I expected that the literary agent would be pleased with this latest plot development. But even she was a bit dismayed.

"It's just so old paradigm," she explained. "I mean, you're trying to create a vision of a better world. Do you really think it should be so violent? You might want to set a better example for youth."

"But you kept telling me: Sex and violence! Sex and violence! You said those are the trends that sell."

"That was last week! Don't you keep up with the times? Celibacy and nonviolence are the latest fashions. It's part of that big spiritual renaissance in this country, and we need to capitalize on it. There are big bucks to be made from spirituality!

"Do you think you could write a book about a shy, retiring, God-fearing virgin who is saving himself for marriage? He could meet a woman at a civil disobedience rally, when they're both laying down their bodies in front of bulldozers (if you're really going to insist on that outdated environmental theme). It will be a beautiful little romance, a slice of life."

"But what about the action and the adventure?"

"Oh, that genre is dead! We don't need another hero. What people are looking for is something that reflects their own life --

something real, with average characters. I mean, if you could have written a manuscript about an unemployed guy from Generation X who still lives at home with his parents, and who suffers from a sense that everything around him is phony -- now that would have sold a million copies! It would have been the Catcher in the Rye for a new generation; it could have explored the difficulties of living as a young adult at the coming of the third millennium, with the sense that the world was coming to an end. Think about how interesting that would be, how much it would relate to people's lives today. Too bad you didn't do that book. I don't know where you came up with this idea for such a violent story."

She shook her head in pity, and departed the room. If only she had known what was coming next.....

Chapter 58

Aurora woke up in an unfamiliar room.

"Are you all right?" asked a man beside her, who was trying to nurse her back to health. "You've gone through some rough times."

"What happened?" she asked. Her memory seemed like it had been erased for a second time.

"Lyze Dammleisz tried to kill you," the man said. "But we managed to catch him just in time. We arrived on the scene right before you were about to get devoured by some pretty hungry reptiles."

"But where am I? Who are you?"

"Oh, I'm sorry," said the polite young man. "I should have introduced myself earlier. My name is Alan Durning. I'm part of the team that is trying to unravel the mystery of who is destroying the Earth. We think we've almost solved the crime, but we need your help."

"<u>My</u> help?"

"Yes, I hope you'll be able to join us upstairs in my laboratory in a few minutes. We've rounded up all of the prime suspects. They're all waiting upstairs as we speak."

"How do you know who are the suspects?" Aurora asked. "Did Lyze Dammleisz reveal who's running the operations?"

"No, he claims he was just following orders. He says he doesn't know who's ultimately in control. We're still looking for the person who's directing the conspiracy. But I've accumulated a vast amount of evidence indicting every single person upstairs."

"So how can I help?" inquired Aurora.

"You know most of the suspects personally."

"What?!?"

"Yes, I hate to break the news to you, but someone you know is playing an instrumental role in the destruction of the Earth."

Chapter 59

Aurora was astonished when she entered Durning's laboratory. When she looked around her, she could not believe her eyes.

Scott Sherman, Sharif Abdullah, John Todd, and Dave Foreman were all sitting around a table.

"B-b-but, I thought you were all dead!" she said. "What happened?"

"We'll explain everything to you later," Durning promised. "Right now we have a much more serious issue to address.

"As you all know, I have been doing a thorough investigation into the environmental crisis. I've been looking into the major questions: Who's responsible? Who's in control?

"And I've come up with conclusive evidence that links every single one of you to the scene of the crime."

The four men were stunned. "What are you talking about?" Dave Foreman demanded to know. "Do you mean to tell me that you're accusing several of the leaders of the environmental movement of betrayal? Don't you have any other serious suspects?"

"Oh, I interrogated some international crime leader named Kayzer Sozse, but I determined that the case against him was too flimsy.

"Damn!" swore my father.

"Yet with one of you in particular, the evidence kept getting stronger, and stronger, and stronger."

The four men looked back and forth at each other nervously, suspiciously, accusingly.

"Yes, I've just unearthed some new information," Durning muttered angrily. "And this time the trail of evidence leads me straight to you, Mr. Sherman."

Chapter 60

Scott felt the cold steel of a pistol against his temple. Durning's assistant tied him down to a chair, while the senior researcher held the gun steady to the detective's skull. One wrong move and this would be the end.

"What proof do you have that I'm guilty of this crime?" challenged Scott. On the verge of death, he had nothing to lose with his defiant stance. "I've done nothing wrong."

"Don't act so innocent with me," Durning lashed out in bitter accusation. "I know the truth about you."

"What are you talking about?" Scott stammered.

"I've been doing some investigating of my own," the senior researcher replied, with a smirk besmirching his face. "Sure, you have a golden reputation -- you're a world-famous war hero, decorated by the President. An international provocateur, single-handedly responsible for the fall of communism across Eastern Europe. A successful private eye, solving some of the most notorious murder cases in the history of the United States. But you can't hide from me. You can't divert attention from yourself, pointing the accusatory finger at all the corporate executives of the world. I may be an amateur detective myself, but I've found plenty of evidence pointing in your direction."

A thousand conflicting thoughts raced through Scott's head. He had entered into a nightmare world where nothing made any sense. He had set out to investigate a crime, and had found himself accused. The valiant hunter had become the prey.

"I've been framed!" he insisted. "You're not going to try to pin this crime on me!"

He flirted with thoughts of escape. He would become a fugitive from justice. Scott would flee the country before he ever served time in prison for a crime he didn't commit.

"Do you use any paper?" Durning asked him. "Do you have furniture made out of wood in your house? Do you mean to tell me that you haven't even used some wooden chopsticks in your life?"

205

"Well, of course, I use paper and wood products," Scott admitted. "But you can't accuse me personally of clearcutting the forests or destroying the life support systems of the planet. It's not my fault! I'm just one individual person."

"But that's exactly the problem," insisted his accuser. "You can't see the destruction your life is causing to the planet! It's all invisible to you, as you enjoy the simple pleasures of life. You're far removed from the consequences of your actions. But that doesn't make you any less responsible or your actions any less devastating.

"50,000 pounds of waste are produced each year to support your lifestyle alone. That implicates you, Mr. Sherman. You're an accomplice in this crime against the earth."

Scott didn't like the direction of this conversation. "I don't throw away 50,000 pounds of waste each year. Your statistics must be screwy. You can't prove a thing against me. I throw away maybe a few pounds of trash each week. I'll have you know that's not a crime in this country. It doesn't cause that much harm to the environment. It's not as if I'm directing a massive conspiracy."

"Don't you see?" Durning insisted. "Well, no, of course, you can't see the damage you're causing. When you flip on the light switch, there is waste being produced to generate the electricity. Somewhere, far away, where you can't see it, perhaps on a Native American reservation, coal is being strip mined to produce light for you. And when you drive a car, do you know how much environmental pollution you belch into this atmosphere? Not to mention the waste created in the production of everything you buy. One small wedding ring generates 14,000 pounds of waste all by itself! So you are guilty, Mr. Sherman. After years of stopping crime, you are now exposed as the criminal."

Scott didn't feel like a cold-blooded murderer. He wasn't aware that his actions were killing off thousands of species and wrecking the ecosystems upon which all life depended. He was innocent. He had not been aware that a crime was in process.

"I have proof of your guilt" Durning asserted. "I happen to know that you drink two cups of coffee each day."

"And that makes me a criminal?" Scott scoffed.

"No, but I'm going to show you how your seemingly innocent actions have devastating consequences all across the planet. I decided to investigate the destruction caused by the apparently innocuous habits of daily life -- things that you do everyday, things that you take for granted. I began with a single cup of coffee.

"Most of the coffee you drink, of course, comes from thousands of miles away from your home, from places like South America. I traced one cup of coffee to its origin in the hills of Colombia.

"The coffee beans had been picked by impoverished Colombian workers on a small mountain farm, where the natural cloud forests had been slashed and clearcut to make way for the coffee plantations. It required the harvesting of 18 coffee trees just to satisfy your individual coffee drinking habits for a year.

"Growing the coffee trees had required the spraying of pesticides, produced in the Rhine River Valley of Germany. The toxic runoffs from the pesticide plants had infested the Rhine, making it one of the most polluted and deadly rivers in the world. The pesticides also poisoned the rivers and ecosystems of the farmlands sprayed in Colombia.

"The beans were shipped from South America in a freighter constructed in Japan, of steel made in Korea, from iron mined on tribal lands in Papua New Guinea. The natives received little compensation for the destruction of their lands from mining, nor for the water contaminated by the mining process."

"The beans were shipped across the Atlantic, thousands of miles into the Gulf of Mexico, where they were finally unloaded in New Orleans. There they were roasted and packaged in four-layer bags of polyethylene, nylon, aluminum, and polyester. The three layers of plastics were produced by oil shipped from Saudi Arabia. Then the plastics were created in factories in Louisana's infamous 'Cancer Corridor,' an area where toxic industries are disproportionately concentrated in poor, African-American neighborhoods."

Scott's mind reeled. It seemed impossible that his single cup of coffee had caused so many unseen consequences, hidden from his view. And there were still more to come. Durning continued to follow his trail of destruction around the world:

"The aluminum layer of the coffee bag was made in the Pacific Northwest, from bauxite strip-mined in Australia and shipped across the Pacific on a barge fueled by oil from Indonesia. The mining of the bauxite had violated the ancestral land of aborigines. The refining of the aluminum was powered by a hydroelectric dam on the Columbia River, construction of which had destroyed the salmon-fishing subsistence economy of native Americans.

"The bags of roasted beans were then trucked thousands of miles across the country to Seattle. The gasoline for the trucks was processed from oil extracted from the Gulf of Mexico. The refining was done at a plant near Philadelphia, where heavy air and water pollution has been linked to cancer clusters, contaminated fish, and a decline of marine wildlife throughout the Delaware River basin.

"By the time I had finished my detective work, I had traced the origins of your single cup of coffee to industries all over the world, and to resources shipped from as far away as Indonesia, Australia, and Russia. The process had burned hundreds of gallons of oil, polluted ecosystems across the globe, and left toxic waste festering on almost every continent and every ocean. All this for a single cup of coffee."

"I plead ignorance! I didn't know about the destructive consequences of my coffee habit," Scott insisted. "I swear I'll give up drinking coffee! It wasn't that good for my health anyway."

"That's an admirable start," Durning conceded. "But coffee is not unique. Almost every one of your economic activities entails widespread destruction across the globe -- destruction that is invisible to you, You claim innocence, but the facts show you to be guilty."

Durning looked at Scott and posed a question the detective did not want to answer:

"If this much destruction was caused by a single cup of coffee, how much other invisible destruction is happening with each of the very simple acts of your life?"

Scott recalled his vision of the clearcut landscape -- the barren stumps extending to the horizon. That had once been a verdant forest, overflowing with life. Now it was turning into a desert -- a parched, dry landscape as barren as the moon. In some ways, he was responsible for that.

"So what are you going to do?" Scott asked. "Will you try to kill me? Or are you going to turn me into the authorities on the charges of devastating the environment?"

"Of course not," replied Durning with a laugh. He withdrew his gun from the detective's temple. "It's not just you. You didn't create this destruction alone. I did it, too! In fact, every single American has contributed to this crisis. Every American who uses paper or wood products is equally as guilty as you. 50,000 pounds of invisible waste is produced each year for each one of us -- it's not simply the actions of one evil person.

"It's like the famous mystery story of the Murder on the Orient Express. There was a murder committed on the luxury train from Venice to Istanbul. When Hercule Poirot, the detective, started to look for the killer, he rounded up a great number of suspects. As he investigated the case, he discovered something remarkable: Everyone was guilty! They had all taken part in the crime!

"All this time you've been trying to track down the people responsible for the destruction of the environment. You've been looking for a villain on whom you could place the blame. But it's not so simple as all that. The most dangerous thing about the environmental crisis is that it's not being caused by a single madman whose plans we can thwart. You can't simply arrest a few people and imagine that the threat will be gone. You want to know 'who done it'? We all done it, Mr. Sherman. We all done it!"

Chapter 61

This reminds me of a dream I had just last week. I dreamt I was an investigator for the police. Somebody had slaughtered Mother Earth, and it was my job to catch the culprits.

I traveled down to the crime scene. There was a chalk outline of a spotted owl on the ground. Forests had been slashed and burned, until all that remained was ashes. Forensics detectives were busy picking up the remnants of what had been a thriving vivarium -- dead dodo birds, decapitated cassowaries, minced minks. They were extinct, stubbed out, dearly departed from the Earth. And who knew where the murderer would strike next? Who would be the next victim?

An anonymous phone call came into the office later that day: "Watch out," he cackled maniacally. "Once all the other animals are gone, then human beings will not survive."

"Who is this?" I demanded, jumping out of my seat and motioning to my colleagues to immediately start a trace. We had to keep the murderer on the line for two minutes in order to determine where the call was originating from.

"It's someone you know," he teased. "Someone very close to you."

The voice did sound vaguely familiar. But where had I heard it before? It was like a strange mixture of every voice I had ever heard -- my brothers, my sister, my father, my mother, my closest friends and colleagues. I could hear elements of their voices all in that one strangely all-encompassing voice.

"Why are you doing this?" I demanded to know. "What is it that you want? What are your demands? What are your motives?"

The killer paused, breathing heavily over the line but without speaking a word. I was afraid I had asked too much. Why would a ruthless serial slaughterer reveal to me his secrets? Would I scare him off, and lose the most vital clues for catching him in the process? In the background, police technicians were frantically tracing the call before the murderer hung up on me.

"I just want to be happy," the criminal finally admitted. "Is there anything wrong with that? Everything that I'm doing is just so I can squeeze a bit of comfort and pleasure out of my years before I die."

I could not restrain my anger. "You madman!" I screamed, knowing that my outburst could wreck all our careful plans to rein in the killer. "Your pleasure is coming at the expense of thousands of other lives! What kind of perverse maniac are you that you find comfort in others' misery? What kind of lunatic would find happiness in the slaughter of thousands of innocent creatures?"

Just as I asked the question, my colleagues interrupted. "We've just succeeded in tracing the call," Sergeant Watson announced, though more with an air of apprehension than one of celebration. "The call is coming from inside the building," he announced. "It's your line. In fact, it's all of our lines. We're all the killers of Mother Earth."

Chapter 62

Scott's handcuffs were removed. The detective was released from his chains.

"You should have seen the fear in your eyes," Durning chortled as he displayed the fake pistol to Scott. "If you had done some better research before flying out here to meet me, you would have known that I'm a faithful adherent of Gandhi's nonviolent philosophy. This was all an act."

"I don't understand," Scott muttered as he examined the false gun. "Why did you set me up like this? Were you just trying to play some sort of cruel practical joke?"

"No, I admit that this seems like a pretty extreme way of making a point. But I wanted to dramatize the truth of the crisis we face: You _are_ guilty of contributing 50,000 pounds of waste each year to the ecological crisis. You as an individual have a devastating impact on the life support system of this planet. Each one of us has this devastating impact."

"So did you have to make this point by tying me up and treating me like a criminal?"

"Sure," said Durning. "You were looking for some sort of conspiracy theory. You were looking to place the blame on some wealthy, powerful corporate executives -- perhaps the heads of the oil companies like Shell and Exxon. You wanted to hold the President or members of Congress responsible for the crime of destroying the planet. Essentially, you were refusing to look at your own complicity.

"Real life isn't like a mystery novel, Mr. Sherman. You can't just find a few evil characters who are responsible for the mayhem. The line of good and evil runs through each of our hearts. We _all_ support the system that is contributing to ecological destruction. We all have to accept responsibility."

"The folks who are fighting us aren't bad people with sinister motives. They just want to protect the country from any threat of change. They can sense that there is a movement to transform the entire system. This jeopardizes everything in which they're invested. They're frightened to death of change, just like the fetal scientist was afraid of leaving the womb. They simply don't realize how much better the future can be! They've never been presented with an alternative to the status quo."

"This is a very compassionate way of looking at the environmental crisis," commented Aurora, who had been watching this whole spectacle.

"Well, the old way of looking at people as our enemies is outdated," said Sharif. "There are no evil people -- just a system that's out of control. People serve the system unwittingly."

"People have been hypnotized to serve the system," added Alan. "It's almost like they've been brainwashed."

"Brainwashed!" Scott exclaimed. "That sounds like conspiracy talk again. Do you mean to tell me that there really is some sort of sinister plan to brainwash the American people?"

"No, you see the system is all the more insidious, because the brainwashing is unconscious. No one is in control! There's no Dr. No, no Goldfinger, no Lex Luther, no nefarious villains at all. The world is a whole lot more complex than in an adventure story."

Chapter 63

I think this latest bit of information is really affecting my sleep. I had another disturbing dream last night.

I was flying over the Earth, with my red cape trailing behind me. People were looking up into the sky, yelling "It's a bird! It's a plane! No, it's Sherman!" I was faster than a speeding locomotive -- or at least, faster than most public transportation in the United States today. I was able to leap a mountain of garbage in a single bound. Now I had to rescue the world from the forces of environmental destruction.

Meanwhile, the evil Lex Luther was plotting to destroy the Earth.

"Why are you bothering to do that?" I asked. "Aren't we doing a good enough job as average Americans?"

Lex looked at me, his eyes green with envy. "That's just it," he complained. "There's no room for an evil villain anymore. Now everybody's part of the problem. They're all accomplices to the crime. Back in the good old days, it used to be so easy for me to try to destroy the world. Things were so clear and morally unambiguous back then. We knew who was good and who was evil. It was very dramatic."

A tear formed in the eyes of Lex Luther. He shook like a little child whose favorite toy has been taken away.

"Do you know how it feels to be in the unemployment line?" he wailed. "Oh, the humiliation of it all! When they asked me my former profession, I felt so embarrassed admitting that I was once responsible for creating wanton mayhem and cavalier destruction."

"Oh, so you were a government worker?" I joked.

"It's not funny," Lex sniffled. "Government bureaucracy wasn't half as efficient as I was at screwing things up in this country. But now everyone wants to get their hands in the action. Everybody gets to play their own little part in destroying the world."

"Democracy in action," I said. "Love it or leave it."

Luther gave me an icy cold stare. "I assume this is your idea of empowerment -- everyone has the power to cause environmental damage, even in the comfort of their own home."

"It does make things more difficult for me," I commiserated. "It was so much easier when I just had to battle against you. I mean, heck, what's a little kryptonite between friends? But now -- now, I've got to do battle with 260 million Americans, all leading wasteful lives of overconsumption. Just yesterday, I got stuck for 45 minutes giving a lecture to the American Manufacturers' Association about the importance of resource recollection and efficiency. It's just not the same as in the good old days when I could go flying around, stopping you from detonating nuclear warheads and drugging the American people. Now they drug themselves."

"What are we going to do, Sherman?" asked Luther. "There's got to be a better way."

"Oh, that's what really saddens me," I continued. "Saving the world has become -- well, it's just not quite as glamorous as in yesteryear. There are no Nazis to fight, no communists.... Even the Klan is in steady retreat."

"There's the militia," Luther offered hopefully. "I applied for a job with them, and they said I was too old. Can you imagine that? Me, Lex Luther -- with a proven track record of terrorism, hatred, and pure, unashamed evil -- and I can't even get a job with the militia. These young people have no respect for the accomplishments of their elders. You would think experience would count for something. But no. They say they're out for fresh blood. They want some new ideas for a new world order. Evidently they think that my brand of terrorism is too passé."

"It is very old paradigm," I had to concede.

"Et tu, Sherman?" Luther stabbed back with his retort. "I thought I could at least count on you for support. All I've got left is an Evildoers Anonymous group. There are just a few of us poor souls, desperately crying out for help. If we didn't have each other, I don't know what I'd do.

"You should have seen just the other day -- I was talking with Dr. Frankenstein. He was complaining how there's no place for a mad scientist anymore. It's not as easy as it used to be to wreak havoc on the Western World."

"There, there," I told him. "There are still a lot of scientists who are doing their part to wreck the planet. Who do you think developed the CFCs that ate up the protective ozone layer? Who do you think came up with all the technologies that are polluting the atmosphere, ravaging the biosphere, and destroying the diversity of life on this planet? It's all people with Ph.D.s and MBAs."

Well, this cheered him up for a little bit. But then he started thinking about all those ethically responsible scientists who are warning humanity about the fate of the earth, and trying to do everything within their power to stop the crisis. He immediately fell back into a depression.

And that's when I woke up. I still haven't dreamt of any solutions yet. How can you solve the environmental crisis when every single one of us contributes to it?

Chapter 64

"I've run out of hope," confessed Aurora. "The odds against us seem too great."

"What are you talking about?" asked Sharif.

"For the past several weeks, I've been collecting wonderful ideas for saving the planet. But now I just don't think that these ideas are realistic. After all, we're fighting against a system that is supported by 250 million Americans.

"There are too many people and businesses who have vested interests in the system. We'll be swatted down like a pesky mosquito if we try to stir up trouble. There's just too much resistance to change."

"Can't we just try to reform the system?" asked Scott.

"No," insisted Sharif. "The system is beyond reform. It's like a runaway train that's speeding north towards the edge of a cliff. People who try to reform the system are like passengers trying to walk southbound on the train. They may congratulate themselves on the progress that they're making. But no matter how far south they walk on the train, they're still part of a system heading for the abyss.

"We've created a horrible monster. This is a system that's leading to the ecological destruction of the planet. This system is deadly, it's irreversible, and it's simply out of control. Everytime we participate in the system, we help breathe life into this leviathan. Even trying to reform the system is helping to give it life. The only way to stop it is to withdraw our support. Instead of fighting the system, protesting it, or trying to reform it, we need to just leave it behind! We need to start building our own southbound train!"

"Give me an example," insisted Aurora. "What exactly do you propose to do? I want a concrete, specific plan of action."

"The best example is what Gandhi did in the struggle for Indian independence," Sharif explained. "For decades he challenged the British authority, but all to little avail. Finally he decided that the best strategy was to ignore the British

217

authority altogether. Indians started organizing their own
village governments, instead of paying attention to the foreign
rulers in their midst. Indians started making their own clothes,
beginning their own industries, and establishing their own self-
reliance. They stopped paying the British taxes and they stopped
heeding the British courts. How long could Britain continue to
rule over India if no one in the country recognized them as a
legitimate authority anymore? Their political system was a
sham; it ceased to have any meaning, because no one in India
believed in it. No one paid it any attention."

Sharif saw the puzzled look on his colleagues' faces, so he
tried to explain it in a different way:

"It's like the economy," Sharif insisted. "It's only real if
we believe in it."

Aurora protested: "How can you deny the reality of the
global economic system? I may not be an expert on international
finance, but I do know one thing for sure: Money controls the
world."

"No," Sharif disagreed. "Our economy is based in fiction.
Do you really think that there are trillions of dollars floating
around? There's not that much currency printed. We don't have
billions and billions of dollars sitting in a safe in Fort Knox.
Most of our money is just imaginary -- little digits on a computer
screen -- but we all believe it's real."

Aurora still didn't understand.

"Don't you see?" Sharif insisted. "Think about the Great
Depression. One day we think the economy is soaring. The next
day stockbrokers are throwing themselves out of windows. What
changed? There's still the same amount of food in the country,
the same amount of physical labor, the same amount of coal and
wood and other natural resources. In other words, we have the
exact same amount of real, material wealth. It's not like we were
hit by a massive earthquake or nuclear bomb. All that changed
was our perceptions! We were held hostage by a ghost!"

Aurora had never thought about any of this before. "I've
got to admit," she said, "I never really did understand economics
very well. In school, I couldn't tell the difference between my

supply and demand. I got slapped around far too many times by the Invisible Hand."

Sharif took out a dollar bill, continuing his explanation of the illusion of economics. "What's the good of this green piece of paper?" he asked. "You can't eat it. You can't wear it to protect you from the cold. It's just a symbol of wealth that we've all agreed to respect as a medium of exchange. If enough people stopped believing that it had any value, then you could no longer buy anything with this piece of paper.

"That's what happened in Germany after the First World War. The German money ceased to have any value. All of a sudden, people had wheelbarrows full of useless paper. Before the war, it could have bought them a house. Now no one believed it had value any more."

"The system of inhumanity is the same way," Sharif insisted. "We believe that the system has control over our lives. But it doesn't even really exist, except as we choose to participate in it and give it our tacit consent!"

Everyone still looked perplexed, so Sharif explained further: "We've already talked about how the system of inhumanity is supported by all our actions. If you eat a hamburger, you help support destruction of a Central American rainforest thousands of miles away. You may not see the connections, but they exist. Rainforests are cleared to make way for cattle grazing, so that consumers in the United States can buy cheap meat from developing nations.

"Similarly, every time you drive a car, you support a system that leads to ecological disaster -- a complex infrastructure of oil refineries, highways, and auto manufacturers, all of which create massive amounts of hazardous wastes.

"Almost every time we participate in the system, we are supporting terrible, invisible destruction like this. Therefore, the best way to solve the problem is to ignore the system altogether. Refuse to participate in it."

"But that's impossible!" Scott cried. "Our standard of living is dependent on the system. I still don't understand why we don't just try to change the system so that it's less destructive to the environment. That's the most sensible path. That's what the existing environmental and social justice organizations are already trying to accomplish. Why don't you work with them, pooling your energy and resources? That seems like a much better strategy than just withdrawing from society."

"No," Sharif argued, "I told you already: the system can't be changed. It's fundamentally flawed. We don't want to sustain a gigantic, anonymous, inhuman beast."

Dave disagreed vehemently. "We can make some important changes in the system," he insisted. "We just have to fight the people who are profiting from the system. Nothing worthwhile comes without a struggle. We need to organize the masses, go out into the streets and protest. This is the way the Civil Rights Movement succeeded. This is the way people gained their independence and liberation all over the world, from South Africa to the Soviet Union."

"What good does it do to protest," asked Sharif, "when there's nobody in control of the system? We all are responsible for the existence of the system. It cannot exist without our participation in it.

"Look at people who spend their whole time protesting the system. Their motto is "Fight the Power." But, if you say that you want to fight the power, you are acknowledging your own powerlessness! You are taking a victim mentality. You insist on having other people take care of your problems. You want to scream and cajole and urge someone else to take action. Instead, here's a better strategy: Just acknowledge that you already have the power. You have the power to create your own system.

"If I want to make the perfect chocolate chip cookie, I don't go out and start protesting at the Keebler Cookie Factory. I don't shout out 'Hey Hey! Ho Ho! Keebler's Cookies Have Got to Go!' I just go out and bake my own cookies.

"Similarly if our goal is to create a better society, why do we spend so much time protesting the old one? We waste our days criticizing everything that's wrong with the old system -- never even acknowledging our own complicity in its maintenance and creation."

"So what's <u>your</u> strategy?" asked Aurora. "What are you going to do besides protesting and criticizing the current system?"

"Let me illustrate my strategy through a parable," Sharif said. "This is one of my favorite stories, and it comes from Malcolm X:

"Malcolm's mentor Elijah Muhammad held up two glasses of water. One of the glasses had dirty, oily, filthy water in it. The other contained pure, pristine, crystal-clear water.

"'Never tell anyone that they have a dirty glass of water,' Elijah Muhammad admonished his apprentice. 'People will just get angry and defensive. They will deny that their water is dirty. They will see you as the enemy, and they will try to fight you. You will earn nothing but their hatred. They will be even more resistant to changing their glass of water.

"'But imagine this much simpler strategy: Instead of criticizing a person's dirty glass of water, just hold up your own clean, pure, pristine glass of water. Then let them choose for themselves which they prefer. You won't have to tell them that yours is better.....'

"Similarly," continued Sharif, "we need to stop criticizing the system. We need to stop dwelling on the problems of our current society, and instead we should just hold up a better vision to the American public. We should present an alternative model of society -- a compelling, creative, beautiful picture of how the world could be.

"All of us have been researching great ideas for creating a new society. Let's start holding them up for everyone in the world to see. Let's not waste our time complaining about all the dirty water we see, and trying to find people to blame or shame. That's been the strategy of too many environmentalists for too long. We've been focusing on the problems, crying out about every injustice we see.

"Instead, let's propose better alternatives. Let's show the world what we have to offer. If we build a better society, billions of people will come."

Chapter 65

"So what is the better vision of society?" asked Scott.

"Have we started to create an exciting picture of a better future?" The visionaries decided to get together and brainstorm all the ideas they had researched. By the end of five minutes, they had already created the following list, summarizing the highlights of a new society:

Ideas for designing a new economy:

More creative, fulfilling work;

More leisure time to spend with family and friends;

Simpler lives -- escaping from the hectic chaos of the rat race;

More emphasis on finding spiritual fulfillment;

Shorter work weeks;

Lower income taxes;

Ending welfare for the rich;

More democracy in the workplace;

Increased worker ownership and control of businesses;

More efficient businesses that save money by reducing pollution;

An economy that restores and heals the natural environment;

An "intelligent product system;"

Industrial ecosystems, where wastes would be minimized;

A reinvestment of money into local communities; and

A philanthropic economy where people would be engaged in good work, helping their fellow humans.

    Ideas for designing better places to
    live:

    Ecological cities, full of gardens, forests,
        parks, and rivers
    Ecological restoration -- returning nature to a
        healthier state
    Harnessing the power of nature, instead of
        fighting against it
    Bioshelters
    Living machines
    Super low energy bills
    Safe, clean, cheap energy (no oil spills or
        nuclear accidents!)
    The elimination of toxic emissions and
        pollution
    Hypercars -- 200 miles to the gallon
    Bioregionalism -- adapting to the "genius of
        the place"
    Permaculture -- growing food naturally without
        pesticides or chemicals
    Improving efficiency -- doubling our wealth
        while cutting our resource use in half

"These ideas are exciting!" Aurora effused. "Why have I
never seen these ideas in a book? Why have we never been offered
this thrilling vision of a positive future? Almost every American
would embrace this new vision if they only had a chance to see it!
But you never hear politicians talk about any of these great
ideas. You never see these ideas presented on the evening news, or
in the mainstream magazines."

"It's true," agreed John. "These ideas are all out there,
but they're mostly underground."

"But there's one important point that we're missing," said
Sharif. "In order to create a new society, we're going to need more
than just redesigning our institutions. Ultimately we have to go
much deeper. We have to change the entire way we see the
world."

Chapter 66

"Wait," said Aurora. "Before you get into that story, I still want to hear about how Scott survived that car crash. In fact, how did any of you survive your predicaments? Dave Foreman had been kidnapped, Sharif had been murdered, and I saw John Todd die right before my eyes! So you're going to have to change the way I see the world right now, because I've always believed that you can't come back from the dead!"

Everyone looked to Scott for an answer.

"Ummmm...." Scott paused nervously, as if he were stalling for time....

How <u>did</u> my character survive the car crash? In fact, how did <u>any</u> of the environmental leaders manage to rise from the graves into which I had condemned them? I was hoping no one would ask me those questions.

Well, there was no putting off the subject any longer. I had to come up with a solution fast. I decided to ask everyone around me for suggestions. I began with the little matter of the deadly explosion on the Oregon highway. How could the detective have possibly lived through that?

"Maybe he jumped out of the car at the last second?" my father suggested.

"No, no, no," argued my mom. "That's so clichéd. It needs to be something much more clever than that. How about this: He wasn't really in the car at all. Actually it was his mysterious twin brother who had disappeared years ago, and who had gone over to the dark side. Yes, it was none other than the elusive villain Kurt von Doppelganger!"

"This is good," said the literary agent, puffing on a cigarette. "This has potential."

"Wait a second," I interrupted. "We all saw Scott Sherman sitting in the car. We know that he was driving the car! Go back and read page 72 of the book. That's out of the question. We can't just all of a sudden substitute some mysterious twin brother who's never even been mentioned obliquely anywhere else in the manuscript."

"So why did you decide to get your hero in a car crash anyway?" my mother asked, feisty after having her suggestion shot down. "Didn't you think about this plot beforehand?"

"It wasn't me!" I insisted. "It was the muse. He spoke through me. I had no control over what happened. Do you think I know where this is going?"

My friend Ellison interrupted. "If we are to take into account Einsteinian physics, it's just possible that your hero may have entered into a space-time warp only moments before the collision."

"Oh, that's realistic," I replied sarcastically. "I'm not writing a science fiction novel here. This is a true story, you know. Well, everything except for the made-up parts."

Rainbow decided to add her two-billion cents to the conversation. "I have an idea!" she exclaimed.

"You know how my hero is going to get out of this car crash alive?" I asked with great anticipation.

"No," she said, "I have an idea for a new line of dolls called the Burnin' Sherman. It would come with its own pyrotechnic exploding car."

"And a fire-retardant suit?" asked Schadenfraude.

"No, no," explained Rainbow. "We want the doll to burn up in the car. That way kids will have to keep buying more and more."

"The symbolism is very profound," commented Ellison. "Ashes to ashes, and all that jazz. Or perhaps it's a hermeneutical question."

"I like the idea of Scott Sherman burning to cinders," added Shoddy helpfully.

"That's not necessary," Ellison suggested. "I think that it's possible to prove that Scott Sherman's car never actually crashed at all, despite the evidence of our eyes."

I started to ask Ellison how that was possible, but then the answer came to me like a revelation. It was all so simple really.

"So how _did_ you survive the car crash?" Aurora repeated her question impatiently.

"It was easy," Scott explained. "You see, there was no crash. It never really happened!"

"What do you mean? There were witnesses to the crash. They found the wreck of the car along the Oregon highway. There were people who claim they saw the fireball. They even found your charred body in the wreckage. I read about it in the papers. I saw it on TV. How could you possibly say it never happened?"

"Do you believe everything you read in the newspapers? How do you know that the news is true? They present it all as objective facts, but the truth of the matter is that everything's biased! Everything represents a subtle point of view, a prism through which reporters reveal their singular perspective on the world."

"But how could reporters be biased when it comes to reporting a car crash? It either happened or it didn't!"

"No, perhaps it never happened, but we staged it to _appear_ as if it did."

"Are you saying that you faked your own death?"

"Of course," said Scott. "I needed to throw my enemies off of my trail. It was convenient for them to think I had been

226

killed, so that I could continue to investigate the crime without fear of being followed."

"I knew it, I knew it!" cried Ellison. "It's one of the oldest devices in the entire genre of mystery and adventure: The author makes you think that the protagonist has perished, only to resurrect him through some miraculous turn of events."

"I read this in a John Grisham novel just last week," my mother interrupted. "Same thing -- a guy supposedly dies in a car crash, but really he just staged the whole thing himself."

This latest piece of news caught the attention of the slick attorney, who suddenly stuck his head inside the window, appearing out of nowhere. "This sounds like a possible copyright infringement," he said with rising excitement. "That's a serious lawsuit, possibly worth millions." He quickly began to dial up the phone number of John Grisham's publishing house on his handy cellular phone.

"Wait a second," I clamored to stop him from completing the call. "I didn't know about that other book, I swear."

"Shut up, you lying philanderer," retorted the attorney as he finished entering the number on his phone.

"Actually," corrected Ellison, "a philanderer is someone who has had many licentious love affairs, adulterous in nature. You probably meant to call Scott a plagiarist."

"Oh sure, that was the initial indictment," the attorney exclaimed with mounting passion. "But maybe I can get more money off this adultery charge! I don't really care anymore if he's some kind of cheating philatelist."

"That's a stamp collector," Ellison pointed out.

"Really?" asked the attorney. "It sounds like our little friend Scott here has lots of interesting hobbies. Maybe I can nail him under some mail fraud statutes, too."

"I'm innocent!" I pleaded. "I deny everything. This is all untrue."

"Oh, look who's suddenly so concerned about the truth," retorted Alan Durning with biting sarcasm. He was obviously still upset about the minor fact that I had never met him in my life, yet here I was, continuing to give him an ever-larger role in the book, attributing negative qualities, such as sarcasm, to his character.

Durning had entered the little party that was now going on in my living room. Half of the characters were making cameo appearances, mingling at this spontaneous get-together to celebrate my return from the dead.

However, there was very little celebration. Instead, I was being cornered by some angry readers. There was a mutiny in the works.

"There's something wrong here," my mother pointed out. "On page 71 of this book, we <u>saw</u> Scott Sherman driving a car to the Portland Rose Garden. We breathlessly followed every second of the car chase. We watched as his enemies pursued him to the death. We were witnesses to the explosion. So how can you tell us now that the crash never really happened? How can you tell us that Scott had a peaceful drive from Seattle and never confronted the killers?"

My father was right behind her, also looking cheated. He was wondering if they could go back to the hospital where I had been born 27 years before, and exchange me for another child.

Lenin and Trotsky were also furious, holding this up as one more example of capitalist duplicity. Death was scheduling an appointment with me in his personal datebook. Even the doctoral student at Stanford, who had been procrastinating on his dissertation, felt quite betrayed. He had stayed with me through the entire manuscript, and now I was pulling a dirty trick.

Meanwhile, the attorney was licking his chops at the legal prospects, hoping to sue me for false representation. Bess Bestsellerstein was ruing the day that she had ever met me. Ellison thought it was a splendid example of postmodern modalities of discourse, but then again Ellison was pretty weird.

I paused, hesitated, and looked at the mob, which was calling for my head on a plate. "Do you want the truth?" I asked.

"Of course we want the truth!" said my mother.

"The truth is very simple: I'm an unreliable narrator."

"In other words, you're lying to us!" accused Lenin. "We can't trust a word you write."

I rose to give an impassioned speech in my defense. "Can you trust anyone?" I asked. "Is there really such a thing as a reliable narrator?"

There was a bit of grumbling at this philosophical digression. Only Ellison seemed intrigued by what I was saying.

"I mean, you read nonfiction books and think they're objective truth. But they're not! They're just a reflection of the author's personal opinions, beliefs, and paradigms. They reflect all of the author's prejudices, conscious and unconscious, and the way the author filters reality. Even the material that authors leave out is significant in revealing their personalities. You learn a lot more about the writer than you do about the subject!"

Someone launched a tomato in my general direction. Other people started throwing eggs, spitballs, and, in one case, a hand grenade. I continued with my sermon:

"What about history books?" I asked. "Do you think those are reliable narratives of what happened in the past? They're just cultural stories masquerading as truth! They leave out so many perspectives and so many events that could offer other versions of truth. And yet most people still accept them as an objective account of what really happened over the past few thousand years."

Losing their patience with me, the angry readers rushed the platform from which I was addressing them. "Let's put him in the cell where he stuck me!" yelled Aurora Borealis.

"If it even really exists," scoffed Shoddy. "It's probably just another unreliable story."

They brusquely seized ahold of me. Then, with a vigilante's sense of justice, they sought their vicious retribution by

---

Well, you don't really want to see this. It gets pretty ugly. Maybe you should just distract yourself from the gruesome reality for a few minutes. As soon as I've healed from my wounds, I'll get back to you.

"And what about the other deaths?" Aurora asked suspiciously. "How did Sharif survive? How about John?"

"Those were all faked, too," Scott replied. "We needed to deceive our enemies. The truth of the matter is that Dave Foreman was never kidnapped. He was in hiding, helping to run the underground movement. Sharif Abdullah never actually died. And the alleged massacre of John Todd and the other visionaries was all staged for your benefit."

"For my benefit?!?" Aurora protested. "You had me scared out of my wits! Meanwhile my life was in real jeopardy!"

"Yes, but we had to tell as few people as possible. We couldn't let our secrets get out. We were working for a higher purpose."

Aurora's anger was subsiding, but she still harbored resentment. She felt like she had been a pawn in a game of deadly intrigue.

"This whole time you've been deceiving me," she accused everyone in the room. "You all claim you're trying to create a better world, and yet you're using these Machiavellian tactics of lies, subterfuge, and duplicity."

Sharif rushed to her defense. He, too, had been unaware of the entire web of deceit that had been spun around the group. In fact, he had not sanctioned the story about his own death. He had been angry when he found out about it.

"Aurora is right," he said. "What is the vision of the future that we are trying to promote? Is it a future based on falsehoods and fibs? Is it a future that rewards dishonesty, in the name of the proper cause?"

Sharif was a mesmerizing speaker. Everyone in the room was rapt in attention as he launched into a soliloquy:

"I imagine a future in which our highest value is Truth. We're not going to create that future by means of deceptions and lies.

"Look at the old system that is causing so much ecological destruction. What is the basis of that system? It's based on a fundamental lie, which everyone believes to be true: the idea that we are all separate from each other. It's the idea that I can gain only if you lose. It's the idea that has formed the foundation of our economic and political structures.

"This is the way so many Americans believe reality to be. They believe that 'it's a dog-eat-dog world' out there. They believe that humans are violent, aggressive, selfish beings. Indeed, they have formed an entire economic system on ruthless competition and the pursuit of self-interest. They think that's natural. They say that competition and violence are the laws of nature. They point to all the instances where predators stalk their prey, and hold that up as an example of the way the world works. In the eyes of most Americans, this is not a belief. It's reality!

"Well, you can imagine why our society is so violent, so competitive, so cutthroat, and so mercenary. If we are convinced that nature is 'red in tooth and claw,' then we are going to act in ways that conform to this belief. We are going to sanction war to achieve our goals. We are going to fight nature everywhere we confront her. We are going to see our lives as a ceaseless struggle against hostile forces. This is the root of environmental destruction. This is why we don't create a society that works with the flow of the natural world. It's all in our consciousness! It's our false and dangerous view of 'reality.'

"But there's a new vision of reality that's available to us. We can choose to believe that the world is a friendly place. We can choose to believe that cooperation is the fundamental law of nature. We can choose to believe that you benefit only when I benefit, too. Indeed, we can choose to believe that you and I are one.

"Now this isn't just some metaphor. It's not just a mystical Buddhist concept. This is a truth that is being discovered by scientists everyday. Our old view of how the world works is disappearing. All our ideas of 'reality' have to change overnight!"

"But how?" asked Scott. "How could that possibly happen?"

"You don't have to wonder how all our ideas of reality could possibly change overnight. For, in fact, it has already happened!"

Chapter 67

"Now what I'm about to tell you may come as a surprise," continued Sharif. "It's the most important news of the 20th century, but almost no one knows about it.

"Around 1920, the smartest people in the world -- brilliant scientists such as Albert Einstein -- discovered something shocking. This was such a dramatic revelation that it would change their lives forever. Nothing would, or could, ever be the same.

"In fact, this news is so important that it could change the course of history. And yet what's remarkable is that its dramatic effects have yet to be felt. Most Americans still remain in the dark. It's a secret to all but a few of us."

"What is it?" Aurora asked. She was enthralled by the story-telling of Sharif.

"These scientists discovered that all our ideas of how the universe worked were totally, irrevocably wrong! Our ideas about the nature of reality were fundamentally mistaken. Everything that we believed to be sacred and true turned out to be a fiction!"

"What do you mean?" Scott demanded to know. He may have been working against the government lately, but there were still certain things that he believed to be sacred and true: God. The family. America. At his core, he was a conservative person, and he didn't like his deepest beliefs being called into question.

"They discovered, for example, that everything in the universe is interconnected. We are all one, at the most fundamental level! It's a scientific truth.

"Before the time of Einstein, everyone believed what their senses told them: that we were all separate, material beings. We believed that the universe was composed of trillions of discrete beings. I am separate from you. This table is separate from both of us. This seems quite obvious. Our eyes have convinced us that we are apart from everyone else. And so we wander through the universe lonely, not knowing whether other people will do us harm or good. Through our senses, we saw everyone and everything as different, as other than ourselves.

"But the new discoveries of science have shown us that we are linked to everyone and everything. Not only do we share the same atoms, but we are interdependent. Our fates, our destinies, are inexorably tied together. I gain only when you gain. I lose when you lose."

"This all sounds very nice and lofty, but give me concrete examples," said Scott.

"These scientists were trying to discover the fundamental building blocks of nature. They wanted to discover the essence of reality. So they investigated deeper and deeper, until they reached some shocking truths:

"As you know, everything in the universe is made up of atoms. But scientists wanted to go even further. What are atoms made of?"

"Protons and electrons?" guessed Aurora, who still remembered a thing or two from her high school physics class.

"That's right. But then scientists decided to look more closely at these protons and electrons. To understand what they discovered, imagine that we enlarged the size of an atom until it's as big as the Capitol dome in Washington D.C., hundreds of meters high and hundreds of meters across. The nucleus of the atom, which includes the proton and neutrons, would be smaller than a a grain of salt. And the electrons would be as small as dust particles, floating at the edge of the dome. In other words, more than 99.999 percent of the atom is empty space. At the core of reality, we find there's just about nothing there!"

Scott looked absolutely perplexed. "So you're telling me that reality just doesn't exist?" he asked, overcome by confusion.

"At the most basic subatomic level, that's right! In fact, this was the conclusion that the greatest minds of the century arrived at after studying all the evidence: 'There is no objective reality in the absence of observation.'

"In other words, a scientist who is studying an atom helps create the atom's existence!"

234

"I knew it," said Schadenfraude. "I knew it! You create your own reality!"

"But these findings don't make any sense," complained Scott.

Sharif agreed: "They are so paradoxical that they shocked even the greatest geniuses of the time, the very people who discovered these truths. Einstein himself said, 'it was as if the ground had been pulled out from under us, with no firm foundation to be seen anywhere.'

"But these findings were just the beginning. There has been a scientific revolution in this century that has transformed the way we understand reality.

"For example, look at the science of cybernetics. In the past few decades, we have come across some startling information --- what one leading thinker called 'the biggest bite out of the Fruit of the Tree of Knowledge in the past 2000 years.'

"Scientists discovered that human beings are not really material objects, separate from the environment. We are more like dynamic, ever-changing streams through which our environment ceaselessly flows."

"What are you talking about?" asked Scott

"Think about a river. We might look at the mighty Mississippi, which appears to be the same river from moment to moment. But, of course, it's not! The water which was in front of our eyes five seconds ago is already flowing downstream. The river is changing at every second. It's more like a dynamic process than a static material object -- more like a verb than a noun.

"Humans are exactly the same, although you might not perceive it. We are changing at every second. In fact, there's not a cell in your body that was there seven years ago! You are constantly receiving food, energy, and information from the environment around you, all of which sustains your life. You have no independent existence. You are just a pattern through which the environment flows! If you were to be deprived of food, light, or even love, you would wither and die.

235

"This confirms the fundamental rule of ecology: Everything is connected to everything else. In fact, the emerging science of chaos goes even further. It shows us that the most seemingly insignificant factor in a system can have a tremendous effect on everything else. It's really true that a single person can change the entire world. Your actions can have major consequences, for good or for bad.

"That's why everything you do is so important. With every action you either support the current system -- the system based on competition, separation, and fear. Or you can choose to create an entirely new system, based on this new vision of reality: a system that is grounded in the idea that all of us are one."

Chapter 68

The trial began at noon. I was roused to consciousness in the morning, given a final meal, and then taken to the courtroom in handcuffs. The protesters had their own sense of vigilante justice, which did not allow for due process of law; nonetheless, they were kind enough to convert the Loca Vista mental hospital ward into a makeshift courtroom.

I looked around at my surroundings: Schadenfraude was lording over the proceedings as the self-appointed judge. I recognized the twelve members of the jury: my Mom and Dad; Rainbow and Ellison; Death, War, and Famine; Bess Bestsellerstein; Phineas Smogg (who looked perturbed that he had played such a small cameo role so far in the book); Robert Cassandra (who looked even more perturbed that he had been killed off and converted into a ghost); and Lenin and Trotsky.

"This isn't a jury of my peers," I complained. "This jury is rigged against me."

"Silence!" ordered Shoddy. "This is the system of law that we've invented. We set our own rules here. I will be the final arbiter of what's fair and just and right."

"Objection!" shouted the opposing attorney, who was dressed in his finest Armani suit for the occasion. "You promised me that I would get to decide what's fair."

"Shhhh!" shushed Shoddy, who was busy counting his hush money as he started the proceedings.

"Would you like to present the case for the prosecution?" Judge Schadenfraude asked the attorney.

"Yes, thank you, your honor. Today we have here a case of the most flagrant act of misrepresentation I have ever seen. The defendant has committed a major crime that his readers can never forgive. He has forever sullied the good name of American fiction.

"How many of you remember the simple days when we could trust writers to lie to us with all sincerity? Those were wonderful times, when an author could create an entire fictional world in which we could believe. The characters that writers created were so real, so true.

"But now we have this pretender -- this impostor who calls himself Scott Sherman -- who has told us a fiction that isn't even true!"

I looked over at the jury to see how they were responding to these damning accusations. My mom was engrossed in a mystery novel, which she had brought to the courtroom. Death was knitting a crochet. Most of the other jury members had fallen into a hypnagogic state, somewhere between wakefulness and dreaming. Only Lenin and Trotsky seemed to be paying much attention, foaming at the mouth in anticipation of my conviction.

"Let me show the members of the jury the first piece of evidence: This is page 72 of the manuscript which the defendant has written. In it we clearly see the hero of the book involved in a car chase. His enemies are pursuing him to the death. His car explodes in a fireball, and the chapter ends with these chilling words: 'There were no survivors.'

"Now we learn, by the defendant's own confession, that he is an unreliable narrator. The hero never was in a car chase on the highway. He never died in a car crash. It was all made up solely to mislead the reader."

This evidence seemed to spell my doom. There was a loud murmur that hummed across the courtroom. People seemed astonished at my brazen act of writing.

"But that's not all, your honor. The defendant has transgressed every literary convention. He has flouted the distinction between fact and fiction at every juncture possible. He is taking the distinguished tradition of American fiction and ruining it by mixing in these actual ideas from visionary people who are trying to save the Earth. Who can tell what's untrue anymore? He's going to endanger the reputation of every writer in the country. Now readers will always have the haunting fear that the words they are reading might actually be true. People don't want to deal with truth! They want to be coddled and comforted; the world may be coming to an end, but at least there will always be a good book on hand so that they don't have to worry about such pesky little details. They can just escape into their own private fantasy worlds. And isn't that what being an American is really all about?"

The attorney added a final rhetorical flourish to sway the emotions of the jury. He ended his soliloquy with a passionate call for justice:

"This writer threatens everything that is not true today. When you can't believe in fiction, what can you believe in? Unless we take immediate action in this courtroom today, the profession of lying for a living will never regain the high stature that it properly enjoys. I urge you to condemn this heretic to death. " His speech moved the judge to tears.

"I rest my case, your honor," he said, and then sat down to thunderous applause from the jury.

Schadenfraude looked at me grimly and said "Have you prepared your closing arguments?"

"My closing arguments? I haven't even had my opening arguments yet!"

"Objection, your honor!" yelled the opposing attorney. "He's trying to confuse the issue by relying on nit-picky procedural details."

"Sustained," said Schadenfraude. "This is my courtroom, and I'll do no more than I have to do to maintain the illusion of justice."

So this was it. it was time for me to defend myself. I had no idea what I might say. So I just opened my mouth and let the words speak through me:

"I have only one thing to say: I am guilty of all the crimes of which I am accused."

The entire jury gasped. They leaned forward in their chairs, listening to how I might exculpate myself. What justifications could I possibly offer for these heinous crimes?

"I wanted to tell a fiction to prove a point. You see, everything in our society is a fiction. That's the whole point of this book. Our political structure is a fiction. Our economic structure is a fiction. Even our legal structure is a fiction. It's not based on any transcendent vision of Justice or Truth; it's just the biases and prejudices of the people who are sitting on the bench."

Schadenfraude started to object, but I had taken his gavel.

"Everything in our current society is just our own invention. It has no basis in reality. It's all a fiction that we've created.

"And if our entire society is a social construction -- if it's all based on fictions -- then we know that it's not universal. It's not inevitable. We can choose alternative visions of society, as different from this one as we can possibly imagine. Once we realize that everything in our current system is a fiction, we have the power to see through it. It loses its magical hold on us. We

240

don't have to believe that this is simply the way things are. There is another way!

"So that's why I decided to blur the thin line between fact and fiction. I wanted to show that everything we believe to be sacred and true is just a belief. It <u>can</u> be changed. We can create a new vision of reality; we can choose new stories to tell, and we can create new truths."

Chapter 69

"We <u>can</u> create a new vision of reality," Sharif agreed. "This can be a vision of the world where the deepest values are love and compassion and unity. It will be a world where humans can develop to their full potential, free from injustice and poverty."

"Those are wonderful ideals," said Scott. "But they're impossible to actually create. You sound like a utopian dreamer. There will always be violence, war, and injustice."

"We can diminish them," argued Sharif. "Some people say that wars are inevitable, but that's only if you believe in the Hobbesian reality where life is a fierce struggle for scarce resources. Humans have a tremendous capacity for acts of goodness, compassion, and love."

"Yes, but those are uncommon traits that are rare and extraordinary," Scott said skeptically. He had been raised in a world in which the threat of nuclear war always hung over his head; life on the planet could be extinguished at any second. He had been trained in the martial arts, learning the ways of deadly deception and intrigue. For him, violence was the reality of the world. He had seen enough killings to make him somewhat immune to the idea that there could be a peaceful alternative.

"You assume that acts of love are uncommon," said Sharif, "because you have been conditioned to only see the acts that confirm your worldview. If you think that life is "nasty, brutish, and short," you will always see the examples that prove your point. Yet, if you expect that the world is full of wonderful acts of forgiveness and compassion, you will be amazed at how those are also all around you.

"It is true that humans have a biological capacity for aggression, violence, and other forms of cruelty. It is one of a possible range of responses to the environment around us. But we also have a capacity for love, kindness, compassion, and goodness. We have the choice about which sets of behaviors and emotions we wish to encourage in the society we create. Do we want to create a world where competition and self-interest are the highest ethics, where we win only at someone else's expense? Or do we want to create a world in which we all win together, in which we live in cooperation with nature, rather than in a state of war? The choice is up to us."

Scott was still doubtful. "I agree with you that we need to create a better society, in which we can diminish the effects of war, injustice, and ecological destruction. But I'm just wondering if it's really possible. I mean, there's never been a society like this before in the world. All of human history has been full of war, violence, and general nastiness."

Sharif disagreed. "I'm reminded of a quote from Gandhi," he said. "A reporter came up to him and asked how the Indians expected to win their freedom from the British without violence. 'Don't you know anything about history?' the reporter asked Gandhi. 'There's never been a successful nonviolent revolution before.' Gandhi simply smiled, and replied: 'I may not know much about history, but you obviously know nothing about human potential. Just because something has not happened in the past does not mean it can't happen in the future!'

"Of course, Gandhi ended up being successful in freeing his country from colonial domination without firing a single shot. He led India through the first major nonviolent revolution in history. Yet, in the 50 years since Gandhi led India to its independence, countless other nations and groups have used nonviolence to gain their freedom. The civil rights movement in the United States, behind Martin Luther King Jr., helped millions of people gain the rights that had been denied to their groups for centuries. The entire Soviet Union and communist bloc came crumbling down without violence, an act that would have surely never been predicted by all the generals stockpiling their nuclear arms. After years of promoting the racist system of apartheid, the South African government was changed into a multiracial democracy, again through a nonviolent revolution. In fact, nonviolence has been gaining freedoms for people all around the globe since the time of Gandhi, helping overthrow military dictatorships all over South America and oppressive regimes in

Asia and Africa. Nonviolence even proved successful when tried against the Nazis in World War II. This is a page in history of which few people are aware.

"So the world is changing fast. New possibilities are opening up everywhere, based on the new vision of reality. Democracy is spreading all over the globe. Women's rights are being increasingly recognized in many countries. Old forms of practice that used to be considered 'acceptable' all over the world -- practices like slavery -- are now considered reprehensible.

"The old vision of the world -- what many people call the 'old paradigm' -- is breaking down. We now know that it doesn't work very well. Most people in America are not satisfied with their lives, despite the fact that they live with more material wealth than all the kings and queens of history. Millions of people are depressed and have attempted suicide in their lives; millions of people have yet to find meaning or purpose.

"But we have yet to see a compelling new vision of a better future. We haven't yet been introduced to an alternative that excites the imagination of the American people.

"So that's what we're going to today: we're going to invent the future."

Chapter 70

"First let's take a trip into the past," said Alan Durning. "There's something fascinating that I want you to see."

"Have you invented a time travel machine?" asked Aurora, only half in jest.

"No, I have a virtual reality machine, in which I can take you back to 1939. I've recreated the exact conditions of that time. When you put on this helmet, you will be experiencing the sights, sounds, and smells of that time. Together we can walk together through the streets of New York, as it appeared 60 years ago."

"But why are we going back to 1939?" asked Dave Foreman.

"This was a crucial period in our nation's history. It was a period of great turmoil and ferment. The nation had been struggling through the Great Depression for ten years already. Millions of honest, hard-working Americans could not find work to sustain themselves. They were standing in bread lines, suffering from poverty, and living in conditions of squalor. The bread basket had turned into a Dust Bowl. The nation was ravaged by despair.

"At the same time, the storm clouds of war loomed ominously on the horizon. In the summer of 1939, it looked like all of Europe might be plunged into a cataclysmic war. Hitler was just months away from launching his blitzkrieg into Poland. The Nazis were about to start the bloodiest, deadliest war in human history, with systematic barbarity that would be unimaginable even to the worst of pessimists. This conflagration would envelop the world, eventually dragging the United States down into the killing abyss. Thousands of young American boys would die in the trenches and battlefields of Europe. Eventually the war would culminate in the development of the atomic bomb -- a weapon so devastating it could destroy the entire Earth.

"This was without question the greatest period of crisis that civilization had ever faced. With all the signs of political and economic disaster around them, Americans were desperately looking for a new vision of the future.

"The organizers of the New York World's Fair in 1939 decided that they would showcase that vision of a better tomorrow. The entire fair was built around the theme of presenting a positive alternative to the civilization that was falling apart around them.

"Now I want you to come on a journey with me. We're about to walk through that vision of a better tomorrow, as imagined by the inventive minds of 1939...."

Chapter 71

Aurora donned her virtual reality helmet. Alan attached electrodes to her body, so that she would have all the physical sensations of actually walking through the World's Fair.

At first, she could see nothing. She was enveloped in darkness. But then Alan switched on the machine, and she was astonished to find herself sixty years in the past. She looked around her and she could see her colleagues -- Scott, Aurora, Dave, Sharif, and Alan -- also walking through the grounds of the fair.

In front of them, thousands of people were waiting in line for an attraction. The line seemed to snake endlessly throughout the fairgrounds.

"What is everyone waiting for?" Aurora asked. "This ride must be fantastic."

"It's not a ride," Alan told her. "Come to the front of the line, and you'll see what everyone's so excited about. Don't worry about cutting in front of all these people waiting patiently; they're just imaginary, anyway."

Aurora was astonished. The people around her looked so real. Everything about the World's Fair seemed so authentic. The atmosphere of 1939 had been captured down to the finest detail.

They eventually came to the front of the line, and saw an amazing spectacle: It was like a radio, but it had a picture screen on it. People could watch moving images flickering across the screen of this box.

"Television!"

"Yes," Alan assented. "The World's Fair of 1939 was the first television broadcast ever. The opening ceremonies were captured on TV, with President Franklin Delano Roosevelt presiding. Of course, virtually nobody had ever seen a television before, let alone owned one. It was a very different world back then. But people were mesmerized by the promise and potential of this new invention."

Alan let his colleagues gape at the scene for a few more minutes, and then he ushered them forward to see another exhibit. It was the "Futurama," sponsored by General Motors, in which visitors to the fair could see a better vision of the future.

What the group saw astonished them: It was a future in which people would no longer have to live in cities. Everyone would live out in these new areas called "suburbs," and then they could drive to work on these new inventions called "highways." As difficult as it seemed to believe, there would be an entire highway system that would connect the country.

Of course, the skeptical visitor of 1939 would doubt that he or she could own a car, in order to drive to work in the city. But the General Motors exhibit promised a future in which everyone might have cars; some families might even have two!

The group of visitors from 1999 looked with amazement at all the other predictions of what the future would be like: there were images of rocket travel into space, as fictional a concept as anyone could imagine; there were images of technological progress entering everyone's homes with such wild ideas as personal computers and fax machines.

"They imagined the future exactly as it is right now!" exclaimed Aurora.

"The best way to predict the future is to invent it," responded Sharif.

"Well, that's the point," said Alan Durning. "That's why I wanted to take you on this visit into the past. You can see that everything we take for granted in the modern world is just a recent invention!

"Look at highways. Those have all been built in the last 50 years. Look at fast food restaurants. There were no McDonalds nor Kentucky Fried Chicken restaurants until just a few decades ago. Now they seem like a permanent part of the landscape everywhere you travel, all over the globe. They serve billions, if not trillions, of customers every single year.

"Shopping malls are also relatively recent constructions, and yet there are now more malls in America than high schools! You might be surprised to know that the whole idea of

248

conspicuous consumption is quite modern. It too was invented in the last 50 years, when marketers determined that they must construct a throwaway society, so that people would constantly need to buy more goods. Before that, there was very much of an ethic of thrift in America; most people reused and recycled as a normal part of life, and they didn't consume materials from all the way around the globe.

"For people who were born since the end of World War II, it seems like this is the way our society always has been. But it's not. We made choices. We invented the future we thought would bring us the American dream. Instead, it brought us the American nightmare -- ecological devastation on a widespread scale, disenfranchisement, exploding cities, pollution, and waste.

Unfortunately, this American pattern of unsustainable development has become the model for the entire world in the past 50 years. You can travel all over America, and see a thousand towns that look exactly alike, whether they are in the Midwest, Southwest, or Northeast. They all have the identical tract houses in suburbs spreading to the horizon, the acres of asphalt, the endless parking lots and paved-over earth. They all have the exact same bland urban spawl, which is ugly as well as environmentally destructive. They have the same chain stores, the same chain fast food restaurants, the same Los Angelization that is eating up the world. And yet still this is the model of economic and urban development that continues to be copied from Bangkok to Buenos Aires. It's urgent that we develop a new vision of where people can live -- a vision that is more in harmony with the natural environment around us. What we decide to do here and now will have radical implications for the future of the planet.

"Think about how much the world has changed in the lifetime of people who were born in 1900. When they entered into this world, there were no airplanes, no computers, no stereos, and no televisions. Very few people had light in their homes. Only the wealthiest of citizens had cars or telephones or radios.

"Women and minorities could not vote; they were treated as second-class citizens, often subjected to harsh injustices. Very few people could travel to foreign countries, so difficult was the journey.

"Look at how much the world has changed in the course of the lifetime of a single person! And the pace of change is accelerating, faster and faster and faster. As technology speeds up and information travels in milliseconds all around the globe, the entire planet is transforming. But the question is: How? How will the world be different when we are our parents' or grandparents' age? Are we careening blindly into the future? Or do we have a compelling vision of the direction in which we want to go?"

"I've seen lots of visions of the future in Hollywood movies," said Aurora. "But they're all bleak and apocalyptic. They all seem to show a future in which we've destroyed our civilization. But I can't remember ever having seen a positive vision offered."

Sharif agreed. "Remember the old Biblical proverb that I mentioned before: 'Where there is no vision, the people perish.' It's frightening how accurate those words are today. We don't have a better vision of the future that has ever been offered in clear, compelling terms to the American people. We're very good at criticizing the dirty glasses of water we see, but we're not very good at holding up the clean, pure alternative.

"Now we can make the choices. We can create this new vision of the future. We can question everything we believed to be a permanent fixture of the landscape. It's all just a fiction, all just a social construction, all an invention of modern times. We can create a world as different from today as we wish to imagine."

"So what would this future look like?" asked Aurora. "In what ways would it be different from the civilization we have today?"

"There's no single answer to those questions," Durning responded. "There would be no master plan that fits all communities, for each area has its own unique qualities -- both cultural and environmental. Each area would blossom into its own distinct and beautiful place.

"Of course, there are many excellent ideas for saving the Earth which apply to any area. I think you all have been investigating some of these visionary concepts: Ecological restoration. Bioregionalism. Redesigning human habitats to flow with the forces of nature....

"I can give you a guided tour through one example of a better future. Let's take another trip through virtual reality...."

Chapter 72

Aurora found herself in an urban oasis. She was right in the middle of a city, but there were trees and flowers everywhere. The human and natural worlds seemed to flow together.

There were no cars in sight. There was no industry, no pollution. The air was clean and pure.

In fact, Aurora was on a pedestrian garden promenade, where people strolled at leisure. It was a haven for artists and musicians and multicultural events. Cafés and restaurants spilled out onto the colorful, sun-drenched streets. Trees, flowerbeds, and vine-covered trellises added serenity and beauty to the active, festive scene. Strains of jazz floated across the avenues, amidst the outdoor market atmosphere of a thriving center of commerce.

It reminded her of a beautiful college campus or a quaint, petite European village -- a place where people could gather in central plazas, where everything was within walking distance, where cars were unnecessary, and where traffic was mostly a thing of the past.

"Do you notice how everything is dense and compact here?" asked Alan. "There's no urban sprawl. The neighborhood contains everything: homes, businesses, schools, shops, and entertainment. If you want to go to a movie, it's within walking distance of your home. If you need to go to the market, it also is centrally located right near you. There's no need to drive several miles to go wherever you need."

They continued to walk through the eco-village. There were small forests and creeks seamlessly flowing into the design of the human habitat. The beauty of nature was a part of the everyday urban experience.

"But this can't possibly be a very big city," Aurora pointed out. "If everyone lives in this one central area, close to the shops and businesses, there can't be more than 5,000 people here. This wouldn't work in Los Angeles or New York."

"Actually, we're trying to get away from the model of monstrous megalopolises like Los Angeles and New York," said

Alan. "In big cities, it's too easy to get lost, to feel anonymous, to be one tiny cog in a huge machine. We want to create smaller, more personalized living areas that are at the right human scale.

"In fact, most of the human habitats throughout history were like this: small African villages, Muslim casbahs with their labyrinthine corridors, Native American settlements, traditional small American towns. Everyone knew each other by name -- there was a true sense of community, a true sense of belonging. Moreover, because the living area was small, the citizens were not divorced from nature."

"But we can't go back to the past," Scott argued. "It would be impossible to revert back to small villages based on bioregions. With the world population skyrocketing into the billions, it seems ludicrous to suggest that everyone could back to small village life. In fact, global civilization is heading the other way: towards giant metropolitan centers with more than 10 million people, sprawling over endless square miles to the reaches of the horizon. What are you suggest that all those people do? We can't just all move out to the countryside; then we would really decimate every last inch of wilderness that remains!"

"Plus, a lot of people like living in big cities," Aurora pointed out. "There's a lot of culture, entertainment, and excitement in the large metropolitan areas that you don't find in small villages. There are also a lot of opportunities in the big city. Oftentimes small towns and villages have very little to offer, and my impression is that residents of a small town, where everyone knows each other, can be provincial, gossipy, and narrow-minded, not very tolerant of people who are different than they are."

As everyone raised their objections, they continued to walk through the city. They passed charming Victorian cottages with children playing outside; they passed a small school where colorful murals had been painted on the walls; they passed a community garden where people were growing many of their own fruits and vegetables.

Alan did not at first respond to the complaints that everyone was voicing. He just let them walk along the narrow tree-lined streets with the red brick paths. He let them stop for a few minutes at the church, where a bride and groom were outside taking wedding photos.

They finally stopped at a rail line, where a sleek modern metro car was pulling into the station. Still Alan was silent, entering the train and motioning for his colleagues to follow. The train started up, left the city boundaries within a minute, and then passed through a thick forest with creeks running through it. Several minutes passed before the metro entered into another small town area on the other side of the forest.

"This is the answer to your objections," said Alan finally. "Cities of millions of people can be divided into many smaller communities; each of these small eco-villages will be surrounded by parks, forests, greenbelts, and recreational areas.

"Public transportation would connect the different centers, so that cars would become unnecessary. There would be dense village clusters; perhaps 10,000 people at most might live around one central area where colorful, exuberant activity thrived: markets, schools, playgrounds, everything necessary for a rich communal life. There might be one central hub in the wheel, where all the major activities would take place -- sports teams, orchestras, playhouses, and cultural events that usually require a city of millions to support them. The mass transit would connect all these villages like spokes in a wheel."

Aurora was enthralled by the visions she saw of this ecologically regenerative future. She loved the small-town charm of each of the villages she passed, and the sense that there was a strong sense of community. But doubts still rose up in her mind. This, after all, was just an imaginary tour of a "virtual city." Could it actually start to happen in the real world?

Chapter 73

Alan Durning knew that a city like this already existed: a successful ecological experiment that was home to three million people.

It was a city in the south of Brazil, called Curitiba. In previous decades, the city had been much like other urban centers of pollution, blight, and overcrowding. But, thanks to the work of an enlightened mayor (as well as an enthusiastic citizenry), the city enjoyed an ecological renaissance. The Brazilians started planting forests, creating parks, and tearing up roads and parking lots. They instituted one of the most efficient, cheap public transportation systems in the country. They closed down polluted thoroughfares to cars, and opened them up to pedestrians.

Bill McKibben had seen this model city grow with great enthusiasm. He described how the city had blossomed: "In twenty years -- even as it tripled in population -- the city went from 2 square feet of green area per inhabitant to more than 150 square feet per inhabitant.... From every single window in Curitiba, I could see as much green as I could concrete. And green begets green; land values around the park have risen sharply, and with them tax revenues."

It was clear that the Brazilians loved to live in a town that had integrated nature into everyday life. As McKibben explained: "In a recent survey, 60 percent of New Yorkers wanted to leave their rich and cosmopolitan city; 99 percent of Curitibans told pollsters they were happy with their town."

Curitiba had safe streets, rich pedestrian plazas, and one of the best public transportation systems in the world -- all at cheap prices. It was a model for cities all across America and all across the world.

Chapter 74

The virtual travelers returned to reality. They took off the helmets that had allowed them to visit an imaginary realm. This vision of the future seemed like a promising beginning. But how would it actually come to take place?

"I'm still doubtful," said Scott. He was used to creating social change through violence and subversion. He had assassinated heads of state, infiltrated mafia hideouts, and overthrown fascist regimes. But he had never dealt with anything like the ecological crisis. This mission was the most difficult he had ever faced. "I love the vision of the future you present, but it just seems like there are too many obstacles. The world is heading towards a future where big is always better. This idea of small eco-villages seems wonderful, but it just seems counter to every trend on the globe."

"That's why it will be such an important task for all of us to spread this alternative vision," said Alan. "Studies have shown that most Americans actually do prefer the images you've just witnessed to the scenes of typical urban areas today. They can recognize that these villages offer a place that is richer in community. They know it's a place where people really matter, where they won't just be anonymous automatons in a technocratic machine culture. They know it's a place where the human spirit can thrive, where people can reach their full potential. They know it's a place that is beautiful and restorative, a place that regenerates the soul.

"Americans really do like the idea of the new reality. They want to see a world in which humans and nature flow together, rather than fight it out. People want to live in a world of compassion, love, and unity. It may sound like lofty ideals to some, but let me tell you this: there is a critical mass of people who are ready to create this new civilization."

And with that, the visionaries left Alan Durning's secret laboratory underneath the old growth forests of the Pacific Northwest. For a long time, we had been hypnotized by fictions about our world -- dangerous fictions that led us to believe that we were separate from each other, separate from nature, and in constant battle with our environment.

It was time to tell a new story about how the world could be....

Chapter 75

My own story was not yet finished. For me, it was judgement day.

The jury had been deliberating for 23 minutes, when they stepped back into the ersatz courtroom. They had nominated Dave Foreman to be the foreman of the jury, even though he wasn't one of the original twelve.

"Have you reached a verdict?" asked Schadenfraude, still delighting in his role as a judge.

"Yes, we have," Dave Foreman replied. He looked down at the card on which my fate was written. He paused for dramatic effect. and then he made the pronouncement:

"We find the defendant not guilty of all the charges leveled against him."

There was great rejoicing in the mental ward, where the decision had been handed down. Actually, I was the only one who rejoiced. The opposing attorney was stunned. "I protest," he said. "I ask that the verdict be dismissed on the grounds that I don't like it. There has been a miscarriage of justice here -- and I should know, since my middle name is 'Miscarriage of Justice.'"

Shoddy, too, was staggered by the results. "He admitted he was guilty!" the judge said to the jury as they filed out of the room. "How could you possibly acquit him?"

"Oh," explained Lenin, as he walked out the door. "We found him not guilty by reason of insanity. I mean, who could ever come up with a crazy story like he told about an ecological crisis? It's the wildest thing I've ever heard." Lenin returned to his business as usual, going to his job as a Wall Street investment counselor.

The men in the white coats came and took me away. I'm back in the same ward where they've always kept me, the same ward where I was when I wrote most of this book.

Fortunately, they allow me some visitors from time to time. My parents came the other day. "That was a really entertaining book," they said. "We laughed a lot, and had a good time." Then they went back to their house in the suburbs, where they drank their Mirage, chased by a coffee.

Rainbow has a new plan that she said was inspired by me. She was concerned about the part of the book where I talked about our society falling apart; she agreed with my assessment that most people are not satisfied with their lives, despite our nation's material wealth.

"I've got a trillion dollar idea," she said to me with great verve. "We don't need to actually transform our civilization. I mean, it just seems like so much work. Why bother?

"Instead of trying to change the world, let's just change our minds! I mean, isn't that the point of your book -- that these stories that we tell ourselves are really just our own private fictions? So there's nothing wrong with the world, really; there's just something wrong with our beliefs about the world!"

I was having difficulty following her logic. "So what are you going to sell people to help them change their beliefs?" I asked.

"I'm contacting the Department of Public Works. You know how they put chlorine in our water supply, so that the water we drink is healthy and free of dangerous bacteria? Well, now I'm going to arrange a contract to put Prozac in the water!"

"Prozac?" I asked.

"You know, the happy drug. This pill will make us mentally healthy. Everyone will go around with a smile on their face, and it won't really matter that it's the end of the world!" She beamed with self-congratulations.

"But wait," I said. "If everyone is happy with their lives, they won't feel the need to buy a million useless products to fill the emptiness inside. You're endangering your own market share!"

A look of horror came across her face, and she quickly went back to the drawing board to come up with new ideas.

The literary agent was the last to see me, before visiting hours were done.

"Congratulations," she said. "You've finished the book. And I think I've found an editor for you."

"Really?" I practically jumped out of my bed. "Someone actually wants to publish my book?"

"Well, yeah, with a few minor changes."

"Changes?"

"Yeah, he wants to take out all the parts where you talk about visionary ideas for saving the Earth. He says that's kind of slow. Those are the parts that readers skip."

"I've already left so many visionary ideas on the cutting room floor," I complained. "The action scenes just kept taking more and more of the book, until finally the ideas just played a minor role. I'll have to write a trilogy just to include them all."

"A trilogy?" Her ears perked up. "That could be profitable."

"Well, life is all about money. Isn't that what you've been trying to tell me this entire time?"

A tear came to her eye. "Oh my goodness," she cried with joy. "You've finally seen the light. It's so rewarding when you reach the end of a book and see that the characters have evolved and grown. You've really undergone a stunning transformation. I love happy endings!"

"Speaking about endings," I said, "I don't think my book is quite finished yet."

"It's not?" she asked, amazed.

"No, this is an epic story and it deserves an epic ending," I bragged. "I mean this is a modern fairy tale. It's a fiction about fictions, and I just think it's missing a certain element that would leave the readers content, as they go back about their business as usual, and forget every message I've tried to convey."

"Oh, I've got an idea," the literary agent said. She whispered something in my ear.

I liked it. I liked it a lot. I decided it was a perfect way to end my story about the end of the world....

And they all lived happily ever after.

Epilogue
Final Truths

Truth intrudes.

In the time it took you to read this book, many of the Earth's most valuable ecosystems were irrevocably destroyed. Of course, you didn't see it. So it didn't <u>really</u> happen.

Or did it?

Sometimes fictions can be more dangerous than the truth.